Aunt Dimity and
The King's Ransom

ALSO BY NANCY ATHERTON

Aunt Dimity and
The King's Ransom

NANCY ATHERTON

VIKING

VIKING

An imprint of Penguin Random House LLC
375 Hudson Street
New York, New York 10014
penguin.com

LIBRARY OF CONGRESS CATALOGING-IN-PUBLICATION DATA
Names: Atherton, Nancy, author.
Title: Aunt Dimity and the king's ransom / Nancy Atherton.
Description: New York : Viking, 2018. | Series: Aunt Dimity ; 23 |
Identifiers: LCCN 2018014593 (print) | LCCN 2018015277 (ebook) |
ISBN 9780525522669 (ebook) | ISBN 9780525522652 (hardcover)
Subjects: LCSH: Dimity, Aunt (Fictitious character)—Fiction. | Women
detectives—England—Fiction. | BISAC: FICTION / Mystery & Detective /
Women Sleuths. | GSAFD: Mystery fiction.
Classification: LCC PS3551.T426 (ebook) | LCC PS3551.T426 A9334 2018 (print)
| DDC 813/.54—dc23
LC record available at https://lccn.loc.gov/2018014593

Printed in the United States of America
1 3 5 7 9 10 8 6 4 2

Set in Perpetua Std
Designed by George Towne

For Mike and Jan Dudding,
my London chums

Aunt Dimity and The King's Ransom

One

It was half past eleven on a blustery Tuesday night in mid-October. My ten-year-old sons were asleep in their room, my baby daughter was asleep in the nursery, and the family cat was asleep in my husband's favorite armchair. After a tumultuous evening involving a dead mouse, an emergency diaper change, and an illicit game of cricket in the living room, my husband and I had retreated to the master bedroom, but we weren't asleep.

Bill was sitting upright against his pillows, perusing a sheaf of densely printed legal documents. It wasn't my idea of a riveting bedtime read, but as an estate attorney with a wealthy and demanding clientele, Bill sometimes had to bring his work to bed with him.

I didn't mind. I was so tired that I wouldn't have cared if Bill had brought his bicycle to bed with him. I wasn't sure why I felt so weary, and I hoped that a good night's sleep would cure whatever ailed me, but in the meantime, I was beat.

I turned off the light in the bathroom, climbed into bed, and flopped back on my pillows with a heavy sigh. At the sound of my sigh, Bill set aside his papers and eyed me warily. Twelve years of married life had taught him to choose his next words with care.

"Something wrong, Lori?" he asked cautiously. "Besides the mouse, the exploding diaper, and the smashed vase, I mean."

"No," I said, staring fixedly at the ceiling. "Nothing's wrong. Not one thing." I sighed again. "My life is perfect."

I wasn't exaggerating. Apart from an occasional domestic disaster, my life was nothing short of a dream come true. My husband was the best of men, my children were as bright as they were healthy, and our cat was an excellent mouser. We lived in a fairy-tale cottage made of honey-colored stone near a picture-postcard village nestled snugly among the rolling hills and the patchwork fields of the Cotswolds, one of England's prettiest rural regions.

Although Bill and I were Americans, as were our twin boys, Will and Rob, and our baby, Bess, we'd lived near the small English village of Finch for more than a decade. Bill ran the international branch of his family's venerable Boston law firm from an office overlooking the village green; Will and Rob attended Morningside School in the nearby market town of Upper Deeping; and I juggled the ever-changing roles of wife, mother, friend, neighbor, and community volunteer. Nineteen-month-old Bess did what nineteen-month-olds do, which meant that Stanley, our sleek black cat, spent much of his time avoiding her.

Bill's father, William Willis, Sr., had made our happiness complete when he'd retired from his position as the head of the family firm and moved to England to be near his grandchildren. A handsome widower with courtly manners and a sizable bank account, Willis, Sr., had broken many a hopeful heart in Finch when he'd met and married his second wife, the well-known watercolorist Amelia Bowen. The pair lived in Fairworth House, a graceful Georgian mansion just up the lane from our cottage.

Finch was no more than a stone's throw from Willis, Sr.'s modest estate, across a humpbacked bridge that spanned the Little Deeping River. A stranger might mistake the village for a somnolent backwater, but those of us who called it home were never at a loss for something to do.

In our spare time we fished from the banks of the Little Deeping, hiked the network of footpaths that crisscrossed the countryside, cycled sedately along the hedge-lined lanes, or took to the bridle paths on horseback. Bird-watching, metal detecting, and gardening were among the most popular hobbies in Finch, but a few of us made quilts or collected model trains or produced paintings that would never be mistaken for Amelia Bowen's.

When it came to communal activities, we were spoiled for choice. Art shows, flower shows, church fetes, and gymkhanas were but a few of the events that dotted the village calendar, and a plethora of committee meetings ensured that each event was well organized and well attended.

When we weren't fishing, hiking, cycling, horseback riding, pursuing our hobbies, or participating in villagewide events, we attended services at St. George's Church; shared pots of tea at Sally Cook's tearoom; shopped at Taxman's Emporium, Finch's grandly named general store; and dozed through committee meetings in the old schoolhouse, which served as our village hall.

Everywhere we went, we gossiped. Gossip was a way of life in Finch, and though it could at times be moderately mean-spirited, it was never cruel. More often than not the village grapevine was simply the most efficient way to spread local news, which was the only news we really cared about.

I simply couldn't imagine a better place to live. My neighbors weren't angels, by any means, but they were fundamentally good. They'd welcomed Bill and me to their tight-knit community with open arms, and they'd opened them even wider to welcome our children. Will and Rob had the run of every cookie jar in Finch, and Bess was treated like everyone's favorite granddaughter. We could depend on our neighbors to come to our aid in any emergency, and they knew that they could always count on us.

I even had a best friend living nearby. Like me, Emma Harris was an American, though, unlike me, she'd married an Englishman. Emma ran the riding school where Will and Rob took lessons and where we boarded their gray ponies, Thunder and Storm. Even-tempered and rational, Emma was in many ways my polar opposite, but in our case as in so many others, opposites attracted.

"My life is perfect," I repeated to Bill. "I have a family who loves me and whom I adore. I live in a beautiful place among wonderful people. I'm valued at home and in my community, and my best friend lives five minutes away. I have no reason—and certainly no right—to complain about anything."

"But . . . ?" Bill coaxed.

"But instead of looking forward to making four dozen butter-scotch brownies for the bake sale on Saturday, I feel like a prisoner who's been sentenced to four dozen years of hard labor," I said, still gazing dully at the ceiling. "I don't know why. I usually enjoy baking."

Bill studied my profile in silence, then hunkered down beside me and whispered in my ear, "Run away with me."

"What?" I said, startled out of my lassitude.

"You need a break," he said, resting his head on his hand. "Even a perfect life gets old after a while. However pleasant a routine, it's still a routine, and routines are meant to be broken. You haven't been away from home since the long weekend we spent at The White Hart in Old Cowerton, and that was way back in July. You need a change of scene, a breath of fresh air, a chance to recharge your batteries."

"Easier said than done," I muttered.

"Most things are," Bill retorted. "This particular thing, however, will be as easy as pie to accomplish."

"I doubt it," I said. "I have an awful lot to do this week. It's not just the bake sale. I have to repaint the palm trees for the Nativity play, bottle jam with Emma, distribute books and magazines at the hospital, sort donations at the thrift shop—and that's on top of everything I have to do at home."

"There isn't much empty space in my datebook, either," Bill said, "but if I can make room in it for a romantic getaway, so can you." He brushed a tousled curl back from my forehead. "I'm not taking no for an answer, Lori."

"Apparently not." I rolled over to face him. "Are you about to reveal a cunning plan?"

"Naturally." He cocked his head toward the sheaf of legal papers he'd placed on the bedside table. "I have to drive down to East Sussex on Thursday to meet with a client. You can come with me. We'll stay at The Mermaid Inn in Rye, and we won't come home until Sunday."

My eyes widened. "The Mermaid Inn? I've always wanted to stay at The Mermaid Inn. It's supposed to be one of England's great historic inns."

"So I've heard," said Bill. "We'll find out together. We'll explore Rye, too. There's a nature reserve on the edge of town that stretches right down to the sea. We can stroll along the shore and search the horizon for pirate ships or wander through Rye's cobbled streets and soak up its history."

I gazed at him rapturously. "A hotel oozing with atmosphere in a town reeking of history, all within sight of the sea? It sounds too good to be true."

"I haven't mentioned the food yet," Bill went on. "The Mermaid Inn's restaurant has a stellar reputation. We can gorge on fine dining there, or we can sample the local fish and chips, or we can have every meal served to us in bed."

"Please don't ask me to decide where we should eat," I said, groaning. "I don't have the energy."

"You will," Bill declared. "Until then, you can leave the decisions to me. How does a luxury suite with a fireplace and a four-poster bed sound?"

"A working fireplace?" I asked hopefully.

"Naturally. Then there's the claw-foot tub, the fluffy towels, the designer toiletries, the chocolates—"

"Stop!" I broke in, smiling. "Don't spoil the surprises!"

"I'll make an online reservation tonight," said Bill, "and I'll speak with Father in the morning. He and Amelia having been champing at the bit to have the children all to themselves for a few days."

"We'll be lucky if they give them back," I said.

"We won't have to worry about Stanley, either," said Bill. "Amelia likes looking after him."

"Amelia spoils him rotten," I said. "He'll feast on salmon, tuna, and minced shrimp while we're gone and go into mourning when we get back. But he'll get over it. He always does."

"We'll take my Mercedes instead of your Range Rover," Bill proposed. "It'll make a nice change for you to travel in a car that isn't equipped with child safety seats."

"Or littered with dinosaurs, cricket bats, and sippy cups," I added. "Good thinking."

"The weather may not be optimal during our getaway," Bill cautioned. "It may be a bit drizzly in Rye."

"If we were afraid of rain, we wouldn't live in England," I reminded him. "And if the weather's too miserable, we'll light a fire in the hearth, curl up in our four-poster, and—"

"Stop," Bill interrupted, nuzzling my neck. "Don't spoil the surprises."

There was a brief intermission during which my gray mood lifted considerably.

When we were able to talk again, Bill's brow furrowed slightly.

"There's only one catch," he said.

"I knew it," I said as my murky mood threatened to return. "I knew there'd be a catch."

"It's a tiny catch," he assured me, "and it has to do with my client."

"Your client?" I said, baffled. "The client you're seeing on Thursday?"

"That's the one," Bill confirmed. "His name is Sir Roger Blayne and he lives in an Elizabethan manor house called Blayne Hall."

"I don't see the catch," I said.

"The catch is that he's a recluse—a serious recluse," Bill explained. "The first time I met with Sir Roger, Father had to come with me to vouch for my identity."

"Charming," I said.

"Our relationship has progressed by leaps and bounds since then," Bill assured me. "Instead of regarding me with distaste, Sir Roger tolerates me."

"Fairly small leaps and bounds, then," I observed drily.

"My point is that Sir Roger sees no one but his physicians, his attorneys, and a handful of faithful retainers," said Bill. "Since you don't fall into any of those categories, I doubt that he'll let you into Blayne Hall."

"I'll wait for you in the car," I suggested.

"I have a better idea," Bill said. "You can drop me off on Sir Roger's doorstep, drive to Rye, check into The Mermaid Inn, and enjoy a long, lazy bubble bath in your claw-foot tub. When I'm done with Sir Roger, his chauffeur can drive me to Rye."

"How far is it from Blayne Hall to Rye?" I queried. I wasn't wildly enthused about driving in the south of England, where the roads tended to resemble green trenches.

"No more than ten miles," Bill replied, "and the route is well signposted."

"Ten miles on well-marked roads?" I said. "That's hardly a catch at all." I snuggled closer to my husband. "I haven't taken a proper bubble bath since Bess was born."

"I may join you in it," he warned.

"I'll keep the water hot for you," I purred.

"Hold that thought," he said. "I have to make a reservation!"

As he rolled out of bed and reached for his laptop, I wrapped my arms around his pillow and heaved a blissful sigh. The elation I felt at the mere thought of running away from home told me that Bill's diagnosis was correct: I was badly in need of a break. I loved Finch dearly, but a change of scene would do me a world of good, especially when the scene encompassed bubble baths, seaside strolls, and a four-poster bed in a romantic inn.

"Who cares if it rains?" I murmured sleepily.

As it turned out, I would.

Two

*E*verything went according to Bill's cunning plan. He and I cleared our schedules, delivered the children to their delighted grandparents after school on Wednesday, and headed south early on Thursday morning. I had surprisingly little difficulty delegating my various duties. My in-laws, friends, neighbors, and fellow volunteers were so eager to see the back of me that I began to suspect that they, too, had noted my need for a holiday.

October's changeable weather compelled me to overpack. By the time I closed my suitcase, I was prepared for just about anything the sky could throw at me, though I was fairly confident that I could rule out a major blizzard.

Bill allowed himself a self-satisfied smirk as he compared his modest overnight bag to my bulging suitcase, but I didn't envy him. While he had to wear a suit and tie to his business meeting, I could travel more comfortably in a whisper-soft cashmere pullover, loose-fitting wool trousers, and buttery leather ankle boots. We both tossed our rain jackets onto the Mercedes' backseat, having learned through soggy experience always to have them within reach.

Since Bill wasn't due to meet with Sir Roger Blayne until midafternoon, we took our time driving south. We had breakfast at our favorite café in Moreton-in-Marsh and rummaged through a secondhand-book store in Woodstock before hopping onto a busy dual carriageway ("highway," in American) that made relatively short work of London's far-flung suburbs.

As soon as we broke free from London's grasp, we resumed our unhurried pace. A series of scenic byways took us past orchards and vineyards, thatched cottages and rambling farmsteads, a few castles and a great many stately homes. By mutual agreement, I quelled the urge to check in with Willis, Sr., every fifteen minutes, and Bill resisted the temptation to touch base with his firm.

It felt positively luxurious to travel in a clean, uncluttered car—no teething rings, no science projects, no long-forgotten juice boxes—but the farther south we drove, the darker and more threatening the sky became. We were enjoying a leisurely lunch at a picturesque riverside pub when the heavens finally opened.

"A bit drizzly?" I said, eyeing the downpour. "Even the swans are running for cover."

"If we were afraid of rain . . . ," Bill intoned.

"We wouldn't live in England," I finished for him. I smiled wryly, then leaned closer to the window beside our table. "Does the river look high to you? Those willows have their toes in the water."

"It does look as if it might be rising," Bill agreed. "Maybe we should take off before the parking lot turns into a lake."

We finished our hazelnut tarts with regrettable speed, paid for our meal, pulled on our jackets, and made a splashy dash for the Mercedes. Once we were on our way, Bill turned up the heat to dry our damp trousers, and I surveyed the countryside through windows streaming with rain.

The foul weather accompanied us all the way to Blayne Hall. The wind snatched at Bill's jacket when he got out of the car, and a spray of raindrops smacked me in the face before he could shut his door.

To keep the rest of me dry, I clambered over the gearshift lever to take his place behind the wheel.

I could tell that my husband was having second thoughts about my solo journey to Rye, and I was having a few of my own, but we kept them to ourselves. Bill had criticized my driving skills once too often for me to accept a sensible suggestion from him to stay put, and I would have eaten raw liver before I admitted to him that I was cowed by the storm.

"I'll call you as soon as I get to The Mermaid Inn," I shouted to Bill through my closed window.

"I'll see you there," he shouted back. "Keep the bathwater warm for me!"

I gave him a cheerful thumbs-up that did not accurately reflect my state of mind.

A faithful retainer emerged from Blayne Hall armed with an enormous black umbrella that immediately blew inside out. Seemingly unfazed by the mishap, he bowed formally to Bill before escorting him into the manor house. I felt slightly bereft as the unflappable servant with the flapping umbrella closed the door behind my husband, but I gathered my courage, turned the car around, and drove back through the puddles pooling in Sir Roger's graveled drive.

When I came to the end of the drive, I hesitated. Bill had explained to me that a right turn would take me to what passed for a major road in East Sussex, while a left turn would keep me on smaller back lanes. To avoid the weather-related traffic jams that were sure to clog the bigger and busier road, I turned left.

The optimist in me believed that the storm wouldn't get worse. The pessimist in me chuckled mirthlessly when it did.

I'd driven no more than five miles when the rain, which had been falling steadily, began to come down in buckets. The drainage ditches on either side of the lane were soon filled to the brim, and though my windshield wipers worked overtime, I could scarcely see roadside signs, much less read them.

The storm didn't deafen me with thunder or blind me with lightning, but I was concerned that it might try to drown me. Whenever I dared to look up from the road, I saw ponds forming in freshly harvested fields, sheep seeking higher ground in waterlogged pastures, and trees flailing wildly in the wind. Gusts battered the car so mercilessly that I had to slow to a crawl while maintaining a white-knuckled grip on the steering wheel.

I began to get seriously nervous when I stopped on a bridge to observe a river that ran through a level stretch of farmland at the base of a broad, flat-topped hill. The raging torrent had not yet burst its banks, but it looked angry enough to smash the bridge to pieces. When six cars crept past me and turned onto a lane that appeared to climb the hill, I followed their taillights. I didn't know where I was going, but it seemed like a good idea to go up.

The mystery lane ascended the hill until it reached the top, where it became a cobbled high street that split a village in two. Knots of scurrying pedestrians brought the vehicles ahead of me to a standstill, so I turned in the direction of a church tower I spotted a short distance away down a side street. After my nerve-racking drive I wanted nothing more than to ride out the storm in a sturdy building.

"Sanctuary," I said under my breath as the church proper came into view. I parked the Mercedes on the grassy verge beside the churchyard wall, switched off the engine, and bellowed a brief but potent prayer of thanksgiving for my safe deliverance. All wasn't exactly right with the world, but it was better than it had been before I'd climbed the hill.

I was about to release my seat belt when my cell phone rang. I pulled the phone out of my shoulder bag, thankful that a call hadn't distracted me while I was wrestling with the steering wheel. I was entirely unsurprised to see Bill's name on the phone's little screen.

"I'm okay, Bill," I said, preempting what I knew would be his first and most urgent question. "I got off the road about five minutes ago. I'm not sure where I am, but I'm about to enter a church in a hilltop village, so I should continue to be okay. Do you know what the heck's going on with the weather?"

"I do," he replied, "and it's not good. According to Sir Roger, an extratropical cyclone is skirting the south coast."

"What's an extratropical cyclone?" I asked.

"Think of it as a hurricane," said Bill. "Blayne Hall is under its outermost bands, but you're closer to the core. If the storm keeps moving, you should be all right. If it stalls, things could get tricky."

"Lucky me," I said. "I guess we should've checked the weather forecast before we left home, huh?"

"We will next time," he said grimly. "Are you sure you're okay?"

"I'll be better when I'm inside the church," I said. "The wind is rocking the car a little."

"I'm coming to get you," he said.

I glanced at the rain and thought fast. I had no intention of allowing my knight in shining armor to ride to my rescue through an extratropical cyclone.

"How?" I demanded. "You don't know where I am. Even if I could give you my precise location, you wouldn't have to come and get me, because I really am okay."

"Lori—" he began, but I cut him off.

"I'm fine, Bill," I insisted. "I'm not floating in a life raft in the middle of the ocean. I'm in a village with shops and houses and at least one church. If I need help, I won't have to send up a flare. I can just knock on a door."

"All right," he said reluctantly, "I'll sit tight for now. But call me as soon as you figure out where you are."

"I will," I promised. "In the meantime, ask Sir Roger to pour you a large whiskey. You need something to steady your nerves."

Bill gave a grudging chuckle and we ended the call.

I sank back in the driver's seat, feeling as if I'd dodged a bullet. I couldn't blame Bill for worrying about me, but the thought of him losing his life in a needless bid to save mine was too terrible to contemplate.

The car shuddered again, so I set the emergency brake, released my seat belt, returned the phone to my shoulder bag, and flexed my tired fingers while I braced myself for the race to the church. It was only then that I noticed a large, hand-painted sign fixed to the churchyard wall almost at eye level.

The sign informed me that I'd arrived at the parish church of St. Alfege, where an exhibition of ecclesiastical needlework was currently on display. I was glad I hadn't seen the sign sooner. I had no idea who St. Alfege was, but I doubted that many churches were named after him. If honesty had compelled me to reveal the church's unusual name to Bill, he would have figured out where I was and come running after me, which was exactly what I didn't want him to do.

The car rocked again and a flurry of raindrops pelted the windscreen. I needed no further inducement to zip up my jacket, pull up my hood, pick up my shoulder bag, and sprint up the path that led to the church's south porch.

The first blast of wet, cold air took my breath away. On top of everything else, the temperature had dropped by a good twenty degrees since our leisurely lunch by the riverside. My decision to wear wool and cashmere suddenly seemed prescient, but the big chill made me wish that I'd worn woolen mittens as well.

I could tell at a glance that St. Alfege's was a very old church. It was short and squat and built of flint rubble masonry with gray limestone dressing. Its roof was clad in overlapping red clay tiles, all of which seemed to be holding their own against the wind, and the stumpy square bell tower reminded me so strongly of St. George's that a wave of homesickness swept over me as I splashed past it. I didn't think St. Alfege's was as beautiful as St. George's—I preferred Cotswold stone to flint rubble—but I had to admit that no church would look its best in the pouring rain.

I crossed the porch gingerly to keep myself from slipping on its wet flagstones, turned the handle on a stout oak door, and staggered into the church. A voluminous sigh of relief escaped me as I pushed the door shut behind me. Though I could still hear the roaring wind and the pounding rain, the wind's roar was muted and the rain was no longer pounding on my head.

I shook myself like a damp puppy, pushed my hood back, and looked around, but I couldn't see very much. Since the sun was unable to show its face, St. Alfege's was illuminated only by the red altar lamp and the flickering flames of a few votive candles set in a wrought-iron candle stand at the far end of the south aisle.

The nave was furnished with laminated wood chairs instead of pews, which, to my eye, detracted somewhat from the timeless beauty of the round Norman arches that separated it from the side aisles. I reckoned that a door on my left was the entrance to the bell tower, but the rest of the church was so shrouded in shadows that it would have been spooky if it hadn't felt so reassuringly solid.

"It'll take more than a cyclone to uproot you from your hill," I said aloud to the sturdy old building.

"It certainly will," said a voice.

That's when things got a bit spooky.

Three

My heart, which hadn't yet recovered from the strain of driving smack dab into a monster storm, nearly jumped out of my chest.

"H-hello?" I faltered, peering into the gloom. "Is . . . is someone there?"

A disembodied head appeared in the wavering light shed by the votive candles.

I gasped and fell back a step, wondering if St. Alfege was the patron saint of horror films, but as the head began to float toward me, I saw that it was firmly attached to the body of a man whose attire made him seem vaguely menacing.

He was dressed all in black—black overcoat, black scarf, black trousers, and thick-soled black brogues—and he clasped a black homburg hat to his chest with black-gloved hands. The gloves struck me as particularly sinister, and though I couldn't hear his footsteps, I could imagine them echoing ominously in the shadows.

Nothing, not even a black-clad stranger with sinister gloves, could have frightened me into abandoning my safe haven. I readied myself to clobber him with my shoulder bag, but when he finally came within clobbering distance, I relaxed. The man was no more menacing than a day-old chick.

He was only a few inches taller than I was—and I wasn't known for my height. He was slightly built, too, and his clothes, while plain, were well tailored. He had wispy white hair, a round, kindly face, and gentle gray eyes that gazed apologetically at me through small, rimless spectacles. Up close, he looked more like a leprechaun than a slasher.

"Forgive me," he said. "I didn't mean to startle you."

"It's not your fault," I responded, thinking that Bill wasn't the only one with unsteady nerves. "I was a little jumpy to begin with. It's quite a storm out there."

"A storm of biblical proportions, I fear," he remarked.

"I hope not," I said. "I forgot to pack my ark."

Smiling, he said, "You're unlikely to need an ark if you're staying in Shepney."

"Shepney?" I said. "Is that where I am?"

"Yes, of course," he replied, looking politely perplexed. "Where did you think you were?"

"I hadn't the vaguest idea," I said. "I was on my way to Rye when the storm exploded."

"It must have been a frightful ordeal," he said, his brow wrinkling sympathetically. He gestured toward the row of chairs nearest to us. "Would you care to sit down?"

"I'd probably be better off sitting than standing," I admitted. "I don't mean to be melodramatic, but my legs are shaking."

"You're not being melodramatic," he asserted. "You're experiencing a natural reaction to a stressful situation." He then demonstrated his good manners by waiting until I was seated to sit beside me.

"I can testify to the stress," I told him. "I've never gone over Niagara Falls in a barrel, but I'm pretty sure I know what it feels like. I had to grip the steering wheel so hard that my hands began to get numb, so I followed some cars up a hill and took refuge in the first church I saw."

"A wise decision," he said, nodding. "I suspect that St. Alfege's has shrugged off hundreds, if not thousands, of storms. I'm confident that it will survive this one as well." He placed his hat on his lap and sighed. "England's weather used to be fairly predictable, with a few extremes. Nowadays it seems to be entirely unpredictable and frequently extreme."

"Are cyclones common around here?" I asked, eyeing him incredulously.

"They're becoming more so," he replied.

"Remind me not to buy a vacation home in East Sussex," I said, shaking my head.

"East Sussex has many charms," he assured me. "I hope you'll return one day, when the weather is less discouraging. I believe you said you were on your way to Rye?"

"My husband will be joining me there this evening," I confirmed. "I should probably call him. I didn't know were I was before, but now that I do, I should let him know."

"Shall I make myself scarce?" he asked.

"Please don't," I said, reaching for my cell phone. "My husband's a worrier. I may need you to back me up when I tell him I'm okay."

Bill answered on the first ring, as if he'd been waiting impatiently for my call.

"Where are you?" he asked without preamble.

"I'm in St. Alfege's Church in the East Sussex village of Shepney," I replied.

"Shepney," he repeated, evidently for Sir Roger's benefit, because there was a short pause before he continued, "Sir Roger informs me that you're about three miles from Rye."

"Good," I said. "I thought I was farther away than that, but three miles is doable, even in the dark. As soon as the storm lets up, I'll hit the road again. In the meantime, there's no need to worry about me. I'm high and dry and I've made a new acquaintance, so I'm not alone. If you don't believe me, I can pass the phone to him."

"I believe you," said Bill. "But no heroics, Lori. Get a room in Shepney if you have to. I can meet you in Rye tomorrow."

"I'll let you know what happens, either way," I promised.

He groaned. "This isn't the romantic getaway we planned, is it, love?"

"You'd better cut back on the whiskey," I said. "It's making you maudlin. Never say die, my dearest. I'll see you in Rye!" I dropped the phone in my shoulder bag, looked ruefully at my companion, and said, "If you want to make God laugh, make plans."

"At least God has a sense of humor," he said. "I'm sure your plans will come right in the end. Do you visit Rye often?"

"I've never been there before," I said.

"If you haven't yet booked a hotel," he said, "I can recommend The Mermaid Inn."

"That's where we're staying," I said happily.

"An excellent choice," he said. "I stayed there many years ago, and I can't praise it too highly. The building is a warren of—"

"Don't tell me!" I cried. I flinched as my words echoed raucously through the church, and immediately lowered my voice. "Sorry, but I'd like to discover the warren for myself."

"You won't be disappointed," he promised. "You must permit me to give you one tip, however. If the chef still has the recipe for celeriac cream soup, ask him to make it for you." He sighed reminiscently. "Once tasted, never forgotten."

"I'll put celeriac cream soup at the top of my wish list," I said.

"Rye is a fascinating town," he went on. "Admittedly, it's too popular for its own good during the summer months, but the crowds will have thinned by now. Are you fond of old churches?"

"Very," I said.

"Then you must visit St. Mary's in Rye," he said with quiet enthusiasm. "It has one of the oldest functioning turret clocks in England. If you climb up to the bell chamber, you'll see the midsixteenth-century mechanism behind the clock face. If you climb higher still, you'll find yourself out of doors, peering over a parapet at the very top of the bell tower. The views are splendid, but you might wish to wait for a fine day to take them in."

"I wouldn't see a whole lot on a day like today," I agreed.

"I seem to recall a rather handsome church cat as well," he said reflectively, "though it's been such a long time since I made his acquaintance that he may have gone to meet his Maker by now."

"If he has, I'll keep an eye out for one of his handsome descendants," I said. "St. Mary's sounds brilliant. It'll be the first place we visit in Rye, after we finish exploring The Mermaid Inn."

"The church in Winchelsea is remarkable, too," he said. "The stone effigies are so delicately carved that they seem to breathe. And Winchelsea is only a short drive from Rye."

"I'm making mental notes as you speak," I told him.

"I'm speaking too much, aren't I?" he said with a self-conscious grimace.

"Not at all," I said. "Even if you were boring me senseless, which you're not, I'd be grateful for the distraction. Thanks to you, I'm thinking about handsome church cats instead of my close encounter with an extratropical cyclone."

"You're too kind." He removed one of his black gloves and extended his hand. "My name is Wyndham, by the way. Christopher Wyndham."

"I'm pleased to meet you, Mr. Wyndham," I said, "but if I were you, I wouldn't shake my hand. It's as cold as a dead fish."

"Here, take my gloves." He began at once to remove the other glove.

"I can't take your gloves," I protested.

"Of course you can," he said, thrusting them at me. "I was going to put them in my pocket anyway. My hands are overheating."

I didn't believe him, but I accepted the chivalrous gesture to avoid hurting his feelings. I was amply rewarded by the warmth that enveloped my frigid fingers as I pulled on the preheated gloves. How I ever could have regarded them as sinister was beyond me.

"Thank you," I said. "My pinkies are dancing for joy, or they will be as soon as they thaw. I'm Lori Shepherd, Mr. Wyndham, but everyone calls me Lori."

"Then you must call me Christopher. Forgive my curiosity, Lori," he continued, "but are you from the United States? Your use of the phrase 'vacation home' suggests that you are, as does your accent."

"Your ears do not deceive you, Christopher," I said. "I was born and raised in Chicago, and my husband is from Boston, but we've lived in England for quite a long time."

"In London?" he inquired, as if he couldn't conceive of an American living anywhere else in England.

"No," I said. "We live in a cottage near a very small village in the Cotswolds. We're raising our children there—twin boys and a baby girl."

"How old are your children?" he asked.

"Will and Rob will turn eleven in March," I told him, "and Bess will turn two in February. She was a bit of a surprise."

"A pleasant one, I'm sure," he said. "How fortunate Will, Rob, and Bess are to grow up in such bucolic surroundings. I live in Winchester. It's a splendid town, but I do enjoy my escapes to the country."

"Was St. Alfege's a port in the storm for you, too, Christopher?" I asked. "Or were you lured here by the needlework exhibition?"

"I came to Shepney to visit St. Alfege's," he replied. "Like you, I'm fond of old churches. The exhibition would have been an added bonus if someone had left the lights on. Unfortunately"—he peered fruitlessly toward a cluster of nebulous shapes in the north aisle—"no one did."

"Not a problem." I reached into my trouser pocket and withdrew a key chain from which dangled a whistle, a miniature Swiss Army knife, and a small but powerful flashlight.

"My word," said Christopher when I held the key chain up for his inspection. "You must have been an exemplary Girl Guide."

"I call it my earthquake survival kit," I said, lowering the key chain. "I put it together after a quake rattled me in New Zealand, and I never travel without it. It won't keep me from being buried in rubble, but it just might help me to get unburied."

"Have you ever had to summon help with the whistle?" Christopher asked interestedly.

"Not yet," I said, "but I use the knife and the flashlight all the time."

"I, too, travel with a torch," he said, "but I foolishly left mine in my hotel room. Are you a needlework aficionado?"

"I am," I said. "A little old lady in my village makes the most exquisite quilts. I never get tired of looking at them. I'm not much of a quilter, but I used to know my way around an embroidery hoop."

"Used to?" he queried.

"I put my needles away when the twins were born," I explained. "I found it too easy to picture Will and Rob with identical puncture wounds." I turned on the flashlight and stood. "My hands are toasty, my legs have stopped shaking, and we have a light source, Christopher. Shall we feast our eyes on the exhibition?"

"We shall," he said, getting to his feet. "Follow me."

The nebulous shapes in the north aisle turned out to be upright, glass-fronted display cases. The first one we reached held a nineteenth-century altar cloth richly embroidered in metallic threads. The threads glittered spectacularly in my flashlight's bright beam.

"Wow," I said in an awed whisper. "Just look at those stitches. They're *perfect*, and you can take it from me that metallic thread is a pain in the neck to work with. It ties itself into knots if you so much as look at it the wrong way." I shook my head. "Whoever embroidered this masterpiece must have had the patience of a saint."

"I find that craftsmen and craftswomen often do their finest work for their places of worship," said Christopher. "To embellish an altar cloth is a form of prayer for such people. I have no doubt that they derive personal satisfaction from creating beautiful objects, but I believe that their ultimate goal is to glorify God."

"It must be," I said. "No one would work that hard for a lousy paycheck." I stepped forward to examine the altar cloth more closely. "Though I suppose some of them just liked to show off. If I could handle metallic threads as skillfully as the woman who praised God with those stitches, I'd have to confess to the sin of pride once a day and twice on Sundays, or risk going straight to hell."

Christopher's robust chuckle sent another round of echoes through the church. He stifled his mirth, then said in a voice still quavering with laughter, "I'm sure your honesty would guarantee your entrance to heaven, Lori."

"Now who's being too kind?" I retorted.

We gazed at the glittering altar cloth for several minutes, then moved to the next display case. It held a kneeler cross-stitched with an apple tree occupied by a red-eyed serpent and flanked by Adam and Eve, whose hands and arms were strategically placed to conceal their respective genders. Though the kneeler was worn and faded, the cross-stitched image was so well executed that I was glad to see it under glass instead of under imminent threat of being squashed by a churchgoer's knees.

"What a treasure," Christopher murmured.

"It doesn't have to glitter to be gold," I agreed.

We were about to move on to the third display case when a siren's wail sounded overhead. As we wheeled around in alarm, every light in the church came on, a door near the altar banged open, and a boy in a bright yellow slicker dashed down the center aisle.

A man in a matching slicker strode after the boy, calling, "Be careful on the stairs, Trevor! You know how uneven they are, and they may be wet!"

The boy disappeared through the door to the bell tower, but the man stopped halfway down the center aisle to wipe rain from his face.

A moment later, a bell began to toll frantically.

"Oh, dear," said Christopher, gazing upward. "I believe there may be a problem."

Four

turned off my flashlight and returned the key chain to my pocket, wondering if the man in the yellow slicker was a rector, a vicar, a verger, or a sexton. He couldn't be a casual passerby, I reasoned, because a casual passerby wouldn't have access to the church's light switches or know about the bell tower's uneven stairs.

The man was tall and slender and several decades younger than Christopher. When he lowered his hood, I saw that he had close-cropped brown hair and a lean, clean-shaven face.

"Good afternoon, Phillip," Christopher called above the combined clamor of the wailing siren and the tolling bell. "Is there something going on that we should know about?"

The young man stiffened, then swung around to face us, looking thunderstruck.

"B-Bishop Wyndham?" he stammered. He opened his mouth, then closed it and sidled hastily toward us between two rows of chairs.

"Bishop?" I said, with a questioning look at my fellow needlework enthusiast.

"Retired," Christopher said quietly. "I try to keep a low profile. If I don't, conscientious young clerics like Phillip think they're on parade."

The conscientious young cleric finished his sideways shuffle and stood staring, dumbfounded, at my new friend, the bishop.

"Lori Shepherd," said Christopher, "please allow me to introduce you to Phillip Lawson, the rector of St. Alfege's and the energetic lead minister in a team ministry that serves three other parishes. Like you, Phillip prefers to be addressed by his Christian name. Phillip, may I present Lori Shepherd? Lori was on her way to Rye when the storm forced her to seek refuge in your church."

The rector glanced at me distractedly, saying, "I'm pleased to meet you, Miss, er, Mrs.——"

"Lori," I put in. "Just Lori."

"Lori," he said before turning to the bishop. "Forgive me, Bishop Wyndham. If I'd known you were coming to Shepney, I would have——"

"You would have made a fuss," Christopher interrupted. "I'm not terribly fond of fusses, Phillip, but I had every intention of looking in on you and your delightful family after evensong. I believe I saw your son Trevor run past us a moment ago. My goodness, Trevor must be"—he paused to consider—"ten years old by now?"

"What a remarkable memory you have, Bishop Wyndham," said Phillip. "Trevor turned ten in April. As my eldest, he has the privilege of ringing the alarm bell, and he guards his privilege jealously." He grinned. "It's the only time he's allowed to run in church."

"May I ask why Trevor is ringing the alarm bell?" Christopher asked.

"It's a village tradition," the rector explained. "In Shepney, a church bell has always been rung in times of crisis. We installed the siren two years ago, but it hasn't gone down well with some of the older members of our congregation. They claim that they hear the bell more clearly than the siren. I'm not quite sure I believe them, but it's better to be safe than sorry. Apart from that, ringing the alarm bell gives Trevor a sense of civic responsibility, which is never a bad thing."

"No indeed," said Christopher. "But why, my dear fellow, is Trevor ringing the alarm bell *now*?" He glanced at the raftered ceiling. "I presume it has something to do with the weather."

"It has everything to do with the weather," Phillip said. "We've had two major storms since August, and rain almost every day in between. The same thing happened last year and the year before, so we know what to expect. It's the result of climate change, of course. All over the world, hundred-year floods have become annual events."

"And in this little corner of the world . . . ?" the bishop prompted.

"The wind should ease off by midnight," said Phillip, "but the ground is already saturated, the river is rising rapidly, and the flood defenses are holding on by a thread. Even as we speak, families from outlying farms and hamlets are evacuating to Shepney." He looked at his wristwatch and asked, "Would you excuse me for a moment?" Without waiting for a reply, he jogged over to the bell tower, leaned through the open door, and bellowed, "That's enough, Trevor! You can come down now!" When the bell continued to ring, he roared, "Privileges can be revoked, Trevor! Come down this instant! *Carefully!*"

The bell rang once more, then fell silent. A few minutes later, the boy joined his father at the bottom of the stairs and they both made their way down the north aisle to the spot where the bishop and I stood. Unsurprisingly, Trevor was tall for his age, brown-haired, and as lanky as his father.

"Hello, Trevor," said Christopher. "I don't know if you remember me, but—"

"You're Bishop Wyndham," Trevor broke in eagerly. "You told me the story about the executioner whose eyeballs popped out when he beheaded St. Alban."

It was a story that would have delighted my bloodthirsty sons. Bishop Wyndham, I decided, was a man who knew his audience.

"This is my friend Lori," Christopher said, tilting his head toward me.

"Pleased to meet you," Trevor mumbled, making it transparently clear that an unknown woman couldn't compete with a bishop who told thrilling tales about headless saints and eyeless executioners. Having observed the niceties, the boy looked up at his father and asked, "Where is everyone, Dad? They should be here by now, shouldn't they?"

"They'll be here shortly," Phillip assured him. "Why don't you keep a lookout for them? They'll come through the south porch." As Trevor left the north aisle to man his post, the rector asked, "Where are you staying, Bishop Wyndham?"

"I have a room at the inn," Christopher replied.

"I suggest you return there immediately," said Phillip. "We've developed an emergency plan, you see. The Hancocks will want to do a head count of their guests. Once they add you to the count, you'll be asked to shelter in place until we sound the all-clear."

"They're here, Dad!" Trevor yelled.

His announcement was still rebounding from the rafters when six men in dripping rain suits entered the church through the same door I'd used. They exchanged bellowed greetings with the rector as they and Trevor began methodically to remove the chairs from the nave and to stack them neatly in the south aisle.

"Part of the emergency plan?" Christopher queried.

Phillip nodded. "The church will be used to store fodder for the farm animals—pigs, chickens, goats, cows, horses, and so on. They're being evacuated to Shepney as well, and it's essential to keep their feed dry."

As if on cue, more men began to stream into St. Alfege's from the south porch. Some were carrying grain sacks on their shoulders while others pushed wheelbarrows filled with flakes of alfalfa hay tightly covered with clear plastic sheeting. It looked as though they'd rehearsed the drill many times, because they moved without hesitation or collision to drop different types of feed in different quadrants of the church before departing to pick up further loads.

"The first two rows of chairs will be left in place for those who wish to attend services," Phillip continued conscientiously, "though I doubt that many will. It's safer for everyone to shelter in place until the worst of the storm has passed." He turned to me. "Are you staying at the inn as well, Lori?"

"I'm not staying anywhere," I replied in a feeble attempt to defy fate. "I'm on my way to Rye."

The rector took a deep breath before saying gently, "I'm sorry, Lori, but there isn't the remotest chance that you'll make it to Rye today. Please believe me when I tell you that it would be dangerous to try. You could lose your life." He shook his head. "I'm afraid you have no choice but to stay here."

"Where?" I said, bewildered. "The inn?"

Christopher shook his head. "It was fully booked when I checked in earlier today."

"There's no room for me at the inn," I murmured, feeling as though I'd stumbled into a rain-drenched Nativity play.

"Can you put Lori up at the rectory, Phillip?" Christopher asked.

"I wish I could, Bishop Wyndham, but I can't," Phillip said regretfully. "It's the emergency plan, you see. Every spare bed in Shepney has already been allocated, either to farming families or to people who work here but live elsewhere. My wife and I are hosting the Bakers—parents, grandparents, four children, two Labradors, and a cockatoo—and as you know, we have three children of our own. I'm truly sorry, but the rectory is full up."

"The emergency plan must include accommodations for visitors like Lori, who were merely passing through," said Christopher.

"It does," said the rector, "but I checked in at the village hall—our emergency headquarters—before I came here. As luck would have it, a rather large tour group from France descended on Shepney today. Their coach should have left by noon, but for some reason their departure was delayed. They've taken the beds reserved for stranded visitors at the inn."

"A camp bed in the vestry, perhaps?" Christopher suggested.

"The vestry's reserved for Joe Turner and his terriers," Phillip replied. "Once we've filled the church with feed, Joe's terriers will perform an essential service. Without them, St. Alfege's would be overrun by rodents."

I glanced squeamishly at the church's unlit corners and said, "Not a problem, Phillip. I brought warm clothes with me. I can bundle up and sleep in my car."

Phillip looked crestfallen, but Christopher wasn't ready to throw in the towel just yet.

"Come with me to the inn, Lori," he said. "Under the circumstances, I'm sure the Hancocks will allow you to stay in one of their public parlors. You'll be safer and more comfortable there than you would be in your car."

"It's worth a try," Phillip said encouragingly.

"I'm game," I said, "but my husband will want to know where I am. What's the inn called?"

"If all goes well," the bishop replied, "you'll be spending the night at The King's Ransom."

I smiled wryly. At that moment I would have given a king's ransom to be sitting quietly before the fire in my room at The Mermaid Inn.

Five

The rector wished me luck, bade the bishop a respectful farewell, and hurried off to stack chairs with his son. I pulled up the hood on my rain jacket and cinched it securely under my chin. Christopher donned his hat and wrapped his wool scarf more snugly around his neck. Though I tried to return his gloves, he wouldn't hear of it.

"I may be old, but I'm not frail," he declared. "And we don't have far to go."

We waited for a gap in the line of fodder toters filing into St. Alfege's, then made our way through the south porch and into the churchyard. I felt even guiltier about the glove situation when Christopher had to clap a bare hand to his hat to keep it from flying away in the swirling wind.

I clapped my hands to my ears. The siren's wail, which had been muted by the church's thick walls, was almost deafening in the churchyard. The wind was howling louder than ever and the driving rain only made matters worse. I had to tug on Christopher's sleeve to draw his attention to Bill's Mercedes, which was blocked on three sides by pickup trucks loaded with animal grub, and on the fourth by the churchyard wall.

"It's just as well we don't have far to go," I shouted. "Unless you can levitate my car, we'll have to walk."

"I leave levitation to a higher power," Christopher bellowed merrily, pointing heavenward. "But never mind. I suspect that a car would be a liability during the current crisis. The high street will no doubt be congested and the car park at The King's Ransom will almost certainly be full." He patted my arm. "Best to leave your car where it is for the time being, Lori. We'll stop to fetch your luggage, then be on our way."

"My luggage," I said hollowly, recalling the all-season wardrobe I'd brought with me and wishing I'd left half of it at home. Though my wheeled suitcase functioned well in airports, I wasn't sure how it would behave on cobbles, especially when it was overloaded. If Christopher hadn't been standing beside me when I opened the Mercedes' trunk, I would have transferred some of my clothing to Bill's overnight bag, but I'd packed a few lacy garments I was reluctant to reveal to a bishop.

"Allow me," he said, reaching for the suitcase with a hand that had turned lobster pink.

"Thanks, Christopher, but I can manage," I said. "I may be a woman, but I'm not a weakling."

I hauled the suitcase out of the trunk before he could get a grip on it, locked the Mercedes, slung my shoulder bag across my body, and leaned into the wind as we walked side by side up the cobbled lane, with the suitcase thudding resentfully behind me.

"So," I said, "you're a bishop."

"A retired bishop," Christopher reiterated. "A retired *suffragan* bishop."

"Suffragan?" I queried.

"I was a mere assistant to the diocesan bishop," he said, "which makes me very small potatoes indeed."

"The rector seems to think otherwise," I said.

"I recommended Phillip for his present position," Christopher explained. "I've always thought very highly of him."

"The feelings are clearly mutual," I observed.

"Phillip has a generous heart," said Christopher.

"He must have," I said. "Only a man with a generous heart would open his home to four adults, four children, two dogs, and a cockatoo. Can you imagine the noise?"

"It will no doubt rival the storm's," said Christopher, chuckling.

I had to walk attentively to avoid twisting an ankle. Though the high street's cobbles were relatively smooth, the side street was paved with irregular rows of vicious, pointy stones made even more treacherous by the pouring rain. The lane's only redeeming feature was that it, like the high street, was level.

"Thank heaven for flat-topped hills," I said, with a meaningful glance at the cobbles.

"Amen," said Christopher. "Shepney sits upon the remnant of what was once a prominent limestone ridge. Eons of erosion reduced the ridge to a relatively modest bump in the landscape."

"A useful bump," I said, "especially during flood season."

"Indeed," he agreed. "It offers wonderful views as well. No place in England is more than forty-five miles from the sea, and Shepney is a good deal closer. On a clear day, one can see the French coastline from St. Alfege's bell tower."

"I'll have to come back on a clear day," I said.

My suitcase's wheels survived the tortuous journey up the lane, but I could almost hear them groan with relief when we turned onto the high street's broad sidewalk. My ankles survived as well, but I made a mental note to change into my hiking boots before I returned to Bill's car.

As Christopher had predicted, the high street was congested, but it wasn't chaotic. Small herds of livestock and a handful of horseback riders mingled with cars, vans, and trucks in a complex ballet directed by traffic monitors who waved long-nosed orange flashlights and wore high-visibility rain gear.

The sidewalks, too, were bustling with purposeful activity. Groups of men and women were clearing away objects the storm might turn into missiles—flowerpots, hanging signs, sandwich boards, café tables and chairs—while across the street a human chain transported boxes, bags, and bottled water from idling vehicles into a large redbrick building with a gabled roof.

"The village hall," Christopher explained, following my gaze.

"Cyclone HQ," I said, nodding. "The emergency operation seems to be very well organized."

"After enduring two major floods in two years, the villagers must have the drill down pat," said Christopher.

"Practice, practice, practice," I murmured.

Conditions weren't optimal for sightseeing, but even through the pounding rain I could tell that Shepney's high street featured a smorgasbord of architectural styles. As we walked along I spotted Tudor, Georgian, and Victorian buildings as well as a few plain-faced modern ones. Similarly, its shops were a mixture of the touristy and the practical. In one short stretch we passed a hardware store, an accountant's office, a bookstore, an eye-catching candy shop, and a shop laden with souvenirs.

"We're almost there," said Christopher. "I think you'll like The King's Ransom, Lori. It isn't as sophisticated as The Mermaid Inn, but it's every bit as interesting. It began life as a medieval alehouse.

It's gone through several rebuilds since then, but its basic structure hasn't changed since Tudor times."

"I hope it has twenty-first-century plumbing," I said.

"I doubt that it would attract many guests if it were still equipped with chamber pots," Christopher observed drily. He stopped before a building that looked as though it had come straight out of a fairy tale. "Here we are, Lori. First impressions?"

The wind's howl seemed to fade into the distance as I stood back to survey the place where—if all went well—I would spend the night I should have spent in Rye. The King's Ransom had come a long way since its days as a simple alehouse. The rambling timber-framed Tudor gem was by far the most interesting building on the high street.

After a pause, during which I took in the overhanging upper stories, the wavy diamond-paned windows, the gnarled grapevine that snaked across the black-and-white facade, and the stained-glass lantern that illuminated the recessed oak door, I turned to Christopher with a broad grin and said, "Wow."

"I thought you'd like it," he said with a satisfied nod. He pointed to an iron bar projecting from an oak beam above the doorway. "They must have removed the inn's sign for safety's sake. I'll have to remember to ask Mrs. Hancock to show it to you. It's quite charming."

"The whole place is charming," I said, "but to be honest, Christopher, I'd rather be in it than in front of it."

"Of course you would," he said and hastened forward to hold the door open for me.

I dragged my suitcase over the threshold and into a narrow corridor lit by wrought-iron hanging lamps that bathed us in a soft and comforting glow. I'd expected the inn to be quieter than the high street, but as soon as Christopher shut the door, the storm's roar was replaced by a hubbub of raised voices. The King's Ransom sounded as if it were bursting at the seams with guests, which made it seem highly unlikely that all would go well for me. It was not a comforting thought.

While Christopher shook the rain from his hat, I lowered my hood and gazed sadly from the corridor's raftered ceiling to its oak-paneled walls to the pattern of small golden roosters on its burgundy carpet. I was certain that, despite Christopher's best efforts, I wouldn't be allowed to stay at the inn long enough to savor its manifold charms.

Keeping a tight grip on my suitcase—and my dwindling hopes—I followed Christopher past a small, overcrowded side parlor to a low-ceilinged, rectangular open space that seemed to be the crossroads for a myriad of hallways, doorways, and staircases, all of which were chockablock with people moving to and from various parts of the inn. To judge by their perplexed expressions, it wasn't an easy place to navigate.

"We've reached the foyer," Christopher explained, stopping just short of the human whirlpool. "I don't know why it's called the foyer, but it is."

The foyer looked as though it had been decorated by a manic antiques dealer. A white marble bust of a mustachioed dandy sat on a wooden stand in one corner; a Jacobean blanket chest stood beneath a bank of wavy windows that overlooked a three-tiered fountain in a tiny enclosed courtyard; and the paneled walls were hung with etchings, paintings, maps, hunting horns, tankards, cutlasses, and blunderbusses.

A petite blond woman dressed in a bulky brown woolen pullover, black jeans, and green Wellington boots stood in the midst of the whirlpool, consulting a clipboard while she answered questions put to her in broken English by four disheveled travelers whose suitcases were twice as big as mine.

The travelers' French accents suggested that they were members of the stranded tour group Phillip Lawson had mentioned. I somehow doubted that they would find solace in knowing that, on a clear day, they could have seen their country's coastline from St. Alfege's bell tower.

"Jean Hancock," Christopher informed me, tilting his head toward the blond woman. "She and her husband, Gavin, bought The King's Ransom just over a year ago. They have two children: Jemima, who's seven, and Nicholas, who's five and a half. You mustn't forget the half, by the way. Nicholas is quite proud of it."

"They always are, at his age," I said, smiling reminiscently.

Mrs. Hancock looked as though she might be in her early thirties. There wasn't a trace of makeup on her pretty face, and she wore her long hair in a sensible pony tail. She appeared to be holding up well under the pressure of presiding over a jam-packed hotel, but she was clearly very busy. When she caught sight of Christopher, however, she asked a dark-haired teenaged girl to deal with the French tourists, excused herself politely, and crossed to speak with him.

"Good afternoon, Mrs. Hancock," he said.

"I suppose it could be worse," she responded. She looked over her shoulder at the dark-haired teenager. "Thank goodness Tessa's parents have a holiday home in Provence. She speaks French like a native." She nodded at Tessa, then flipped through the sheets of paper on her clipboard, pulled a pen from behind her ear, and crossed something out with a flourish. "There. I've completed our head count. Yours was the only unticked name on my list, Bishop Wyndham."

"I'm terribly sorry, Mrs. Hancock," said Christopher. "I didn't realize—"

"Do you mind if we talk in the office?" Mrs. Hancock interrupted. "I can scarcely hear myself think out here, and I should look in on the children. I didn't want to leave them alone in our flat, so I stowed them in the office to keep them from being trampled underfoot."

"A prudent precaution," said Christopher.

I parked my suitcase beside the blanket chest and trailed after the bishop as Mrs. Hancock led us through another corridor and down a short flight of stairs to a room with linoleum flooring and distinctly nonantique furnishings: a massive metal desk, a handful of battered office chairs, and a row of gunmetal-gray filing cabinets.

Two flaxen-haired children in brightly striped woolen pullovers sat at the desk, tongues between their teeth, drawing vigorously with crayons. The girl was working on a landscape in which most of the kelly-green countryside was covered with aquamarine water. The boy seemed to be illustrating the wind's power by drawing a triangular roof tilted at an extreme angle from a square house.

"Hi, Mum," the children chorused as their mother closed the door behind us. They glanced shyly at me from beneath their long lashes, but their faces lit up when they saw Christopher. He was evidently as popular with them as he was with the rector's son.

Mrs. Hancock motioned for Christopher and me to sit in two of the office chairs, then dropped her clipboard on a filing cabinet and walked around the desk to hug her children.

"Steve made an apple crumble," she informed them. "I told him to save two big bowls of it for you because you've well and truly earned a treat. You've been as good as gold."

I ducked my head to hide my smile. As a parent, I appreciated the value of bribery.

"Carry on with your artwork," Mrs. Hancock continued, "while I chat with Bishop Wyndham and . . ." She regarded me questioningly.

"Lori Shepherd," I said. "But everyone calls me Lori."

"Lori," said Mrs. Hancock, "meet Jemima and Nicholas."

"Hi," I said to the children. "I like your pictures."

"Thank you," said Jemima. "May I call you Lori?"

"You may," I said.

Nicholas, who seemed to be less at ease around strangers than his sister, remained silent.

Mrs. Hancock ruffled her son's hair affectionately, then came out from behind the desk and sank with a groan into a third office chair. "I can't begin to describe how wonderful it feels to be off my feet. I haven't had a proper sit-down since dawn."

"I didn't intend to make your job more difficult by missing the head count," Christopher said contritely. "I'd no idea that the situation had become life threatening until I spoke with Phillip Lawson at St. Alfege's."

"I imagine he took forever to come to the point," said Mrs. Hancock, rolling her eyes. "His sermons—" She broke off abruptly, as if remembering that whatever she said about the rector's sermons would eventually be repeated by her offspring. "I'm just glad you're safe, Bishop."

"I may be safe, but Lori isn't," said Christopher. "Lori was driving to Rye when the storm inspired her to seek shelter in the church. I realize that your guest rooms are fully booked, Mrs. Hancock, but I was rather hoping that you might have a sofa to spare for her in one of your public parlors. She has nowhere else to go."

Mrs. Hancock emitted another groan. "I'm sorry, Lori, but don't have a square inch of floor space to spare in the parlors, let alone a sofa. A coachload of French tourists—"

"Phillip Lawson told us about the tour group," I broke in, "and I saw for myself how crowded the inn is. Please don't worry about me, Mrs. Hancock. I can sleep in my—"

"You mustn't sleep in your car," Christopher interrupted, frowning fretfully. "Cars tumble about in cyclones. You could be seriously, perhaps fatally, injured." His frown vanished suddenly. "I know what we'll do. You'll take my bed and I'll sleep on the floor in my room."

"I'm not kicking you out of your bed, Christopher," I protested. "I'll sleep on a chair in St. Alfege's before I—"

"You can't sleep in the church," he objected.

"Why not?" I demanded. "It won't tumble about in the cyclone."

"True," he said, "but the sights and sounds of Mr. Turner's terriers gleefully dismembering rodents may make it difficult for you to nod off."

He had a point, but I refused to acknowledge it.

"I'm not taking your bed," I said stubbornly. "End of discussion."

"There's a bed in the attic," said Jemima.

Christopher and I stared at the little girl for a moment, then looked at her mother.

"Is there a bed in the attic, Mrs. Hancock?" he inquired.

"Well . . . yes," she said doubtfully. "In a manner of speaking."

"Desperate times . . ." said the bishop.

"You'd have to be desperate to sleep in our attic," said Mrs. Hancock. "It doesn't have heat or running water, and there are no electrical outlets. It has a smoke detector, of course, but if, God forbid, a fire blocked the staircase, you'd have to climb through a window to reach the fire escape."

"I'm fairly agile," I said.

"Lori's not a weakling," Christopher added, with a teasing glance in my direction. If he hadn't been a man of the cloth, I would have elbowed him.

"Then there's the dust," Mrs. Hancock went on. "The attic must be an inch thick in dust. It's been used as a general dumping ground for ages, and we haven't even begun to sort it out. There's a wardrobe that looks as if it's been there ever since the inn was built. It's empty, thank heavens, but I'd have to excavate the bed before you could use it, Lori."

I didn't want to add another chore to her already considerable workload, but I didn't want ride out the storm in the Mercedes, either. As Christopher had pointed out, a car wasn't the safest place to be during a cyclone.

"I can do the dusting and the excavating," I said readily. "I have three children, Mrs. Hancock, and two of them are ten-year-old boys who can turn a room upside down faster than a force-nine gale. I'm no stranger to housework."

"Why don't you look at the attic before you make up your mind?" Mrs. Hancock proposed.

"Excellent," said Christopher, as though the matter were settled. "I'm very grateful to you, Mrs. Hancock."

"Don't thank me yet," she cautioned.

"With faith we can move mountains," he replied serenely. "Have you altered this evening's dinner schedule?"

"We've had to do a little juggling," Mrs. Hancock acknowledged, "but we haven't changed your reservation, Bishop Wyndham."

"May Lori join me?" he asked. "If Shepney's emergency plan calls for strict rationing, we can share my portion."

Mrs. Hancock laughed. "We won't have to ration the food supply, Bishop Wyndham. We're surrounded by some of the most fertile farmland in England. Most of our evacuees are farmers. They bring enough provisions with them to feed the entire village for at least a month."

"It sounds as though Shepney is preparing for a siege," he marveled.

"We are," Mrs. Hancock said firmly. "The waters usually recede after two or three days, but it can take much longer to repair the roads and to clear them of debris."

"How much longer?" I asked, wondering if I'd make it home in time for Christmas.

"It depends on the amount of damage and debris," she replied with unassailable logic. "However long it takes, you won't go hungry. The inn's larders are full and our backup generator will keep spoilage at bay when the power outages start. Our goal during any emergency is to feed as many people as we can seat. It reduces the pressure on the community kitchen in the village hall. Shall I add your name to the bishop's reservation, Lori?"

"Yes, please," I said, "but only if he allows me to return his gloves!"

I held the black leather gloves out to him. He accepted them meekly and pulled them onto his pink hands as he stood.

"I'll meet you in the dining room at eight o'clock, Lori," he said. "Until then, you'll find me at St. Alfege's, assisting Phillip Lawson. I doubt that he'll allow me to carry sacks of grain, but I can at least relieve him of his obligation to conduct evensong."

"Will you come back in time to tell us a story?" Jemima inquired. Her brother gazed at Christopher with wide, hopeful eyes.

"Of course I will," said the bishop. "I'll tell you all about St. Alfege."

He thanked Mrs. Hancock again, then left the office. She got to her feet and rummaged through a desk drawer until she found an ornate iron key.

"It looks like something out of *The Count of Monte Cristo*, doesn't it?" she said, displaying the heavy key in the palm of her hand. "A locked door is the only thing that keeps guests from wandering into the attic by accident. Heaven knows what they'd make of the dust." She slipped the key into her pocket and turned to the children. "Lori and I are going to the attic. Want to meet us there?"

Jemima and Nicholas bolted from their chairs and galloped past us like a pair of frisky yearlings released into a pasture.

"They've been stuck in here since lunchtime, poor things," she said. "They need to stretch their legs."

"Aren't you worried about them being trampled?" I asked.

"They'll take the staff staircase," she replied. "It won't be as busy as the central staircase."

She tapped the children's artwork into a neat pile and began to clear the desk of crayons.

"They seem very fond of the bishop," I observed.

"We're all fond of the bishop," said Mrs. Hancock, depositing crayons in an empty biscuit tin. "He used to stay at the rectory when he visited Shepney, but since his retirement, he's chosen to stay with us." She gave me a knowing look. "I think he grew a little tired of being treated like a national treasure."

"How do you treat him?" I asked.

"Like a cherished friend," she replied. Her brow wrinkled as she corrected herself. "A cherished friend with an odd taste in children's tales. The last time he was here, he told the children a gruesome story about a beheaded saint whose executioner's eyes fell out. I'm sure he meant well, but Jemima and Nicholas were up half the night, trying to keep their eyeballs from rolling onto their pillows."

"Maybe St. Alfege's story isn't as gruesome," I said.

"Are you kidding?" she retorted. "St. Alfege was hacked to death by Vikings."

"Oh, dear," I said, trying not to laugh.

She closed the biscuit tin and squared her shoulders. "I'll have a word with the bishop when he gets back from the church. I simply refuse to cope with night terrors on top of everything else!"

I nodded sympathetically and followed her out of the office, blithely unaware of the night terrors that awaited me at The King's Ransom.

Six

Mrs. Hancock and I went back the way we came. "We'll take the central staircase," she said. "If you do decide to stay with us, you should know your way around."

"Is there a map of the inn?" I asked, hoping to be helpful.

She chuckled wearily. "We ran out of maps yesterday and we haven't had time to print more."

"Not a problem," I said. "I prefer trial and error. It's more exciting than using a map."

As we wormed our way across the teeming foyer, Mrs. Hancock identified doorways and passageways with a speed born of familiarity. I tried to memorize her fleeting words, but the confused tangle of voices and the rain pummeling the bank of wavy windows made it difficult to concentrate.

"Reception, dining room, pub, small parlor, large parlor, and Captain Pigg's parlor," she said. "That's Pigg with two *g*'s, by the way, and before you ask, Captain Pigg was an eighteenth-century brigand who quaffed so much ale at The King's Ransom that they named a room after him."

"A great honor," I said. "Hold on a minute. Let me grab my bag."

"Don't bother," she told me. "I'll have one of the porters bring it up to you—if you decide to stay."

The pummeling rain had only increased my determination to stay at the inn, but I happily left the suitcase where it was and stuck close to Mrs. Hancock as we began our ascent to the attic.

It wasn't a straightforward journey. When we reached the top of the central staircase, we had to walk down a carpeted corridor lined with guest rooms to reach another staircase, which led to another carpeted corridor lined with guest rooms. There were steps within each corridor as well, but only two or three of them at a time, so they hardly counted as staircases. Even so, I felt sorry for the poor porter who would be tasked with lugging my luggage up to the attic—but not sorry enough to run down and fetch it myself.

As we made our way through the inn's upper stories, I began to understand why so many of the people I'd seen in the foyer looked lost. The inn was a veritable maze. The corridors jogged to the left or to the right at seemingly random intervals. We passed landings that served no apparent purpose, windows set at differing heights in unexpected places, and several oddly shaped alcoves that were too small to accommodate furniture. Though the alcoves were prettily decorated with dried flowers and pieces of old china, the reason for their existence eluded me.

"Your staff must have an excellent sense of direction," I commented. "I'm beginning to wish I'd brought bread crumbs with me to mark the trail back to the ground floor."

"It takes a bit of getting used to," Mrs. Hancock conceded. "The inn is a collection of buildings that were cobbled together over several hundred years. It gives new meaning to the word 'retrofit.'"

As we hustled up another three-step mini staircase, I spotted Jemima and Nicholas waiting for us at the far end of the corridor. We were halfway there when Mrs. Hancock came to a halt.

"I shall now let you in on the worst-kept secret in Shepney." She pointed at a door on her left labeled PRIVATE. "You see before you the entrance to our flat."

"You live on the premises?" I said, surprised.

"My husband and I consider it a privilege to live in a historic building," she said, walking on. "The children love it, and it makes our job easier. We don't encourage guests to wake us in the middle of the night, but we're here if they need us."

The children were standing in front of a deeply burnished oak door that was also labeled PRIVATE. While they fidgeted impatiently, Mrs. Hancock gave me two more navigational tips.

"The staff staircase," she said, indicating a door opposite the oak door. "It'll get you to the ground floor faster than the central staircase, but you might have a hard time finding the foyer once you get there." She then opened an unmarked door in an alcove to the right of the burnished oak door. "I can't offer you a full bathroom, Lori, but if you decide to stay with us, you can use the staff powder room. A previous owner carved out a space for it to save Housekeeping the bother of running all the way down to the ground floor when nature calls."

I peered into a timber-framed recess furnished with a wall-mounted towel rack, a pedestal sink, and an old-fashioned chain-and-cistern toilet.

"It beats using a chamber pot," I said, recalling Christopher's comment about the inn's plumbing. "And it definitely beats climbing out of my car in the dark to search for a place to"—I glanced at the children—"answer nature's call. Thank you, Mrs. Hancock. The powder room will do nicely."

She inserted the ornate key into the oak door's keyhole and turned it. The lock gave a satisfying click and the door swung outward on creaking hinges to reveal a flight of stairs that would not have looked out of place in a dungeon. The bare wooden steps were worn into a U shape, as if a thousand farmers in hobnailed boots had clambered up and down them, and they disappeared into a darkness that was deeply uninviting.

"Our grand plan is to turn the attic into a guest suite," said Mrs. Hancock. "We should get around to it in a couple of centuries."

She pressed a wall switch just inside the doorway. The dim light cast by a dusty ceiling lamp made the staircase seem marginally less forbidding, but no less hazardous. I let Jemima and Nicholas dash past me, waited for Mrs. Hancock to close the creaking door, and followed her up the stairs at a measured pace. Having saved my ankles from the vicious cobbles, I did not intend to sprain one on the U-shaped steps.

"You can go in," Mrs. Hancock called to her son and daughter, "but do try not to get *too* filthy, will you?"

A pool of light illuminated a landing at the head of the stairs as the children opened a second door and let themselves into the attic.

"We never lock the upstairs door," Mrs. Hancock informed me, "and the light switch is on the right, between the door and the wardrobe." She hesitated. "You do know what a wardrobe is, don't you? Your accent tells me that you're from America, so . . ." Her voice trailed off on a doubtful note.

"I know what a wardrobe is," I assured her. "I hang my clothes in one at home."

"I didn't realize that wardrobes were common in the States," she said.

"They're not," I said, "but I live in the Cotswolds."

"I'll bet you wish you were there right now," she said.

I was pretty sure that every tourist in Shepney wished they were somewhere else at the moment, but it seemed like an impolite thing to say to a woman who lived in the village, so I kept my thoughts to myself.

"Here we are," said Mrs. Hancock when we reached the landing. "It isn't much, but it's yours for as long as you need it—if you want it."

I'm not sure what I expected to see in the attic—a napping vampire, perhaps, or three witches stirring a cauldron—but what I did see was more appealing than it had any right to be. The overhead light filled the room with weird shadows, the curtainless dormer windows were crusted with dirt, and cobwebs hung like bridal veils from the roughly plastered walls, but the ceiling was ribbed with hand-hewn oak beams, the floorboards were as solid as a ship's planks, and the contents, while a tad overwhelming, were undeniably fascinating.

A rattan peacock chair in need of repairs stood between a marble-topped washstand that had seen better days and a teak bookcase filled with old books. A gramophone sat atop a stately wireless set that had in all likelihood broadcast the outbreak of the First World War. The ponderous mahogany wardrobe Jean had mentioned took up an inordinate amount of wall space beside the door, dwarfing a pine chest of drawers and a freestanding corner cupboard.

Birdcages, reed baskets, and wooden tennis rackets hung from the crossbeams, and every level surface was cluttered with odds and ends: bamboo fishing poles, furled parasols, hickory golf clubs, lamps without lampshades, lampshades without lamps, tarnished silver teapots, china figurines, basins, ewers, and a croquet set that looked as if it had last been used at an Edwardian garden party.

Those were merely the items I saw at first glance. A second glance confirmed that the attic was as full of stuff as the inn was full of guests.

Christopher might believe that faith could move mountains, but I had no trouble understanding why the Hancocks hadn't yet transformed the room into a guest suite. In addition to faith, they would have needed a front loader and a crane to shift the vast amount of delightful detritus that had been dumped there.

"It's not as big as I thought it would be," I said.

"You're looking at only half of the attic," Mrs. Hancock explained. "The other half has its own staircase. We use it for storage, but we left this half as we found it."

While Jemima stroked the bristly mane of a three-legged rocking horse and Nicholas played with a toy biplane that had evidently suffered several crash landings, Mrs. Hancock cleared a path to a cream-colored iron bedstead that was buried beneath a pile of bandboxes.

"The inn's hat collection," she said drily, nodding at the bandboxes. "There's a mattress on the bed, but I can't vouch for its condition."

"I'm sure it'll be fine," I said, though I wasn't sure at all.

"You're not bothered by the dust?" she asked.

"Not one bit," I replied. To show that my mind was made up, I dropped my shoulder bag on an octagonal occasional table and hung my rain jacket on a hook in the mahogany wardrobe.

"Welcome to The King's Ransom," said Mrs. Hancock. She returned the ornate key to her pocket. "For safety's sake, I'll leave the downstairs door unlocked during your stay."

"I wouldn't want to fiddle with it in an emergency," I agreed, "but how will I keep wandering guests from bursting in on me?"

"The 'private' sign should do the trick," she said. "I'll be back in a minute with bedding and whatever else I can think of to make you more comfortable, and I'll send up your bag. Oh, and before I forget . . ." She pointed at a dirt-encrusted window on the far side of the bed. "The fire escape is through there."

"Let's hope I won't have to use it," I said.

She raised crossed fingers, then headed for the staircase, saying, "Nicholas? Jemima? Come with me, please. Lori has work to do, and you need to wash your hands."

The children raced ahead of her down the stairs. Jemima's exultant cry of "Apple crumble!" floated up to me before the creaking door signaled their departure.

The storm's roar seemed to grow louder once I was alone, and the room's temperature seemed to drop. I allowed myself three seconds to mourn the loss of my suite at The Mermaid Inn, then got to work.

My excavation of the bed led to the discovery of a thin but serviceable mattress with no discernible lumps, nests, or signs of insect life. The mattress rested on woven cotton webbing rather than springs or wooden slats, and though the webbing looked as if it had been manufactured during the Industrial Revolution, it was still strong enough to take my weight when I tested it with a brief but energetic lie-down.

I would have needed a month or more to clean the attic properly, so I let sleeping dust lie and tackled the tasks I could accomplish in a reasonable amount of time. After some vigorous clearing and shifting, I created a horseshoe-shaped room-within-a-room composed of the bed, the octagonal occasional table, a Windsor armchair, and the pine dresser.

The pine dresser required the most effort, as the drawers were full of seashells, but I got there in the end. The finishing touch came in the shape of a rather good Turkish carpet, which had lain hidden in a pile of lesser rugs until I resurrected it and used it to fill the U-shaped space between the bed and the dresser.

With my main goal accomplished and Mrs. Hancock nowhere in sight, I decided to call Bill. I had my cell phone in my hand when the oak door creaked.

"I'm back!" shouted Mrs. Hancock, presumably to avoid startling me. "Sorry we took so long. We were waylaid. *Repeatedly.*"

With a sigh, I put my phone back into my shoulder bag, dropped the bag onto the octagonal table, and turned to face the landing door. Mrs. Hancock entered the attic a moment later, her arms full of pillows and bedclothes. She was accompanied by a short, stocky man with flaxen hair who gripped my suitcase in one hand and a tall, battery-operated camping lantern in the other. Though a pillow concealed the lower half of my hostess's face, I had the pleasure of seeing her eyebrows rise as she surveyed my "room."

"Good heavens," she said. "You have been busy."

"Bravo," said the man, sounding equally impressed. "You've brought order out of chaos. Where would you like your suitcase?"

"On top of the chest of drawers, please," I said, stepping forward to take the camping lantern from him. "Sorry it's so heavy."

"Not a problem." The man lifted the bag as effortlessly as my sons lifted their saddle blankets and laid it flat on the chest of drawers. "It's that time of year, isn't it? You have to be prepared for anything."

"You do," I said earnestly, wishing Bill were there to hear him.

"I'm Gavin Hancock, by the way," he said, "Jean's husband."

"I'm very glad to meet you, Mr. Hancock," I said, shaking his proffered hand.

"Gavin, please," he said.

"And Jean," Mrs. Hancock added. "The bishop is more particular about formal titles than we are."

I set the lantern on the octagonal table. I would have made the bed as well, but Jean beat me to it. While she tucked a perfectly creased hospital corner under the thin mattress, Gavin drew me aside.

"You can use the lantern to light your way to bed after you turn out the overhead light," he said. "We've left towels for you in the powder room, and we'll send a thermos of hot cocoa up with you after dinner. It's the closest we can come to providing you with central heating."

"As long as I can't see my breath, I'll be okay," I said, "but I never say no to hot cocoa. Where should I charge my cell phone?"

"Use one of the power strips in the office," Gavin advised. "Avoid the wall outlets, unless you want to fry your mobile. There'll be a power surge when the generator kicks in."

I nodded, then gazed pensively at my suitcase. "If I'm going to be here for a few days, I guess I should unpack."

"I would if I were you," he said. He nodded at the pine chest of drawers. "Is there room in the dresser for your things?"

"There is now," I told him. "I had to empty it before I could move it."

"Ah, yes," he said, nodding. "The seashell collection."

"Done," said Jean, crossing to stand beside her husband.

I swung around to admire her handiwork and felt a somewhat embarrassing flood of emotion. The piled pillows and the plump duvet made my sad little nook look almost homey.

"You've been so kind," I said, blinking rapidly. "I . . . I don't know how to thank you."

"No tears," Jean said with mock severity. "They'll turn the dust on your face into mud."

"If you want to thank us——" Gavin began.

Jean cut him off with a wifely frown, muttering, "Hasn't she done enough?"

"No, she hasn't," I insisted, stiffening my upper lip. "Please, tell me what I can do."

"The truth is, Lori, we could use some help in the kitchen tonight," said Gavin. "We're shorthanded because we sent most of our crew to the village hall to set up the community kitchen. Every guest we've approached has turned us down for one reason or another. We wouldn't expect you to prepare meals, but if you could chop a few onions, you'd lighten our chef's workload."

"I love chopping onions," I said staunchly. "After I call my husband, I'll report for kitchen duty."

"You're a star," said Gavin, beaming at me.

"Don't forget your dinner date with the bishop," said Jean. "He'll be expecting you in"—she consulted her wristwatch—"two hours. And don't bother to dress for dinner. No one else will."

They departed, thudding swiftly down the worn wooden steps and closing the creaking oak door behind them.

Since my phone call to Bill was long overdue, I left the unpacking for later. I pulled my cell phone from my shoulder bag and sat in the Windsor armchair while I debated what sort of update to give my husband. It seemed unwise to give him an accurate one. The thought of his wife sleeping on the top floor of an ancient multistory building during a storm that could rip roofs to shreds would only torture him. To keep him from swimming to my rescue, I decided to describe my makeshift lodgings in general terms and to save the dusty details for a sunnier day.

I'd scarcely finished pressing speed dial when he answered.

"Where are you, Lori?" he asked, his voice taut with anxiety. "Are you all right?"

"I'm still fine and I'm still in Shepney," I responded. "I found a room at an inn called The King's Ransom."

"Thank heavens," he said. "I'll let Father and Amelia know you're safe."

"Have you spoken with them?" I asked.

"Several times," he replied. "All is well at Fairworth House. It's been windy in Finch, but they haven't seen a drop of rain."

"I wish I could say the same for Shepney," I said. "It looks as though I may be here for a few days, Bill. The roads around Shepney are either flooded or on the verge of flooding."

"The roads around Blayne Hall are flooded, too," he said, "so we're both marooned."

You're marooned in considerably more comfortable circumstances than I am, I thought enviously, but aloud I said, "What will you do for clothes? Your overnight bag is in the Mercedes."

"Sir Roger's valet loaned me some of his," said Bill. "Quentin's suits reek of mothballs, but we're about the same size, so they don't fit too badly. Quentin will do my laundry as well, and he stocked my bathroom with everything from scented bath salts to fresh razor blades."

I pictured my bare-bones powder room and could not repress a moan.

"What's wrong?" he asked alertly.

"I miss you," I said, which was true in general terms. "It's lonely being here without you."

"Look in the outside pocket on your suitcase," he said. "The large pocket."

"Why?" I asked.

"You'll see," he replied.

I rose from the armchair, unzipped the large outside pocket on my suitcase, and withdrew from it a book bound in blue leather.

"Oh, Bill," I said, feeling a lump rise in my throat.

"I smuggled it into your suitcase when you weren't looking," he said. "I thought you might like to chat with a friend while you waited for me in Rye."

His remark would have baffled a stranger, but I understood it.

"You've won the Best Husband of the Year award yet again," I said. "I'll call you in the morning with the latest news from The King's Ransom."

"Sleep well, love," he said.

"You, too," I told him, and rang off.

I returned the phone to my shoulder bag and sank onto the Windsor armchair with the blue book cradled in my hands. The onions could wait, I told myself. I needed a quiet moment to chat with a friend.

Seven

$\mathcal{F}$'d often smiled over a book. Depending on the story, I'd also wept, gasped, giggled, or fallen asleep. The only book that had ever made me want to sit down for a cozy chat, however, was the one Bill had smuggled into my suitcase. It had once belonged to an Englishwoman named Dimity Westwood, and it was as unique as she was.

Dimity Westwood had been my late mother's closest friend. The two women had met in London while serving their respective countries during the Second World War. They'd been very young, very brave, and very frightened, but the dangers, the hardships, and the pots of tea they'd shared had created a bond of affection between them that was never broken.

After the war in Europe ended and my mother sailed back to the States, she and Dimity strengthened their friendship by sending hundreds of letters back and forth across the Atlantic. When my father's sudden death left her bereft, my mother found solace in those letters. They became a refuge for her, a retreat from the sometimes daunting challenges of teaching full time while raising a rambunctious daughter on her own.

My mother was extremely protective of her refuge. She told no one about it, not even me. As a child, I knew Dimity Westwood only as Aunt Dimity, the fictional heroine of a series of bedtime stories

invented by my mother. I didn't learn about the real Dimity Westwood until after both she and my mother had died.

It was then that my fictional heroine became a real heroine. At
the lowest point in my life, Dimity Westwood bequeathed to me a
comfortable fortune, a honey-colored cottage in the Cotswolds, the
precious correspondence she'd exchanged with my mother, and a
blue leather–bound journal filled with blank pages.

It was through the blue journal that I finally came to know my
benefactress. Whenever I opened it, Aunt Dimity's handwriting
would appear, an old-fashioned copperplate taught in the village
school at a time when smithies still outnumbered petrol stations. I
nearly jumped out of my skin the first time it happened, but I quickly
discovered that I had nothing to fear from Aunt Dimity. Her sole
desire was to be as good a friend to me as she'd been to my mother.

Neither she nor I could explain how she managed to bridge the
gap between the earthly and the ethereal, but as sheets of rain lashed
the windows and gusting winds buffeted the roof, I knew one thing
for certain: If I couldn't share my attic with Bill, there was no one I'd
rather share it with than Aunt Dimity.

I opened the journal and said, "Dimity? I can't talk for long, but I
wanted to touch base with you before I reported for kitchen duty."

The sight of Aunt Dimity's fine copperplate curling gracefully
across the page made me yearn to be in the study at home, curled in
one of the tall leather armchairs, with a fire dancing in the hearth, a
cup of tea at my elbow, and the blue journal resting in my lap.

*Good evening, Lori. Why must you report for kitchen duty? Have you
joined the army?*

"No," I said wistfully. "I ran away from home and into the arms of
an extratropical cyclone." I gave Aunt Dimity a speedy synopsis of

my travels and travails, then sat back, confident that she would respond with soothing words of consolation. It instantly became apparent that my confidence was misplaced.

How lucky you've been, my dear!

"Lucky?" I echoed in disbelief.

The cyclone didn't kill you, the bishop befriended you, and the Hancocks went out of their way to house you. I'd call that lucky, wouldn't you?

"I suppose so," I said doubtfully, "but—"

I hope you weren't expecting me to commiserate with you over your less-than-luxurious sleeping arrangements, my dear. I regret that your romantic getaway was so rudely interrupted, but I must confess that I feel sorrier for Bill than I do for you.

"I don't feel sorry for him," I grumbled, thinking of the scented bath salts.

You should. While you're making new friends in a lively village, he's sequestered in a remote country house with a recluse who merely tolerates him.

"On the other hand—" I began, but Aunt Dimity cut me off again.

What is more, you have the comfort of wearing your own clothes, whereas your poor husband is condemned to wearing borrowed suits that stink of mothballs.

"Well," I said grudgingly, "when you put it like that . . ."

I do put it like that. Oh, yes, Lori, you've been very lucky indeed, as I'm sure you'll realize after you've had time to think about it. Now, run along and make yourself useful. There's no better cure for self-pity than to lend a hand to those in need. I'll be here to keep you company when you get back.

After Aunt Dimity's handwriting had faded from the page, I shook off my melancholy mood and got to my feet. I placed the journal on the octagonal table, dug my toiletry bag out of my suitcase, grabbed my shoulder bag, and headed downstairs to make myself useful. There was nothing quite like a scolding from the Great Beyond to stiffen one's backbone.

I paused in the powder room to pull cobwebs from my hair, beat small clouds of dust from my cashmere sweater, and wash my grubby face and hands. When I was as presentable as I could be without access to a shower or a bathtub or a valet who would do my laundry for me, I parked my toiletry bag on top of the cistern and set out in search of the kitchen.

A glance at my watch told me that I'd already used twenty minutes of the two-hour countdown to my dinner date with the bishop. Having forgotten the lesson I should have learned from my recent experience with shortcuts, I decided to shorten my journey through the inn by taking the staff staircase. It seemed like a good idea at first. Instead of zigging and zagging all over the place, the staff staircase took me straight down to the ground floor. As Jean Hancock had foretold, however, I had trouble finding my way around once I got there.

Nothing was familiar. The corridor at the bottom of the staff staircase was well lit but as plain as porridge. The utilitarian carpet and the bare plaster walls suggested that I was even further behind the scenes than I'd been in the office. The door at the end of the corridor was clearly an exit, so I didn't touch it. A second door led to a laundry room, a third to a vast linen closet, and a fourth was locked.

I detected delectable aromas outside the fifth door, but I also heard a heated argument taking place on the other side of it. I could tell that two men were involved, but since they were speaking rapid-fire French, I wasn't sure why they were arguing. The man with the gravelly voice had a dreadful accent, while the man with the silky voice spoke French as if it were his mother tongue. The Finch-trained snoop in me caught the words *le prix, un escroc,* and *non, non, non!* before I ordered myself to stop eavesdropping.

I hadn't taken more than two backward steps when a fat little man with dark wavy hair and a pencil mustache flung the door wide and swept past me, hastily tucking a white packet inside his blue blazer. I shrank back another two steps as a man in a black short-sleeved chef's coat filled the doorway. He seemed to be seven feet tall and built of granite. Though he, too, had a dark mustache, his was connected by two rivulets of facial hair to a scruffy goatee. He wore a red bandana on his shaved head, pirate style, and every visible inch of skin below his jawline was covered in tattoos.

I fully expected him to bellow "Be off, ye landlubber!" and to threaten me with a hook, but he merely folded his muscular arms and growled, "Lost?"

"I'm looking for the k-kitchen," I stammered, fighting the urge to run for my life. "Gavin Hancock told me that the kitchen crew was shorthanded, so I volunteered mine." I held up my hands and wiggled my fingers in a weak attempt at humor, but the tattooed man remained stone-faced.

"To do what?" he asked.

"Prep work?" I said, grasping at a phrase I'd heard but never used. "Chopping onions, peeling potatoes, whatever needs doing."

His lip curled disdainfully, as if it pained him to deal with amateurs. He must have felt compelled to go along with his boss's wishes, however, because he turned his brawny back on me and muttered, "This way."

I followed him through a large storeroom to a second door that opened into a hot, humid, and tormentingly fragrant professional kitchen. Steam rose from an array of stockpots and saucepans while a skeleton crew of two weedy young men toiled over sauté pans, cutting boards, and mixing bowls. They raised their heads briefly at my entrance, then quickly lowered them again.

Silently, the tattooed man showed me where to stow my shoulder bag, led me to a stainless-steel sink, and motioned for me to wash my hands. I didn't feel the need to inform him that I'd already washed them. He then led me to a stainless-steel counter, dumped a pile of parsnips in front of me, and handed me a vegetable peeler.

"Peels here, parsnips there," he explained succinctly, plopping a plastic bucket and an empty stockpot on either side of the parsnip pile. "I'm Steve."

"I'm Lori," I said, but Steve had already walked away.

Steve? I thought wonderingly as I got to work with the peeler. I was certain that Jean Hancock had credited her children's apple crumble to someone called Steve. The thought of the tattooed man preparing a special treat for Jemima and Nicholas made him seem slightly less scary, but only slightly.

Apart from Steve barking commands at the weedy young men, the only voices I heard for the next ninety minutes belonged to the waitstaff calling out orders. Steve evidently discouraged casual chit-chat in his kitchen. I wasn't surprised. There was so much to do that the only thing I found surprising was that Steve had abandoned his post to argue with the fat little Frenchman.

Not even Aunt Dimity could have described my stint in the kitchen as "making friends in a lively village." When I finished peeling the parsnips, Steve gave me carrots to peel. When I finished peeling the carrots, he gave me beets and a pair of latex gloves to keep the beet juice from staining my hands while I wielded the peeler. As the minutes crept by, I began to feel as if I *had* joined the army. I could have danced for joy when Gavin Hancock appeared at my side to escort me to the bishop's table.

"Is it eight o'clock already?" I said, feigning shock.

"On the dot," he replied.

I left the latex gloves on the counter, retrieved my bag, and fled the kitchen, throwing a relieved "Bye, Steve!" over my shoulder as I left. He did not respond.

"I didn't see your mobile in the office," Gavin said as he led me through a pair of swinging doors and down another corridor.

"I couldn't find the office," I told him.

"Give it to me," he said. "I'll charge it and return it to you after you finish your meal. The bishop's been asking for you."

"Bless him," I said, handing over my cell phone.

"Bless *you*," he countered. "You're the only guest who answered our call for help, and we're very grateful. Don't even try to pay for your meals while you're here, Lori. They're on the house. Consider it a small recompense for services rendered."

"I can't accept free meals," I protested. "You've already given me a place to stay."

"We put you in the attic," he said, giving me a sidelong look. "You owe us nothing."

The dining room was long, narrow, softly lit, and splendidly atmospheric. Small tables draped in white linen sat on either side of an aisle that ended at a bank of large diamond-paned windows. Heads turned nervously as rain crashed against the windows like ocean waves.

A pair of slender oak columns in the aisle supported a low ceiling striped with exposed beams. Dozens of gilt-framed oil portraits hung from the paneled walls, and silver bowls, urns, and loving cups added a subtle gleam to the dark oak mantel of a beautifully carved stone fireplace. Since a roaring fire would have scorched the diners seated with their backs to the hearth, it was decorated, like the upstairs alcoves, with dried flowers and pieces of china.

Every chair but one was taken, and murmured conversations in both French and English filled the air. Though I scanned the room for the fat little Frenchman, I didn't see him. I wondered idly if he was a guest at the inn or an unwelcome intruder, but before I could mention him to Gavin, I spotted Christopher waving to me from a table beside the windows. He rose to his feet politely while Gavin seated me.

"Due to a staff shortage, we've had to reduce the number of items on our menu tonight," Gavin explained, "but we haven't reduced the quality. Here's Tessa. She'll take good care of you."

He departed, and the dark-haired teenager whose parents owned a holiday home in Provence welcomed us warmly, filled our water glasses, and handed menus to us. I ignored mine. Christopher's clerical collar had reminded me of his mission of mercy at St. Alfege's.

"Did you have a good turnout for evensong?" I asked.

"Yes, indeed," he replied, laying his menu aside. "Two worshippers attended the service—double the number I anticipated. Mrs. Hancock tells me you've worked wonders with the attic."

"The bar was set pretty low," I said without thinking. To prevent him from offering to swap rooms with me, I hastily amended my statement and changed the subject. "But it beats sleeping in my car. Did you get back from the church in time to tell Jemima and Nicholas about St. Alfege?"

The blush that suffused the bishop's kindly face suggested that Jean Hancock had had a word with him about the level of gore in his bedtime stories.

"I told them about St. Alfege's remarkable life," he replied, "but at Mrs. Hancock's behest, I refrained from mentioning his death. She thought it might upset them."

"They may not be used to hearing stories about saints who were hacked to death by Vikings," I suggested.

"St. Alfege wasn't merely hacked to death," Christopher said earnestly. "He was kidnapped by Danish raiders and held for ransom. When he refused to allow his people to pay the extortionate sum required to free him, the Danes beat him with ox bones and ax handles until one of them took pity on him and killed him with a resounding blow to the head." He peered at me beseechingly. "Young Trevor Lawson found the story fascinating. It helped him to see the patron saint of his father's church in a whole new light."

I didn't have the heart to tell him that the average ten-year-old boy would find the marauding Danes vastly more fascinating than the martyred saint, so I focused on the disparity in the children's ages.

"Trevor Lawson is older than Jemima and Nicholas," I pointed out gently.

"Mrs. Hancock said much the same thing," he acknowledged. "I shall henceforth be more selective in the stories I share with Jemima and Nicholas." He opened his menu. "Mr. Hancock told me of your volunteer work in the kitchen. Did you assist with any of tonight's dishes?"

"I peeled parsnips," I replied. "And carrots. And beets. Lots of beets."

"I'm sure your efforts were appreciated," he said.

I didn't share his certainty, but I let the matter slide. After studying my menu, I ordered the crab and smoked sea trout roulade as an entrée and the filet of beef as a main course. I would have ordered a bottle of wine as well, but it seemed inadvisable to attempt the long trek to the attic on wobbly legs. Christopher ordered the same entrée and main course, so we were a bit confused when Tessa presented us with bowls of soup.

"Cream of parsnip soup," she informed us. "With the chef's compliments."

"The fruits of your labor," said Christopher, smiling. "The chef must have a sense of humor."

"Have you met Steve?" I asked, eyeing him skeptically.

"I have not yet had the privilege," he replied.

"I didn't think so," I said. "He's not a laugh-a-minute kind of guy." I blew on my soup to cool it before adding thoughtfully, "He has a temper, though."

"Oh, dear," said Christopher. "Did he criticize your work?"

"He hardly said two words to me," I said, "but I overheard him arguing with a Frenchman, in French, in a storeroom. He sounded furious, but the Frenchman flounced out before Steve could deck him."

"The French tend to be fussy about their food," Christopher observed, "and chefs tend to resent fussy patrons."

"I don't think they were arguing about food," I told him. "One of them called the other a crook—*un escroc*—and said something about the price—*le prix*—of something."

"Perhaps the Frenchman was objecting to the price of his meals," said Christopher. "It would be harsh to describe overpriced dishes as theft, but as I said, the French tend to be fussy about food."

"I'm glad I'm not French," I said. "I'm happy when someone else cooks for me."

For the next two hours I was very happy. Our meal more than justified the hard work of Steve and his weedy sous chefs. The cream of parsnip soup was exquisite, the roulade was divine, and the beef was as tender as it was flavorful. When it came time to order dessert, I was disappointed to learn from Tessa that the kitchen had run out of apple crumble. She recommended the nutmeg custard tart with caramel sauce and toffee shards, however, and it proved to be an extremely satisfactory substitute.

"For a big scary dude, Steve sure can cook," I said after Tessa had cleared the table. "That was one of the finest meals I've ever eaten."

"The cream of parsnip soup compares favorably with the cream of celeriac soup served at The Mermaid Inn," said Christopher, as if he could give Steve no higher praise. "Shall we conclude our repast with a pot of tea, or perhaps a brandy?"

"I'd love to," I said, "but it's getting late and I still have to unpack."

"Of course," he said. "Would you care to join me for breakfast? I booked a table for nine o'clock."

"Thank you for inviting me," I said. "I'll be there."

"Splendid," he said. "I don't mind eating alone, but I prefer congenial company."

"So do I," I said, beaming at him.

We rose to leave. I would have forgotten my cell phone if Tessa hadn't rushed up to me with it as well as the thermos of hot cocoa Gavin Hancock had promised. I explained the thermos to Christopher as we made our way to the foyer. He thought it an eminently practical way to compensate for the lack of heat in the attic.

"I have an extra blanket in my room," he began, but I refused the offer before he made it.

"Thanks, Christopher, but I don't need your extra blanket," I said. "The Hancocks gave me a nice fluffy duvet. Between it and the hot cocoa, I should be as snug as a bug tonight."

"I'm very pleased to hear it," he said.

The foyer wasn't nearly as crowded as it had been when I'd arrived at the inn, but the thrum of voices coming from the public parlors made me realize how fortunate I was to have the attic all to myself. Aunt Dimity, I thought, would applaud my change of heart, though I could also imagine *I told you so* scrolling across a page in the blue journal.

Since I had no pressing appointments to keep, I returned to my dusty digs via the central staircase. I suspected Christopher of gallantry when he accompanied me all the way to the top floor, but my suspicion was unfounded. His room happened to be directly across the corridor from the Hancocks' flat.

"Mrs. Hancock offered me ground-floor accommodations," he explained, lowering his voice to avoid disturbing the family, "but I requested a room higher up because of—"

"The views?" I interjected playfully.

"On a clear day, they would be magnificent," he confirmed. He put his key in the lock, then hesitated. "I intend to volunteer at the village hall after breakfast tomorrow. I wonder if you . . . ?" He regarded me diffidently as his words trailed off.

"As long as they don't ask me to peel vegetables," I said, "you can count me in."

He nodded happily, said good night, and let himself into his room.

I headed for the powder room, reviewing the pleasant evening I'd spent with the bishop. There were, I thought, quite a few plus sides to being marooned at The King's Ransom, not the least of which was Steve's cooking.

If it hadn't been for the bath salts, I would have felt sorry for Bill.

Eight

*F*was rinsing my toothbrush in the pedestal sink when someone knocked on the powder room door. I hastened to make way for a staff member whose needs were greater than mine, but instead of a desperate housekeeper, Jean Hancock stood in the corridor, holding her daughter's hand. Jean was still in her day clothes, but I was stricken with guilt when I saw that Jemima was clad in pajamas and pink bedroom slippers.

"Bishop Wyndham and I didn't wake Jemima with our chatter, did we?" I asked contritely.

"It wasn't you," Jean replied stoically. "It's the storm. My little night owls haven't been able to settle. I probably should have let them race up and down the high street all day, but it's too late to wear them out now." She sighed a sigh I'd sighed many times before. "Jemima would like to speak with you." A mother's sixth sense prompted Jean to look over her shoulder just as Nicholas poked his tousled head out of their flat. She released her daughter's hand and strode back to her son, whispering sternly, "Didn't I tell you to stay in bed?"

Jemima paid no attention to her brother's misbehavior. Her unblinking gaze remained fixed on my face, and her grave expression suggested that she had something of great import to say to me. To prime the conversational pump, I pointed at the stuffed animal she held in the crook of her arm, a small pink pig sprinkled sparingly with smudgy black dots.

"Who's this?" I asked.

"Captain Pigg," she replied.

"Like the parlor downstairs?" I asked.

"Yes, but my Captain Pigg isn't a pirate," she explained carefully. "He's a Gloucester Old Spot."

"So I see," I said, having encountered the venerable breed during family outings at the Cotswold Farm Park. "I have a pink bunny named Reginald. He's been my best buddy for as long as I can remember. I'd introduce him to you, but I left him at home."

"Mr. Turner gave Captain Pigg to me," she went on, as if I hadn't spoken. "He raises Gloucester Old Spots on his farm. He likes them because they're good mummies and daddies, and they don't get in a flap when his dogs bark."

"What a lovely gift," I said, wondering if the Mr. Turner who raised praiseworthy pigs was the same Mr. Turner whose terriers were gleefully dismembering rats in St. Alfege's.

"I want you to have Captain Pigg," she said suddenly, holding the little pig out to me, "for if you get scared in the attic."

Though her words caught me off guard, they helped me to understand why she'd prefaced the presentation with a primer on Gloucester Old Spots.

"Because he'll look after me?" I hazarded. "And he won't get in a flap even if I do?"

She nodded somberly. Her concern for me was so touching that I accepted the pig without cavil.

"I'm very grateful, Jemima," I said. "I'll take good care of Captain Pigg, but there's nothing to be afraid of in the attic."

"Not during the day," she said solemnly, "but at night the lady who died in your bed comes back."

"The . . . who?" I said. Before I could fashion a less addled response, Jemima turned and padded up the corridor to let herself into the family flat. I stared at her in astonishment, then looked down at Captain Pigg. "The bishop wouldn't tell her a ghost story, would he?"

I couldn't read Captain Pigg's gleaming black eyes as easily as I read Reginald's, but he seemed doubtful.

"I'll ask him tomorrow." I shook my head. "Jean won't be happy if the answer is yes."

On that point, the pig clearly agreed.

Another stab of guilt assailed me when I opened the creaking oak door, but since an oil can was one of the few things I hadn't brought with me, I could do nothing to silence its hinges. I made it to the landing without tripping or slipping on the worn wooden steps, opened the landing door, and closed it behind me as I flicked on the overhead light. The wind was still roaring and the rain was still pounding, but the inn's burly roof beams bore the assault with admirable indifference.

Unlike the roof beams, I was a tiny bit shaken. Try as I might, I couldn't keep myself from glancing uneasily at the iron bedstead as I deposited Captain Pigg, the thermos, and my cell phone on the octagonal table. Though it stood to reason that such an old bed would have witnessed a death or two, it wasn't the sort of thing I cared to contemplate while I was drifting off to sleep in a cobwebby attic.

I emptied my trouser pockets into my shoulder bag, slung it over the back of the Windsor armchair, and began to unpack. With a sigh, I passed over the lacy garments and pulled out a set of long underwear. I'd planned to wear the unglamorous underclothes while exploring the nature reserve in Rye. In Shepney, they'd impersonate pajamas.

When I finished unpacking, I stowed my suitcase in the mahogany wardrobe and got ready for bed. The dormer windows were so grimy that I didn't bother to cover them before I donned my ersatz pajamas. Finally, I set the alarm on my cell phone, turned on the camping lantern, turned out the overhead light, and crawled under the plump duvet.

The camping lantern was useful, but it did little to calm my nerves. The shadows it cast were even weirder than those cast by the overhead light, so I switched it off quickly, telling myself that I could catch up with Aunt Dimity before I joined the bishop for breakfast.

I said good night to Captain Pigg, pulled the duvet to my chin, and snuggled into the pile of pillows. Between the storm, the exceedingly strange surroundings, and the dead lady who walked by night, I thought I would have as much trouble settling as the Hancock children, but my eyes refused to stay open. The long day had finally caught up with me. In a twinkling, I was asleep.

I woke in impenetrable darkness. The taste of dust on my lips and the rain's steady patter brought my sleep-muddled thoughts into focus. I wasn't at home. I was in a dead woman's bed in the attic of an ancient inn. A cyclone had upset my plans and turned me into a refugee.

The pattering rain caught my attention. Rain didn't patter during a cyclone, I told myself. It crashed, dashed, and splashed, but it didn't patter. Why was it pattering now?

I pondered the question drowsily until it dawned on me that the wind was no longer driving the rain against the dormer windows. I vaguely recalled someone—the young rector at St. Alfege's?—saying that the wind would ease off by midnight. Had his prediction come true? I wondered. Was it the witching hour?

Instead of reaching for my cell phone to verify the time, I smiled into the darkness. Whether it was the witching hour or not, I hadn't been awakened by Jemima's ghost. I'd simply grown so accustomed to the wind's roar that its absence had pulled me from sleep. If I relaxed, the rain's rhythmic drumming would make it easy for me to find my way back to dreamland. I was halfway there when the oak door creaked.

I sat upright, instantly awake, and peered pointlessly into the gloom. Faintly, at the outermost edges of my hearing, I detected the sound of a measured footstep upon the stairs. I was absolutely certain that neither Bishop Wyndham nor the Hancocks would sneak up on me in the dead of night, but I couldn't bring myself to believe that a wandering guest would be stupid enough to tackle the U-shaped stairs in the dark.

I waited on tenterhooks for a strip of light to appear beneath the landing door, but the darkness remained absolute. With a trembling hand, I groped blindly for the camping lantern, found it, and switched it on.

"Hello?" I called, half blinded by the lantern's glare. "Who's there?"

No one answered. I listened hard for retreating footsteps but heard nothing.

Fear segued rapidly into annoyance.

"If you're playing games with me," I shouted, swinging my legs over the side of the bed, "I can guarantee that you'll live to regret it."

I got up, grabbed the lantern, and marched furiously to the landing door. I was ready to give a tongue-lashing of epic proportions to the moron who'd ignored the PRIVATE sign, but when I stepped onto the landing with the lantern held high, I saw no one. The staircase was empty and the oak door was shut.

The oak door had closed without creaking.

A chill trickled down my spine. Was Jemima's dead lady playing games with me?

I backed slowly into the attic, shut the landing door, and returned the lantern to the octagonal table. To keep my feet from freezing, I crawled back under the duvet. To ward off the trickling chill, I reached for the blue journal.

"You're a fine fellow," I said to Captain Pigg, "but you don't have the kind of expertise I require right now."

I gave the little pig a pat on the head, then heaped my pillows into a pile behind me. The iron bedstead squeaked softly when I leaned against the pillows with the open journal propped on my bent knees.

"Aunt Dimity?" I said.

As Aunt Dimity's handwriting began to loop and curl across the page, I thanked my husband silently but fervently for providing me with a companion who could answer the question that was foremost in my mind.

You're up late, my dear.

"Not by choice," I said.

Did the storm wake you?

"Sort of," I said. "I woke the first time because the wind had stopped blowing, but the second time . . ." I glanced nervously at the landing door, chided myself for being nervous, and shifted my gaze resolutely to the blue journal. "Is The King's Ransom haunted, Dimity?"

Of course it is. If I owned The King's Ransom, I'd post a plaque on the door, proclaiming it one of the most haunted inns in England. Haunted inns attract such interesting guests!

"I'm sure they do," I said, "but could you be a little more specific? About the ghosts, I mean."

Where shall I begin? There's a jolly drunkard in the pub and a rather maudlin one in room sixteen. A pair of dashing rogues in room five engage in sword fights when the mood strikes them. The young boy in the dining room sings the lullabies his mother sang to him, but only when he has the room to himself. The gray lady in room twenty drifts about every now and then, looking pensive and attenuated, and the black dog wanders freely throughout the inn, searching for his master. Shall I go on?

I gave my bed another apprehensive glance. I didn't mind the inn's extreme hauntedness, but I wasn't entirely happy with the thought of a dead lady rising from the bed in which I was sleeping, while I was sleeping in it. "What about the lady who died in my bed?"

No one died in your bed, Lori. A building as old as The King's Ransom is bound to accrue its fair share of ghosts, but none of them inhabit the attic, not even the black dog. Why would you think otherwise?

"Jemima Hancock told me that the lady who died in my bed comes back at night," I explained.

If I recall correctly, Jemima Hancock is seven years old.

"She is," I said defensively, "but she seemed very sure of herself. She gave me a stuffed animal—a Gloucester Old Spot named Captain Pigg—to protect me from the . . . the lady."

I can't imagine why Jemima would name her brave pig after the jolly drunkard in the pub.

"Captain Pigg haunts the pub?" I said. "You'd think he'd haunt the parlor named in his honor."

You'll find the late Captain Pigg in the pub nowadays, though I don't know why you'd want to. He couldn't protect you if his afterlife depended on it. He does nothing but dance hornpipes and quaff brandy.

"Jean Hancock told me he quaffed ale," I said.

During his lifetime he quaffed a wide variety of alcoholic beverages, but brandy was his favorite tipple then as it is now. Which is beside the point. The point being: You're a grown woman. You should know better than to believe a fantastic tale told by a seven-year-old.

"I do know better," I insisted, "but a few things happened tonight that made Jemima's tale seem credible." I described the sounds I'd heard and my failure to discover an earthly reason for them.

Strange noises are to be expected in a very old building during a powerful storm, Lori, and they can be amplified by an overactive imagination. Need I remind you that you were unnerved by Bishop Wyndham's sinister gloves?

It would have been futile to deny that my imagination sometimes ran away with me, so I stuck to the facts.

"I didn't hear a *strange* noise," I protested. "I heard a *recognizable* noise."

Are you certain the oak door creaked? It might have been the bed. Iron bedsteads tend to creak, and your ears were very near the bed frame.

"My bed squeaks a little," I admitted, "but not enough to wake me when I was half asleep with my head buried in pillows. The door's hinges are loud and distinctive, Dimity. And they *didn't* creak when it closed."

It may have creaked while you were shouting. May I posit a scenario that doesn't rely on Jemima's dramatic testimony?

"Posit away," I said.

An innocent, possibly inebriated guest opened the oak door by mistake and ran away in alarm when an angry stranger bellowed at him. He was probably more frightened than you were by the encounter. Heaven knows I'd leave in a hurry if you bellowed at me.

I managed a weak chuckle. "I suppose you're right, Dimity. If the attic doesn't have its own ghost, the sounds I heard must have been made by a guest."

You must tell the Hancocks about Jemima's warning, Lori. I'm certain they'll wish to discover who told their daughter about the dead lady in the attic.

"It may have been Bishop Wyndham," I said reluctantly. "He wouldn't tell her a ghost story intentionally, but she may have misunderstood one of his gruesome bedtime stories."

Why on earth would a retired bishop tell gruesome stories to children?

"It's his way of making religion more interesting," I explained. "In a way, it does. Children are more likely to remember a saint who died horribly than one who died in his sleep."

Most will remember the horrible death more clearly than the saintly life that preceded it.

"Will and Rob would," I acknowledged, "but they might become interested in the saint's life when they're older. Jean Hancock asked Christopher to tone down his stories, but the damage may already have been done. I'll find out tomorrow. He may have inadvertently said the wrong thing to Jemima, or he may be as innocent as the wandering guest who scared me tonight."

Have I put your mind at ease on that score, my dear?

"You have," I said. "Thanks, Dimity."

You're welcome, Lori. Now go to sleep!

The graceful lines of royal-blue ink faded from the page. With a mind very much at ease, I closed the journal, returned it to the octagonal table, and said a second good night to Captain Pigg. His friendly pink face was the last thing I saw before I turned off the camping lantern, burrowed into the pillows, and found my way back to dreamland.

Some time later, when the distant sound of children's laughter pulled me from slumber, I opened one eye, saw that it was half past two in the morning, and went back to sleep. I could leave it to the Hancocks to deal with their mischievous offspring. I was off duty.

$\mathcal{N}$ine

o further diversions disrupted my first night at The King's Ransom. I woke in time to preempt my alarm, refreshed and ready to face the day. The gray light leaking through the rain-streaked dormer windows indicated that I would face another wet day, however, so I ran down to the powder room to conduct my morning ablutions, then ran back up to fortify myself with hot cocoa while I dressed in the clothes I would have worn had my husband and I strolled hand in hand through Rye's nature reserve in the rain.

Since I'd already caught up with Aunt Dimity, I left the blue journal unopened on the octagonal table and picked up my cell phone instead. A small, mean-spirited part of me hoped that an early call would rouse Bill from his comfortable slumber, but the better angel of my nature was glad to hear that he was already awake.

We had a relatively brief conversation because I edited out any reference to jolly, maudlin, sword-fighting, singing, or pensive ghosts, and somehow forgot to mention the one that didn't exist. I could just about tolerate Aunt Dimity making fun of my overactive imagination, but I wasn't angelic enough to put up with Bill's teasing.

After confirming that my husband was still elegantly trapped by the floodwaters surrounding Blayne Hall, and promising to touch base with him in the evening, I rang Willis, Sr. My father-in-law assured me that Will, Rob, and Bess were flourishing, and when I spoke with Will and Rob, I knew what he meant.

Far from being distressed by my absence, my sons were having such a good time at Fairworth House that they *could* wait for me to come home. Bess restored my flagging morale by telling me that, while she loved Grandma and Grandpa to bits and pieces, she missed me terribly and wanted nothing more than to throw her dimpled arms around my neck and give me a dribbly kiss. Bill would have challenged my interpretation of her comments, but he wasn't as fluent in toddler as I was.

At half past eight I grabbed my shoulder bag from the back of the Windsor armchair, retrieved my rain jacket from the mahogany wardrobe, tucked the empty thermos under my arm, and headed for the central staircase. I felt a pang of parental sympathy for Jean and Gavin Hancock as I passed their door. I suspected that their children's late-night antics would have them second-guessing their decision to reproduce.

I didn't see the bishop or the Hancocks on my way down to the bustling foyer, but as I was turning toward the dining room, a familiar figure barged into me. I wheeled around, prepared to exchange polite apologies with the fat little Frenchman, but he continued to plow a path through the foyer, seemingly impervious to the indignant glares his jostled victims aimed at him.

His victims had progressed to muttered imprecations when Tessa emerged from the small parlor with an armload of damp bath towels. I sidled up to her and nodded at the Frenchman's retreating back.

"Do you know who that man is?" I asked.

"It's Monsieur Renault from Marseille," she said, utilizing the accent she'd acquired in Provence.

"Is Monsieur Renault with the tour group?" I asked.

"For the time being," she replied. "He's visited Shepney two or three times a year for the past few years, but this is his first visit since the Hancocks took over. From what I hear, he'll have to book his trips with a different coach company from now on."

Having learned the art of gossip from the experts in my village, I employed the tried-and-true techniques of raising my eyebrows, folding my arms, leaning closer to my news source, and saying in a confidential murmur, "What's he done?"

"It's his fault the tour group is stuck here," she explained, lowering her voice. "He went missing for a few hours, and by the time he showed up, the roads were closed. To add insult to injury, he has a guest room all to himself. While the rest of the group is sleeping rough in the parlors, he's got a private room with a proper bed."

"How did he manage to snag a room?" I asked.

"He always reserves one ahead of time." She giggled. "While everyone else is doing the walking tour, he takes a nap!"

My eyebrows rose. "Couldn't he nap on the bus?"

"He could, but he doesn't," she said. "He always gets the same room, too. Room thirty-four. He says it's restful."

"It must be," I said. "He slept soundly enough to be late for the bus."

"Oh, he didn't oversleep," said Tessa. "Jean knocked on his door, and when he didn't answer, she went in to make sure he hadn't been taken ill." She gave me a significant look. "He wasn't there. No one knows where he was."

"His fellow travelers must be ready to tar and feather him," I said. "Steve doesn't seem to think much of him, either. I heard them arguing in the kitchen yesterday."

"Monsieur Renault was in the kitchen?" Tessa said, her eyes widening. "I'm surprised Steve didn't throw him out on his ear. He has a strict rule barring guests from entering the kitchen during work hours."

"I thought he might," I said, nodding. "He let me help out, but only because Gavin sent me."

"Don't let it bother you," said Tessa. "Steve's a great chef, but I wouldn't put him in charge of guest relations. He's better with purees and pastries than he is with people." She shifted the towels from one arm to the other and asked apologetically, "Do you mind if I get on? I'm working in the laundry *and* the dining room this morning."

"Sorry," I said, stepping out of her way. "See you later."

The dining room crowd was fairly evenly divided between those who had a proper bed and those who'd slept rough in the parlors. It wasn't hard to figure out who was who: The former looked well rested and the latter looked disheveled, disgruntled, and groggy. Had I been Monsieur Renault, I would have eaten breakfast in my room.

Christopher was waiting for me at "our" table near the windows. As if he, too, wished to spare himself a trip upstairs, he'd brought his hat, scarf, gloves, and overcoat with him. In marked contrast to the graceless Frenchman, he again stood as I approached and waited until I was seated to seat himself.

I'd been unable to fully appreciate the view from the dining room at night, and the gray morning light revealed that there wasn't much of a view to appreciate. Disappointingly, the dining room's bank of windows overlooked the inn's parking lot.

"Not your sort of thing at all," I said, looking askance at the uninspiring vista.

"Cars must be parked somewhere," Christopher observed philosophically, handing me a menu. "I trust you slept well?"

"Better than the Hancocks," I replied. "They must have been up half the night, chasing after Jemima and Nicholas."

"You heard them, too," he said, nodding. "I must confess that I couldn't identify the noises I heard until I recollected my proximity to the Hancocks' flat."

"I had no trouble identifying it," I said. "It's the sound of children driving their parents crazy. Have you seen Jean or Gavin this morning?"

"I have not," said Christopher. "They must be working behind the scenes to keep the inn ticking along like a well-oiled machine."

"Speaking of which," I said, "I wish they'd oil the hinges on my door. An unidentified guest opened it last night, then ran away. The creak gave me a fright."

"I heard it, too," said Christopher. "I heard footsteps as well. I assumed you were, ahcm, availing yourself of the facilities."

"Nope," I said, shaking my head. "I was half asleep." I smiled. "I imagine the Hancocks feel more than half asleep this morning. Or maybe they're availing themselves of some extra shut-eye."

"I doubt it," said Christopher. "Not at the same time, at any rate. One or the other would have had to take Jemima and Nicholas to school."

"To school?" I said. "The school is open?"

"It's not a school in the strict sense of the word," he clarified. "Shepney's village school closed twenty years ago, but the villagers put the building to use as an informal school when the need arises. I'm told it frees the parents to man the barricades, so to speak, and it helps the children to maintain a sense of normalcy in times of crisis."

"The villagers should give seminars on how to cope with a natural disaster," I said. "They've factored everything into their emergency plan."

A towel-free Tessa arrived to take our orders. To show that I had nothing against the French in general—and because it sounded heavenly—I ordered the strawberry-stuffed French toast and a pot of tea. Christopher's request was less indulgent than mine, but no less Francophone: fresh-baked croissants and a pot of hot chocolate.

Tessa took my thermos with her when she left, promising to refill and return it at dinnertime. After she'd gone, I fiddled with my cutlery while I contemplated the best way to express my concerns to the bishop without hurting his feelings.

"You're very quiet this morning, Lori," he observed.

"Sorry," I said, and took the bull gently by the horns. "I know that Jean asked you to dial down the gore in the stories you share with her children, but something happened last night that made me wonder if you . . ." I described Captain Pigg and the reason Jemima gave for presenting him to me, then asked cautiously, "You haven't told Jemima a ghost story, have you?"

"Certainly not," he replied, looking distressed. "The only ghost I've mentioned to the Hancock children is the Holy Ghost."

"Could Jemima have twisted any of your stories into one that features a dead lady who walks by night?" I asked.

"I've told Jemima precisely two bedtime stories," he replied, sounding mildly vexed, "and they contained no reference whatsoever to a zombie in the attic. They couldn't have. St. Alban and St. Alfege died several centuries before the inn was built. Jemima must have heard the unpleasant tale from someone other than myself." He turned his gaze toward the rain-drenched parking lot, murmuring pensively, "I wonder who?"

"A building as old as The King's Ransom is bound to accrue its fair share of ghost stories," I said, adjusting Aunt Dimity's statement to suit the bishop's sensibilities. "Jemima may have overheard a guest or a staff member discussing the inn's supernatural side."

"It's incumbent upon us to disabuse the poor child of the notion that dead people are flitting about the inn," he said. "She lives here, after all, and—"

"Not our job," I interrupted firmly. "I'll let Jean and Gavin know what's going on, but it's up to them to decide what to do about it."

"You're quite right," Christopher conceded humbly. "I shall butt out."

I was still chuckling over his choice of words when our breakfasts arrived. My French toast was sinfully scrumptious and Christopher declared that his croissants would pass muster with even the fussiest Frenchman. While we ate, he gave me the weather report—"Wet."— and the welcome news that, although the cyclone had left a trail of destruction along the south coast, the damage had been moderate, no ships had been lost at sea, and no one had been killed or seriously injured—so far.

The hazards of being caught out in the storm were brought home to me when Christopher delivered his most alarming piece of news.

"Shepney's high-water rescue team had to retrieve a family of four from a semisubmerged car this morning," he said, as we lingered over our hot beverages. "Like you, they were trying to reach Rye. Their vehicle is a total loss, I'm afraid, but they're safe and sound at the village hall."

"Thank goodness," I said with feeling. "And God bless the rescue team. If Phillip Lawson hadn't kept me off the road, they might have had to retrieve me—or my corpse—from Bill's half-submerged car."

"As a member of the team, Phillip has a vested interest in preventing tragedies," Christopher informed me.

"Vested interest or no, he saved my bacon," I said. "I've been on the receiving end of an awful lot of kindness since I stumbled into St. Alfege's. I'm glad you came up with a way for me to give back." I grinned slyly as I drew a pair of waterproof hiking gloves from my shoulder bag and put them on. "I'm ready to go when you are."

"You certainly are," he said, smiling. "Village hall, here we come."

"Mum's the word if we see Jean or Gavin," I warned as we readied ourselves to venture outdoors. "They're short on sleep and scrambling to cover a lot of bases. I'll tell them about Jemima's ghost when the right moment presents itself."

Christopher pretended to zip his lips, but they didn't stay zipped for long. The moment we left the inn, he glanced up and exclaimed with great pleasure, "The sign! They've rehung the sign!"

The sign that had been removed the previous day for safety's sake now hung by chains from the iron bar implanted in the oak beam above the inn's recessed front door. The sign was an oblong wooden board upon which the inn's name had been painted in curlicued gold letters above a carved and painted bas-relief of an old wooden barrel filled to spilling with bright gold coins.

"Charming, isn't it?" said Christopher as raindrops streamed down his upturned face. "I've never seen another one like it."

"It's delightful," I agreed. "Well worth the wait."

I felt a little giddy. A sugary breakfast, a slight improvement in the weather, and the knowledge that I'd escaped a watery grave filled me with a sense of energetic well-being. Though the rain fell steadily, it no longer fell hard enough to bruise my skull, and the air, however damp, was fresher and cleaner than the air I'd breathed in the attic.

When Christopher urged me to admire the inn's frontage all over again, I was happy to oblige.

"The effect is incomplete without the sign," he asserted, patting his face dry with a neatly folded white handkerchief.

"Like spaghetti without meatballs," I said, "or the *Mona Lisa* without a smile."

"You're teasing me," he said ruefully.

"Maybe a little," I admitted as we walked on, "but I do like the sign. The gold coins in the barrel must be the king's ransom."

"Indeed," he said, "but I regret to say that I have been unable to identify the king."

"Charles the Second?" I guessed. "He rambled around the south of England while he was dodging Cromwell's army, didn't he?"

"Yes," said Christopher, "but he didn't ramble as far east as Shepney, and he was never held to ransom. I asked the Hancocks who the king was, but they didn't know."

"We need a local historian," I said.

"Perhaps we'll meet one in the village hall," said Christopher.

"If we don't, we'll conduct a house-to-house search for one," I joked. "I can't leave Shepney without solving the inn's most impenetrable mystery!"

"I'd prefer to solve the inn's other mystery," Christopher said quietly.

"What other mystery?" I asked.

A determined gleam lit his blue eyes as he turned his collar up and shoved his gloved hands into his pockets. "I want to know why Jemima believes in ghosts."

Ten

Shepney seemed to lead a charmed existence. I couldn't vouch for the entire village or for the farmland that surrounded Shepney's hill, but the high street appeared to be miraculously unscathed. Every window we passed was intact, and the flapping tarpaulins I associated with roof damage were notable for their absence. If it hadn't been for some truly impressive puddles, I wouldn't have known that a cyclone had blown through the village.

Though the rain continued unabated, the cyclone's windy phase was clearly over. Many hanging signs had been rehung, and sandwich boards scrawled with menus or with vivid sale notices stood once again outside their places of business. The café tables and chairs had not yet reappeared, but the flowerpots had. Mums, nasturtiums, asters, and Michaelmas daisies raised cheerful faces to the lowering sky. I hoped they had good drainage.

Despite, or perhaps because of, the state of emergency, a holiday atmosphere pervaded Shepney's high street. Every parking spot was taken, presumably by evacuees, and the shops were as crowded as the inn's foyer. In true English fashion, people clustered on the sidewalks beneath small forests of umbrellas to pass the time of day with friends and neighbors.

A pair of traffic monitors in high-visibility gear patrolled the high street, but there was virtually no traffic for them to patrol. Road closures remained in effect, ensuring that the only vehicles to leave or to enter the village were emergency vehicles. A ripple of cheers and energetic applause greeted a forest-green Range Rover as it cruised down the street, towing a rubber dinghy on a trailer. I wondered if the dinghy had played a role in rescuing the family of four from its half-drowned car.

I saw no one else in high-visibility gear until we entered the village hall, where loose-fitting lime-green vests distinguished the helpers from the helped. The helpers buzzing around the lobby reminded me of the sturdy middle-aged women who ran Finch's multitudinous village events. They dashed past us, intent upon their duties, while we followed a series of hand-lettered signs that led us to the INFORMATION / VOLUNTEER SIGN-UP table in the corridor that divided the building in two.

A sturdy middle-aged woman with tightly curled gray hair sat behind the table, dispensing answers to questions put to her with varying degrees of urgency. Though "Where's the toilet?" seemed to be the most common query, I overheard several others while Christopher and I waited to volunteer.

"Is the bell tower open, Rebecca?" a grizzled old man asked the woman. "I can see my farm from there. I want to know if it's underwater."

"You know very well that your farm's underwater, Jack," Rebecca replied tartly. "The only question is: How deep? I should be able to answer it after the spotters come in from their rounds."

"What about the bell tower?" he demanded stubbornly.

"You can put the bell tower right out of your mind, Jack Stanton," Rebecca said sternly. "Your wife would have my head if I encouraged you to climb those stairs. You'd give yourself a stroke, and the medical team has better things to do than to look after a foolish old man who made himself ill. Connie Fordyce's baby is due any minute. Do you expect her to deliver it by herself? Come back at noon and I'll give you the spotters' report."

The old man was replaced instantly by a flustered mother accompanied by three bickering children. Rebecca gave her directions to the schoolhouse and explained patiently that the children did not have to be registered at the school in order to attend classes.

"When you've dropped them off, come back for a cup of tea, dear," Rebecca advised her. "You look as though you could use one."

The mother agreed wholeheartedly and herded her brawling brood toward the front door.

"Bishop Wyndham!" Rebecca exclaimed, beckoning us to come forward. "I heard you were in town. Sorry about the cyclone."

"I don't hold you personally responsible for it, Mrs. Hanson," said Christopher, shaking her hand. "I intended to leave Shepney this morning, but Mother Nature altered my plans."

"Mother Nature has changed everyone's plans." Rebecca tilted her head toward the flustered mother. "That poor woman was on her way to Hastings with her family when the storm hit. They've been stuck here since yesterday morning. Her husband keeps volunteering to wash dishes. If you ask me, he does it just to get away from the kiddies. You're lodging at The King's Ransom, aren't you?"

"I am," he replied.

"Sick of the rector fawning over you?" Rebecca said shrewdly.

"The rectory is full up," the bishop said with exquisite diplomacy. "May I introduce my friend Lori Shepherd? She was on her way to Rye when the storm interrupted her journey."

"Where are you lodging, Lori?" Rebecca asked, suddenly alert.

"At the inn," I replied. "The Hancocks found a bed for me in the attic."

Rebecca consulted a clipboard. "Here you are—here you *both* are. Bishop Wyndham and Lori Shepherd at The King's Ransom." She looked up. "We try to keep track of everyone in Shepney during an emergency."

"Good idea," I said, oddly reassured by the knowledge that my name was on her list.

"If it's not too much trouble, Mrs. Hanson," said Christopher, "I would very much like to know what spotters are."

"We send teams out to keep an eye on the floodwaters," said Rebecca. "They report back every hour on the hour. It's the kind of job locals do best. They know who lives where, so they can give each landowner an accurate report on the state of his or her property."

"A cogent explanation," said Christopher. "Thank you. Lori and I would be useless as spotters, of course, but we're keen to help in some other way."

"I've got just the job for you, Bishop," said Rebecca. She flagged down another middle-aged woman in a lime-green vest. "Susan? Here's Bishop Wyndham, come to volunteer. Take him to the back room, will you?"

"And Lori?" Christopher inquired.

Rebecca favored me with an appraising look. She must have decided that I was as sturdy as she was because she said, "You can work a shift clearing tables, dear. Susan'll take you to the dining hall, and Kenneth Cartwright will show you the ropes."

Christopher and I added our signatures to Rebecca's volunteer list, then accompanied Susan to a cloakroom, where we left our wet coats; to a locker room, where I left my wet shoulder bag; and to the dining hall, where the bishop and I parted ways. Susan was too busy fawning over her esteemed guest to introduce me to Kenneth Cartwright, so I entered the dining hall alone, hoping to find someone who would point him out to me.

The proscenium stage at one end of the dining hall indicated that the room wasn't normally occupied by people consuming hearty meals at rectangular folding tables. The air was redolent with the mouthwatering scents of fried bacon and sizzling sausages, as well as the din of families, friends, and stranded strangers making the best of a bad situation.

I scanned the room until I spotted a gangly teenaged boy clearing a table that looked as if it had recently been vacated by a hoard of barbarians—or a trio of bickering children. The boy had a mussed thatch of light brown hair, dark brown eyes, and a long, delicate nose that suited his long, thin face. He wore a bibbed cotton apron over a khaki shirt and blue jeans, and he appeared to be lost in thought, as though he were pondering ponderous matters while he loaded a plastic tub with dirty dishes. When I realized that he was the only person at work in the dining hall, I crossed to speak with him.

"Kenneth Cartwright?" I said tentatively.

"You serve yourself," he said, raising his left hand to indicate a table set up as a breakfast buffet. Since his shirtsleeves were rolled to his elbows, I couldn't help but notice the misshapen human skull tattooed on his forearm. The stark image seemed at odds with his subdued demeanor, but I refrained from commenting on it. Teenagers, I knew, could be sensitive about such things.

"I've already eaten breakfast," I explained. "My name is Lori and I'm here to help. Rebecca Hanson said you'd show me the ropes."

Kenneth stopped loading his tub and gazed shyly at me.

"I'll get you an apron," he said.

After donning a bibbed apron plucked from a pile in the kitchen, I pushed up my sleeves and got to work. I filled plastic tubs with dishes, carted them to the steamy kitchen, and, by dint of throwing questions at Kenneth, discovered that he was fourteen years old, that he was a student at Winchester College, and that he'd been given leave to return home from his boarding school for his mother's birthday, a leave the cyclone had extended indefinitely. I chatted with my bashful coworker for nearly an hour before I asked him about his tattoo. Bill would have been amazed by my restraint.

"What's with the skull?" I said as we cleared opposite sides of the same table. "Are you in a gang?"

"No," he replied, blushing crimson. "It's not a real tattoo. Mum would have killed me if I'd gotten a real tattoo, so I did it myself with henna."

"It's striking," I said admiringly. "Why a skull?"

"I . . . I want to be a paleontologist." He spoke defiantly, as if he expected me to laugh at him. When I didn't, he extended his arm across the table to allow me to see his faux tattoo more clearly. "It's a forensic artist's reconstruction of Lucy's skull."

Hoping fervently that he hadn't needed a forensic artist to reconstruct a dead girlfriend's skull, I searched my memory for a Lucy related to the study of fossils. It took me less than two seconds to come up with one of the many scraps of knowledge my magpie mind had accumulated over the years.

"Lucy, the hominid?" I hazarded.

"*Australopithecus afarensis*," he said, nodding eagerly.

"The fossilized human skeleton discovered by Donald Johanson in Ethiopia," I said as one scrap led to another, "and named Lucy after the Beatles' song 'Lucy in the Sky with Diamonds.'"

"How do you know about Dr. Johanson?" Kenneth asked, sounding flabbergasted.

"We were both born and raised in Chicago," I replied. "I've never met Dr. Johanson, but as a fellow Chicagoan, I take pride in his accomplishments."

My scraps of knowledge served me well. From that moment on, Kenneth treated me like a trusted friend. He spoke with unbridled enthusiasm about his lifelong fascination with paleontology and confessed that it hadn't won him much respect in Shepney.

"People here thought I was a weirdo," he told me, "because I used to look for bones when I was little."

"Not in the churchyard, I hope," I said, adding a smile to show my sensitive young friend that I was jesting.

"The churchyard was the only place I didn't look," he said. "I used to climb all over the hill, hunting for animal bones—foxes, rabbits, birds, sometimes a sheep. I wanted to train my eye to recognize bones in a natural setting, the way Dr. Johanson saw Lucy's bones in Ethiopia." He blushed again and ducked his head. "I'll never make a discovery as momentous as his, but I'd like to try."

"Don't sell yourself short," I said. "I'm sure Dr. Johanson was as awed by his predecessors as you are by him. With a lot of hard work and a little luck, you could find yourself on the top rung of the paleontological ladder. Before you launch your career, though, I'd like you to promise me one thing."

"What?" he asked, coming to a standstill.

"Promise me that you won't get a real tattoo," I said.

"You sound like my mum," he said with a hint of age-appropriate sulkiness in his voice. "Why shouldn't I get a real tattoo?"

"Because," I replied, "a *professional* paleontologist doesn't need one."

He nodded thoughtfully, as if I'd said something profound. His mother, I told myself, would thank me one day.

"Also," I continued in a lighter tone, "you don't want to end up looking like Steve."

It wasn't the longest shot I'd ever taken. I reckoned that someone like Steve would stand out in a village like Shepney.

"You've met Steve, have you?" Kenneth said guardedly, resuming his work.

"I have," I said. "I peeled parsnips for him last night at The King's Ransom."

"Only an idiot would want to end up like him," Kenneth muttered.

I eyed my dish-filled tub and said, "I wouldn't mind having his muscles right now."

"Do you know how he got them?" Kenneth asked.

"Lifting weights?" I said.

"He lifted weights, all right," said Kenneth. "There wasn't much else for him to do while he was in prison."

The sight of Monsieur Renault tucking a white packet inside his blue blazer returned to me unbidden. I hadn't thought of the white packet since the fat little Frenchman had scurried past me after his contretemps with Steve, but Kenneth's words brought it vividly to mind. What was in the packet, I wondered, and why had Monsieur Renault brought it to the kitchen? Was he peddling wares from a past Steve was trying to escape?

I lowered my gaze to conceal my thoughts while saying casually, "I didn't know Steve had been in prison."

"That's where he learned to cook," Kenneth informed me.

"He must have graduated with honors," I said. "He's a phenomenal chef. Why was he put away?"

"Sorry, Lori, but I'm not supposed to talk about it," Kenneth replied reluctantly. "If I do, it'll get back to my mum—everything does—and she'll kill me."

"Did she tell you why Steve is off limits?" I asked.

He heaved a long-suffering sigh, as if abiding by his mother's strictures was a burden he had to bear. "Mum says it's not easy for a man to find his way in the world after he comes out of prison, and we shouldn't make it harder for him by turning his past mistakes into cheap gossip. She says as long as the Hancocks are okay with him, we should be, too."

"I'd like to meet your mother," I said, quelling my hunger for cheap gossip. "She sounds like a wise woman."

"Do you think so?" he said doubtfully.

"I do," I declared on behalf of all mothers everywhere.

"Dad says I get my brains from her," said Kenneth. "She's a statistician. Dad's a poet."

I was about to point out that poets had brains, too, when a flurry of activity signaled a shift change. A trio of kitchen helpers swapped breakfast dishes for lunch items on the buffet table, and two sturdy middle-aged women relieved Kenneth and me of our tubs and our aprons. Bishop Wyndham attracted the most attention, however, when he entered the dining hall at the head of an eye-catching procession.

"Lori!" he called. "We've been invited to lunch!"

Eleven

he bishop led a slow-moving parade of five elderly men and women, none of whom were fully ambulatory. Two used walkers, two used canes, and one zipped into the dining hall in a snazzy electric wheelchair. The speed demon rolled ahead of the group to lay claim to an empty table, while the others tottered along at a snail's pace.

I nodded at Christopher to acknowledge the lunch invitation, then turned to Kenneth.

"Join us," I said. "Bishop Wyndham lives in Winchester. He'd love to hear your take on the town."

"I wouldn't be able to get a word in edgewise with that lot," he said grumpily, eyeing the bishop's shuffling chums. "They never stop talking. Besides, Mum asked me to come home for lunch."

"Time spent with you is the best birthday gift you could give her," I told him. "Mums miss their little boys after they send them off to boarding school."

"I'm not—" He cut his angry protest short and grinned ruefully. "I suppose I'll always be her little boy, won't I?"

"There's no escaping it," I confirmed. "Mums are funny that way. Will you be back here again tomorrow?"

"I'm in it for the duration," he said, "whether I want to be or not."

"I'm glad you were here today." I pushed my sleeves down and extended a hand to shake his. "When you make your momentous discovery, I'll be proud to say that I once spent a couple of hours in Dr. Cartwright's company."

He blushed to his roots, mumbled an adorably tongue-tied good-bye, and left the dining hall. I watched him go, thinking of how much I missed my own little boys, then hurried over to help Christopher, whose companions were proving to be a handful.

Though the woman in the wheelchair was capable of independent movement, the others required our assistance. We steadied them as they seated themselves at the table. We parked their walkers in a corner, where no one would trip over them. We took their lunch orders—which were more like lunch demands, barked peremptorily without a "please" or a "thank you"—and we fetched the items they requested from the buffet.

Once we'd seen to their needs, we saw to our own. Christopher selected a bowl of split pea soup dotted with bite-sized chunks of smoked ham hock, and I helped myself to lentil stew, thick slices of crusty bread, and an enticing wedge of chocolate cake. Our lunch-mates put their forks down and bowed their heads over their frail, folded hands while Christopher said grace.

It was a rare moment of tranquillity. Kenneth hadn't overstated the group's garrulity. When Christopher attempted to introduce them, they cut him off and introduced themselves, adding such a wealth of detail to their autobiographies that I could scarcely keep track of it all. We weren't expected to contribute to the conversations that followed, either, which made for a strangely restful meal. While they talked—and talked and talked—we ate.

Sibyl Fordyce, the wheelchair champion, informed me that her granddaughter was due to give birth shortly, triggering a loud and vivid discussion of birthing techniques that drew aghast looks from diners at adjacent tables. Henrietta Hanson bragged that her daughter Rebecca was in charge of Shepney's entire emergency operation, to which George Turner replied acidly that his son Joe didn't take orders from Rebecca.

"Your gal doesn't know the first thing about terriers," Mr. Turner declared, "or rat catching."

"I should hope not," sniffed Mrs. Hanson.

Meanwhile, Leona Dodd kept up a running commentary on her meal, decrying its inferiority to a meal she'd enjoyed in the dining hall during the previous year's flood. Her unflattering observations about the ingredients, the recipes, and the volunteer cooks were received with a mixture of irritation and resignation by the women overseeing the buffet, and she lost all credibility when she requested second helpings of each item on her plate.

Howard Bakewell made his mark by disagreeing with everyone about everything.

"You put up with this for two hours?" I murmured to Christopher, who was seated beside me.

"Was it only two hours?" he murmured in return.

Despite his telling response, he continued to display the patience of a saint. He smiled, nodded, and shrugged off interruptions that would have driven me up a wall. I wanted to give him a standing ovation when he managed to ask if anyone knew who the king in The King's Ransom was. Unsurprisingly, his question ignited a firestorm of dissension as the quarrelsome quintet proposed five different answers, then argued over which one was correct.

Was "the king's ransom" a corruption of a French phrase that had nothing to do with kings? Was it a corruption of a Latin phrase? Did it refer to the inn's original owner, a man named Robert Leroy, whose very existence was called into question by the indefatigable Mr. Bakewell? Or was it a snide tribute to King John II of France, who was held to ransom by the English crown during the Hundred Years' War?

"The answer is lost in the mists of time," Leona Dodd intoned, raising her voice to drown out the others.

"You ought to know, Leona," Mr. Turner shot back with a rumbling chuckle. "You've been lost in the mists of time for the past decade."

"Look who's talking!" Mrs. Dodd retorted. "You'd forget your head if it wasn't screwed on."

The sniping became so overheated that an innocent bystander must have lodged a noise complaint at the information desk, because Rebecca Hanson marched into the dining hall to break up the fight. As she folded her arms and glowered at the combatants, it struck me that the elder Mrs. Hanson was about to receive the same type of scolding she'd given her daughter in days gone by.

"What's all this, then?" Rebecca asked, sounding like a censorious constable. "Making a ruckus? Disturbing the peace? Annoying every living soul within fifty yards of you?" She clucked her tongue in disgust. "A fine way to behave before the bishop." Old Mrs. Hanson opened her mouth to speak, but Rebecca silenced her with a raised finger, a gesture she'd no doubt learned at her mother's knee. "Bishop Wyndham is your guest of honor! Is this how you honor him? By acting like a pack of hooligans? You should be ashamed of yourselves." She swelled with indignation as she continued, "I want to hear an apology from each of you. When you're done saying sorry to the bishop, I'm taking you back to your room. You're not fit to be seen in public." She turned her gimlet gaze on her mother. "You first, Mum."

Christopher graciously accepted the mandatory apologies, and the five geriatric rowdies were escorted from the dining hall under Rebecca Hanson's reproachful eye.

"Hasn't it gone quiet?" I said, when Christopher and I were alone. "Can I get you a headache tablet? Or a cold compress for your forehead?"

"A cup of tea will suffice," said Christopher, refreshing himself with a sip from his cup. "Tell me about your morning."

"It was less challenging than yours," I said, digging into my chocolate cake. "I was paired up with a shy young man who yearns to become a paleontologist."

"Kenneth Cartwright." Christopher nodded. "I put in a good word for him when he applied for Winchester. After he was admitted, his parents asked me to keep an eye on him. I do so, but from a discreet distance. I wouldn't want Kenneth to regard me as a spy."

"He'd make a good spy," I said. "I spent half the morning trying to get him to talk. It was worth the effort, though. You won't believe what he told me about—" I broke off as Rebecca Hanson sat in an empty chair across from us.

"I'm sorry for sending you into the lion's den, Bishop Wyndham," she said. "I thought you'd be a good influence on my mother and her pals, but they're beyond influencing."

"We all become set in our ways," Christopher said with characteristic graciousness.

"They'll have to become unset before I let them eat in the dining hall again," Rebecca declared.

"While I have you here, Mrs. Hanson," said Christopher, "I wonder if I might put a question to you?"

"Ask as many questions as you like, Bishop Wyndham," she said.

"I have only one," he said, smiling. "Do you know why the inn is called The King's Ransom?"

Rebecca winced apologetically. "I wish I did. I've heard a dozen different stories, but I've never bothered to find out which one is true."

"Maybe Mrs. Dodd was right," I said. "Maybe the answer is lost in the mists of time."

"I wouldn't take Leona Dodd's word for it," said Rebecca, rolling her eyes. "She'll say anything to make an impression." She thought for a moment, then said, "Horatio Best may be able to help you. East Sussex is his specialist subject."

"Where might we find Mr. Best?" the bishop inquired.

"At his bookshop," said Rebecca. "He opened it about six months ago. He calls it his dream project. It's on the high street, opposite the village hall."

"Best Books," I said, turning to Christopher. "We passed it yesterday, on our way to the inn."

"Ah, yes," he said, nodding. "Between the sweet shop and the accountant's office. I assumed the name was a form of advertising."

"It is," said Rebecca with a small chuckle. "Horatio isn't a shrinking violet. He'll be the first to tell you that no one knows more about our little corner of England than he does. It's not a hollow boast, either. He taught history for twenty years at Battle Abbey School."

"A preparatory school overlooking the ground where the Battle of Hastings was fought," Christopher explained to me.

"In 1066, when the invading Normans defeated the Saxons, killed King Harold with an arrow through the eye, and altered the course of English history," I said, reaping the rewards of assisting my sons with a recent school project.

"Full marks," said Christopher, as if he sensed how pleased I was with my erudition. "You are correct in every particular." He turned back to Rebecca. "Thank you, Mrs. Hanson. Battle Abbey School is a fine institution. I look forward to meeting Mr. Best."

"I should warn you that he's a bit . . . eccentric." She shrugged. "Well, he'd have to be, to open a bookshop in Shepney." She glanced at the wall clock above the buffet table and jumped to her feet. "Sorry, must dash. The volunteer who's covering for me has a hair appointment in five minutes, though what good a perm will do her in this weather is anyone's guess. Thanks, both of you, for helping us out today. If it weren't for decent folk like you, Shepney would be up a flooded creek without a paddle." She reached across the table to pat Christopher's hand. "You are hereby exempt from volunteering again, Bishop Wyndham. You, too, Lori. You've both sacrificed enough."

"Nonsense," Christopher protested. "Service is a privilege, not a sacrifice."

"You're still exempt," she reiterated.

She patted his hand again, then scurried out of the dining hall. Christopher took another sip of tea, and I renewed my attack on the chocolate cake.

"It seems we've found our local historian," he observed.

"An eccentric bookstore owner," I said. "Sounds about right."

"I'm rather fond of eccentrics," he said.

"So am I," I said, "as long as they're not armed and dangerous."

"They seldom are," said Christopher. "They can be obsessive, but their obsessions are usually harmless. I wonder how eccentric Mr. Best is." He rested his elbows on the table, tented his fingers over his teacup, and looked thoughtfully at nothing in particular. "I wonder if he would tell ghost stories to a child."

"There's one way to find out," I said, licking my fork and wishing I had the nerve to lick my plate. "Let's ask him."

Twelve

hristopher and I deposited our dishes in a plastic tub, collected our things from the cloakroom and the locker room, and set out in search of the eccentric Mr. Best. The dreary, wet day we'd left behind when we'd entered the village hall was still dreary and wet when we emerged from it. Raindrops pelted the glistening cobbles and dripped from Christopher's hat brim as we crossed the high street and let ourselves into the bookshop. I couldn't tell how he felt about Mr. Best's dream project, but for me, it was love at first sight.

There was nothing corporate about Best Books. The place smelled of rain and old bindings. Its pine shelves looked as though they'd been hammered together in someone's garage rather than ordered en masse from a factory, and the wall posters behind the checkout counter touted local events instead of the latest best sellers. A flint-eyed professional would have frowned upon the uneven lighting, but I thought it added to Best Books' allure. While some parts of the shop were as bright as day, others were best explored with a flashlight.

The bookshelves were arranged in bays on either side of a center aisle that required some agility to negotiate as it was scattered with cardboard boxes filled with books. Books covered the wooden tables at the front of the shop, and the wide floorboards beneath the tables were all but hidden by bags of books.

Horatio Best clearly had no interest in selling toys, games, puzzles, greeting cards, calendars, tote bags, T-shirts, or collectible bookmarks. His shop was packed to the rafters with nothing but new and used books. Paperbacks sat beside hardcovers on shelves labeled by topic, with fiction to the left, nonfiction to the right, and children's books cleverly placed on lower shelves, where young readers could reach them.

The shop wasn't packed to the rafters with customers, but it was exceedingly busy. Men, women, boys, and girls reached over, around, and in some cases under one another for volumes that caught their eyes. Some chatted excitedly about a find, some stood in silence while skimming a chapter or two, and a few small children sat on step stools, their noses buried in colorful picture books.

"I could spend all day here," I said, lowering the hood on my rain jacket.

"Indeed," said Christopher, removing his hat. "It's the sort of place that invites burrowing."

I heaved a contented sigh and murmured, "Exactly."

We waited for a lull at the checkout counter to ask the purple-haired young woman behind it if we could speak with Mr. Best.

"You'll find him in History," she said. She pointed toward the rear of the shop. "It's the oversized section, all the way at the back."

"Is Mr. Best with a customer?" I inquired, not wishing to intrude on a business transaction.

"Oh, no," the young woman said easily. "Horatio always hangs about in History." She laughed. "He says it's his natural habitat. And you may as well call him Horatio. You'll find he insists on it."

We thanked her and wound our way up the center aisle, taking care to avoid bumping into customers and tripping over boxes. It was much harder for me to avoid giving in to temptation. The thought of my bulging suitcase was the only thing that prevented me from bringing an armload of books back with me to the inn.

The sound of a distinctive voice reached us as we approached the last bay. It was an attractive voice, deep, resonant, and unabashedly theatrical—the voice of a born storyteller. When I peered into the bay, I saw that the voice belonged to a short, round-bellied man whose attire could be described as eccentric. In addition to a black frock coat and loose-fitting gray pinstriped trousers, he wore an intricately knotted neck cloth, a green-and-gold striped waistcoat, red socks, and a pair of monogrammed black suede bedroom slippers.

The man had a broad, flabby face, a bulbous nose, a wide mouth, and small, pouchy eyes. Though his gray hair was sparse on the top of his head, the rest of it flowed to his shirt collar in flyaway waves. He held a decaying leather-bound book in one hand, leaving the other free to gesticulate gracefully as he held forth on the subject of Queen Boudicca's revolt against the Romans.

A young couple stood listening to him with the strained expressions of polite hostages who wished desperately to escape their captivity without giving offense to their captor.

"There you have it," the plump orator concluded. "I do hope I've answered your question."

"I don't remember what our question was," said the young woman, turning her bewildered face toward the young man. "Do you, Jake?"

"Yes, I do, Linda," the young man said hastily. "And Mr. Best—"

"Horatio, please," Mr. Best insisted.

"And *Horatio* answered our question," Jake stated firmly, his eyes boring into Linda's.

"Yes, yes he did," said Linda, nodding rapidly as she and Jake backed out of the bay. "Thank you, Mr., er, Horatio, but we really must be going."

"Adieu, adieu," said Horatio, raising a pudgy hand in farewell. "Parting is such sweet sorrow." He caught sight of Christopher and me hovering in the aisle. "But journeys end in lovers meeting! Come in, come in!" He eased his considerable bulk into a high-backed leather armchair and motioned for us to perch on a pair of four-legged wooden stools. "Horatio Best, at your service. I am the pro-prietor of this establishment, and though I cannot claim an intimate familiarity with every tome under its roof, I will try my best to point you in the right direction. I believe I would be correct in saying that you, madam, are a stranded traveler."

"Does it show?" I asked, wondering if I looked as unkempt as the French tourists who'd spent the night sleeping on floors and sofas.

"Not at all," he assured me. "I've made it my business to know everyone who lives within a ten-mile radius of Shepney, but I do not, my dear madam, know you."

"I'm Lori Shepherd," I said, "and this is—"

"You need not introduce your companion," Horatio interrupted. "His fame precedes him." His chin multiplied briefly as he made a neck bow to Christopher. "You are, of course, Bishop Wyndham. Word of your visit has spread throughout Shepney with the speed of a plummeting falcon. It is an honor to meet you, sir. If the shop weren't so crowded, I would give you a guided tour of my humble demesne, but the power is out in the village and very few of my neighbors own generators. I had one installed in my shop because the writing is writ large on the wall: Mother Earth will continue to pun-ish us with floods, famines, and fires until we learn to behave as custodians of the natural world rather than as its conquerors."

"Most interesting," said Christopher. "But what has a power outage to do with an increase in business?"

"The two are inextricably linked, my dear bishop." Horatio leaned forward and spoke in a low, quavering voice. "Imagine, if you will, the horror that engulfs a modern family when they realize that they cannot"—he made a moue of distaste—"charge their electronic devices. Their mobiles, tablets, laptops, and desktops are useless! Panic sets in. Without a screen to watch or keys to tap, all harmony is at an end. The ties that bind are on the verge of snapping when someone recalls a dim and distant memory of"—he thrust the dilapidated book into the air as his voice rose in strength and power—"the original virtual-reality device! A wondrous device that will allow them to go anywhere at any time with anyone they choose. A device powered by the imagination, a device gravity cannot shatter, a device that decays organically, leaving no toxic sludge behind to poison our precious planet!" He lowered the book, leaned back in his chair, and concluded matter-of-factly, "At which point they visit my shop."

"I see," said Christopher. "Thank you. I hadn't realized how beneficial a cyclone could be for a business such as yours."

"As the river rises, so, too, do my profits," said Horatio. "Still, the river is kinder to us than the angry sea is to coastal communities."

"A couple moved to my village from the coast because of coastal erosion," I piped up. "They were afraid their cottage would fall into the sea."

"Though our storms have become more frequent and more catastrophic in recent years, the coastline has always been vulnerable to the sea's depredations," Horatio informed us. "Old Winchelsea was a port town of enormous importance, with more than fifty inns and a populace numbering in the thousands, yet it was whittled away by sea incursions until 1287, when it vanished completely beneath the waves and the shifting sands."

"It vanished completely?" I said doubtfully.

"Down to the last brick and cobble," Horatio declared. "The hardy souls who survived the catastrophe moved inland and built a new town, also called Winchelsea, with a tidal harbor on the River Brede. The revived Winchelsea flourished until the 1520s, when the cumulative effects of French raids, the Black Death, and the unrelenting silting of its harbor brought its glory days to an end. Today it is considered by some to be the smallest town in England. If you have not yet visited Winchelsea, I recommend that you do so. It's a paltry three-mile drive from Shepney and, though small, it pulses with history."

"I'll add it to my must-visit list," I said. "But while we're here—"

My words were drowned out by Horatio's. Once he was on a roll, he simply kept rolling.

"Then there's Rye," he went on. "Rye, too, was a prosperous and powerful port town until its harbor was cut off from the sea by the same powerful storm that destroyed Old Winchelsea. Though efforts were made to keep the harbor open, the costs of repeated dredging became prohibitive, and Rye's significance as a center of sea trade faded. It remains, however, a town rich in beauty and history, and it, too, is well worth a visit. It takes less than ten minutes to drive from Rye to Winchelsea. If you visit one, you owe it to yourself to visit the other."

"I concur," said Christopher. "Rye and Winchelsea are fascinating places. However, Lori and I hoped you might answer a question about—"

"The sea has played an indirect but vital role in Shepney's history as well," Horatio went on. "As you may know, the town's name is a combination of Old English words meaning 'sheep island.' Its lofty position has allowed it to—" He broke off, his roll brought to a sudden halt by a loud squawk and a series of thuds.

With a grunt, he heaved himself up from his chair and stepped into the aisle. I slid from my perch to follow him and saw a man even fatter than Horatio sprawled on the floor beside an overturned step stool surrounded by scattered books.

"Dennis Dodd!" Horatio thundered. "Have you forgotten to monitor your insulin levels again? Need I remind you that low blood sugar makes you dizzy?" He rushed forward to help Mr. Dodd to his feet, saying with real concern, "My dear fellow, are you all right?"

"Bruised pride, but nothing worse," said Mr. Dodd, though he looked shaken. "I'm sorry, Horatio. I'll tidy up."

"Ursula will tidy up," Horatio said sternly, gripping Mr. Dodd's arm. "You'll come with me to the back room for a nice cup of tea and a biscuit. You're lucky you didn't break your neck, you old fool." As he and Mr. Dodd passed us, he said, "Pray excuse me. My diabetic friend requires my undivided attention. Come back tomorrow morning with your question. The shop opens at ten. It will be less crowded then." He threw the last two sentences over his shoulder as he guided Mr. Dodd through a door at the rear of the shop.

Christopher and I retreated to the History bay.

"Shall we return tomorrow?" he asked.

"Unless we find someone else who knows why The King's Ransom is called The King's Ransom before then," I said, "we shall."

"Good," said Christopher. "Now that I've been released from volunteering, I'll have an ample amount of free time to devote to our quest."

"A quest we might have finished today if Mr. Dodd hadn't taken a tumble," I said. "Is it selfish of me to resent him? Horatio was just getting around to telling us about Shepney when . . . *bam!*"

"It is selfish," he replied, "but understandable. I, too, feel a certain amount of frustration. Had Mr. Best—"

"Horatio," I said, wagging an index finger at him. "Mr. Best insists."

"Had Horatio gone on for a few more minutes," he said, smiling, "we could have steered him toward the answer we're seeking."

"We'll just have to steer him tomorrow." I stared at the empty armchair for a moment, then asked, "What about the other mystery? Does Horatio Best strike you as the type of chap who'd frighten children for fun?"

"He's a performer," Christopher acknowledged, "but he's also a teacher. I believe he prefers fact to fiction. I doubt that he would recount a ghostly tale without adding footnotes to explain the historical significance of the events that inspired it."

"I don't know any seven-year-olds who would sit still for the kind of long-winded footnotes Horatio would add," I said. "He'd bore them to tears and take all the fun out of being scared. No, I think we can scratch our local historian off the suspect list."

"There's one way to find out who the guilty party is," said Christopher.

Our eyes met as we chorused, "We'll ask Jemima."

Thirteen

The sun had sunk low in the sky by the time we left Best Books. Sunsets came early in England in mid-October, but the relentless rain made the twilight seem darker than usual. Conversely, the shop windows seemed brighter. The high-street merchants had evidently seen the same writing on the wall as Horatio Best and equipped their businesses with generators.

As the bishop and I turned toward The King's Ransom, we spotted Jean Hancock coming out of the souvenir shop. Though I couldn't imagine why someone who lived and worked in Shepney would feel the need to buy souvenirs, a reusable shopping bag dangled from her wrist. She paused in the doorway to open a pink umbrella, then strode jauntily down the high street toward the inn. For a sleep-deprived woman, she looked astoundingly chipper.

"I'm impressed," I said to Christopher. "If my children kept me up half the night, I'd be dragging."

"Perhaps she's learned to tune them out," he said. "I'm told most parents do."

"She wouldn't tune them out at bedtime," I assured him. "There'd be too big a price to pay come morning." A fresh suspicion darted into my mind. "Let's catch up with her. I'd like to know if Jemima told her about the dead lady—or vice versa."

Christopher's eyebrows rose. "Why would Mrs. Hancock fill her daughter's head with such nonsense?"

"To discourage her kiddies from sneaking up to the attic and getting their clean clothes filthy," I said. "They know where she keeps the key. If I were seven years old, I'd find the inn's attic irresistible."

"We're all vulnerable to the lure of the forbidden," said Christopher, lengthening his stride.

Jean Hancock stopped before the candy shop's window to survey a display of bonbons that had been wrapped in gold foil and artfully stacked in pyramids. When she saw our reflections bearing down on her, she turned to greet us. She seemed even perkier up close than she had at a distance.

"Porcini," she announced, indicating her shopping bag. "Steve ran short and everyone else was busy, so I nipped out to the souvenir shop to buy some."

"Porcini mushrooms?" I said, mystified. "At a souvenir shop?"

"Karen Bakewell—the shop owner—keeps a few bits and bobs on hand for our local gourmets," she explained. "Dried mushrooms, crystallized ginger, properly aged balsamic vinegar . . . all sorts of tasty things." A smile lit her face as she looked at me. "I'm glad I ran into you, Lori. I've been wanting to thank you."

"For what?" I asked.

"I don't know what you said to Jemima last night," she said, "but whatever it was, I'm grateful to you for saying it."

"I didn't say much," I told her. "Jemima did most of the talking."

"You must have a calming presence, then," she said. "After she spoke with you, she went straight to bed—and she persuaded Nicholas to go to bed, too. They slept through the rest of the night without making a peep. Thanks to you, Gavin and I got the forty winks we needed instead of the two we expected."

"Jemima and Nicholas didn't keep you up late?" I asked.

"The storm kept them up a little later than usual," she admitted, "but once Jemima came back to the flat, they went off to bed, no problem."

"If Jemima and Nicholas slept through the night," I said, "why did I hear them laughing at half past two in the morning?"

"I don't know what you heard, Lori, but it wasn't my children laughing," she said. "Perhaps you were dreaming."

"I heard them, too, Mrs. Hancock," said Christopher. "I was awakened at half past two by the sound of children laughing. I'm quite certain of the time. I looked at my travel clock."

"It must have been the wind," said Jean. "The inn makes all sorts of queer noises in a high wind. I can promise you that my children were sound asleep at half past two." She gave me another grateful look, then said, "I'm sorry, but I must get back to the inn. The children will be home from school soon and Steve needs his porcini!"

She strode away from us with a definite bounce in her step, leaving Christopher and me to exchange puzzled glances.

"It could have been the wind," he said dubiously.

"The wind died down around midnight," I said. "When the rainfall changed from horizontal to vertical, I woke up."

"Perhaps we heard someone else's children laughing," he theorized. "The inn may funnel sounds from one floor to the next. It's a very old building. It must be filled with hollow spots where the walls don't quite meet."

"It's possible, I suppose, but—" I broke off and banged a fist against my forehead. "I am *such* an idiot, Christopher! I forgot to tell Jean about Jemima's dead lady!"

"It's not too late," he said. "She hasn't gone far."

Fortunately, Jean had paused to chat with a woman whose otterhound seemed unfazed by the rain. The dog walker departed and we hastened forward, coming up on either side of Jean as she sped toward the inn.

"We meet again," she said brightly.

"Hi," I said. "There's something I forgot to mention when we were talking just now, and it's something you ought to know."

I rapidly recounted Jemima's warning about the lady who died in my bed. The faster I spoke, the more slowly Jean walked until, finally, she came to a halt.

Christopher and I stopped, too, and waited for her reaction.

"Jemima gave Captain Pigg to you because she thinks he'll protect you from a ghost in our attic?" she said, her brow furrowing.

"Captain Pigg's a Gloucester Old Spot," I explained. "They're known for looking after their piglets." I studied her perturbed expression and said, "I take it the story is new to you."

"Entirely new," she confirmed. She giggled suddenly. "Captain Pigg and the dead lady. It sounds like a singing group—or a creepy fairy tale."

"A fairy tale you did not tell to Jemima," I said, just to be sure.

"When Gavin and I set up house in The King's Ransom," she said, "we eliminated fairy tales from our repertoire. The building is spooky enough without adding evil witches, helpless orphans, and ravenous wolves to the mix." She smiled wryly. "Horse stories and dog stories are much safer. I won't deny that some of them bring a tear to the eye, but at least they're grounded in reality."

"I do hope you'll believe me when I say that there are no ghosts in the stories I've shared with your children," Christopher said gravely.

"Of course I believe you," said Jean. "Jemima's more than capable of making up her own ghost stories. She has a vivid imagination, and

we do live in a spooky building." She sighed. "She's scrupulously honest, though. If I ask her where the story came from, she'll tell me the
truth. Come on," she said, gesturing for us to accompany her as she
resumed her homeward stroll. "It's time for me to have a chat with
my children. They'll be in the dining room. Steve always has a snack
waiting for them when they come home from school."

"We'll understand if you wish to speak with them privately," said
Christopher.

"You brought the situation to my attention," said Jean. "You've
earned the right to hear what Jemima has to say."

The sun slipped below the horizon as we approached The King's
Ransom. The stained-glass lantern above the recessed entrance cast
a soft light on the inn's wooden sign as well as its front door. I glanced
at the sign's coin-filled barrel and felt another guilty twinge of re-
sentment toward Mr. Dodd for his ill-timed accident. I was certain
that Horatio Best knew what the coins signified. If Mr. Dodd had
treated his diabetes with more respect, I might have known, too.

We left our wet things behind the reception desk and made a beeline for the dining room. As we passed through the foyer, I detected a
change in the sounds coming from the public parlors. Instead of
moans, groans, and grumbles, I heard softly spoken conversations
taking place. The French tourists, it seemed, were becoming recon-
ciled to their fate.

Tessa was setting tables for dinner when we entered the dining
room. Jemima and Nicholas were there, too, drinking milk and
munching on chocolate chip cookies at a table near the stone hearth.

"Tessa," said Jean, holding the shopping bag out to the teenager, "would you please deliver these mushrooms to Steve, along with my apologies for their late arrival?" She smiled mischievously. "I dawdled on the high street."

Tessa grinned, took the bag from her, and disappeared into the kitchen corridor. Jean kissed her children's rosy cheeks before seating herself at the table. When Christopher and I hung back, she motioned for us to join her. Christopher pulled up a chair and sat next to Jemima, but I sat beside Nicholas. I wanted to watch Jemima's face as she responded to her mother's questions.

Jean took it slowly. She asked the children about their day at the informal school and listened to their replies before she switched gears.

"Jemima," she said, sounding curious rather than accusatory, "why did you loan Captain Pigg to Lori?"

"For if she got scared in the attic," Jemima replied.

"Why would Lori get scared in the attic?" Jean asked.

"Because at night the lady who died in her bed comes back," said Jemima, dunking a cookie in her milk.

"I see." Jean nodded. "Who told you about the lady?"

"Trevor Lawson," said Jemima, keeping a watchful eye on her cookie.

"The rector's son?" Jean looked briefly at Christopher and me, and we nodded minutely to show that we knew who Trevor Lawson was.

"Yes," said Jemima.

"When did Trevor tell you about the lady?" Jean asked.

"When he came by with the parish magazine." Jemima transferred the cookie from the milk to her mouth and swallowed a satisfyingly saturated bite of it before adding, "The day before Lori came. The day after the rain started."

"That would be Wednesday," Jean said, nodding. "Trevor always delivers the parish magazine on Wednesdays. Why didn't you tell me or Daddy about Trevor's story?"

Jemima looked into her mother's eyes and replied with transparent honesty, "I thought you knew."

"Well, we didn't know. Because the story isn't true," Jean said. "Trevor's been playing a joke on you, darling. You know how he likes to play jokes, don't you? Remember when he rang the church bell very late at night and upset everyone?"

Jemima nodded, and Nicholas, who'd been following the conversation mutely but attentively, quickly imitated his big sister.

"Ringing the bell was a naughty thing to do," Jean went on. "It was naughty of Trevor to tell you such a silly story, too. It's always naughty to say things that aren't true, isn't it?"

"Yes, Mummy," said Jemima.

"There's no one in the attic but Lori," Jean said firmly. "No one died in her bed. And dead people can't be bothered to hang about in dusty old attics. They'd much rather stay in Heaven. Okay?"

"Okay," said Jemima.

"If Trevor says anything silly to you again," said Jean, "you'll tell me or Daddy about it straightaway. All right?"

"All right," Jemima agreed. "Can we set tables with Tessa after we finish our snack?"

Jean shot a questioning look at Tessa, who'd returned from delivering the porcini to Steve. Tessa nodded good-naturedly, and Jean mouthed the word "thanks."

"If you drink up every last drop of your milk," she said to Jemima, "you may set tables with Tessa."

She stroked her daughter's blond hair and ruffled her son's, then gestured for us to come with her as she rose to her feet and retreated to the foyer.

"Trevor Lawson," she said with a reluctant smile. "I should have known. Forgive me, Bishop Wyndham, but Trevor's a typical rector's son. He's always trying to prove that he isn't a goody two-shoes. Nearly every prank in the village can be traced back to him."

"Like ringing the church bell very late at night?" Christopher asked.

"He rang it at two o'clock in the morning!" Jean exclaimed. "Frightened poor old Mrs. Dodd half out of her wits. Will you be taking evensong again this evening?"

"I will," he said.

"I'd be grateful if you'd drop a word in the rector's ear about Trevor's latest stunt," she said. "I'd do it myself, but evenings tend to be rather hectic around here."

"I've noticed," said Christopher. "I'll convey your concerns to Phillip."

"I'll come with you," I told him, before turning to Jean. "Unless I'm needed in the kitchen."

"Thanks," she said, "but you'll be relieved to know that your services are no longer required. Once our crew finished setting up the kitchen in the village hall, they returned to their proper jobs. A table for two will be ready for you whenever you get back." She pursed her lips thoughtfully. "In the meantime, I'll ring a few parents. Trevor's story will spread like wildfire unless we stomp on it right away. I wouldn't want it to keep the village children from coming over to play with Jemima and Nicholas."

"Don't worry, Jean," I said. "I have two ten-year-old sons at home. I can give the rector some useful tips on how to deal with naughty boys."

Fourteen

Jean asked us to wait in reception while she fetched a pair of flashlights from the office. As she handed them to us, she told us we'd need them.

"You'll be able to find your way along the high street easily enough," she explained, "but Church Lane will be as dark as a tomb. There's been a villagewide power outage, and no one who lives on Church Lane has a generator."

Although Christopher and I had already heard about the power outage from Horatio Best, we hadn't yet experienced its effects first-hand. We thanked Jean for the flashlights and set out for St. Alfege's.

"Do you attend evensong when you're at home, Lori?" Christopher inquired.

"Not as often as I'd like," I said. "I find it comforting to sit quietly in church at the end of a busy day, but my days are so busy that I rarely have time to sit quietly at home, let alone at church. I make time for it when I can, though. I like the prayer toward the end of the service, the one that asks God to defend us from the perils and dangers of this night."

"An oldie but a goody," he agreed, "though I hope most sincerely that you face neither perils nor dangers *this* night."

"I thought I was facing some last night," I admitted. "I don't mind telling you that Trevor's story freaked me out a little. I did everything but look under my bed for monsters. I won't mind seeing the village prankster get his just deserts."

"What would be his just deserts?" asked Christopher.

"If he were mine," I said, "I'd haul him in front of every child who heard his story and make him tell the truth to each of them. Then I'd make him apologize for being a big fat liar." I pursed my lips judiciously. "Then I'd ground him for a week."

"Spoken like the mother of two young boys," said Christopher.

"Spoken like my mother's daughter," I corrected him. "My father wasn't a rector, but my mother was a schoolteacher. I didn't have it easy when I was in her class. I wasn't as naughty as Trevor, but I can remember pulling a few stunts to prove that I wasn't teacher's pet."

"You must empathize with Trevor," Christopher observed.

"I do," I said. "If I didn't, I'd ground him for *two* weeks."

Christopher's hearty chuckle turned heads as we retraced our steps to St. Alfege's. Rain glittered like tinsel in the light from the high street's shop windows, and though Church Lane was enveloped in gloom, it wasn't quite tomblike. Flickering shadows in cottage windows suggested that the residents had stocked up on candles for a rainy—a very rainy—day.

The lane's vicious cobbles were still pointy and slick, but my hiking boots, my borrowed flashlight, and the fact that I wasn't dragging a hefty suitcase behind me allowed me to stride across them with confidence. When Bill's car came into view, I was relieved to see that it was undamaged and pleased to note that it was no longer blocked by pickup trucks loaded with animal feed. I had no desire to move the Mercedes, but it looked so wet and lonely that I gave it a reassuring pat as we walked by.

Some of St. Alfege's windows flickered, while others shone steadily, indicating to me that it was lit by a combination of candles and other less primitive light sources. The flints embedded in the church's thick walls glinted like rain-washed gems in the beams from our flashlights as we hurried up the churchyard path and through the stout oak door in the south porch.

St. Alfege's looked like a monastic barn. Neatly piled sacks of grain covered the nave's flagstone floor, and stacked hay bales encircled the round pillars that supported the Norman arches. Pitchforks, shovels, and a miscellany of other farming implements leaned against the wall on either side of the bell tower door.

A dozen wheelbarrows shared the north aisle with the ecclesiastical needlework exhibition, and five laminated wooden chairs near the wrought-iron candle stand in the south aisle supported a huge roll of plastic sheeting that was used, no doubt, to keep the feed as dry as possible while it was transported to the refugee farm animals.

The church smelled different, too. There was a hint of holy hayloft in the air as the familiar scents of beeswax, incense, old hymnbooks, and furniture polish mingled with the hay's musty fragrance and the metallic tang of machine oil.

The only part of the church that looked like a church was up front, where, as Phillip Lawson had promised, two rows of chairs had been left in place before the chancel. While the nave was dimly illuminated by camping lanterns similar to the one that stood beside my bed at The King's Ransom, the altar was candlelit. It should have been a sight to warm the heart on a cold, wet evening, but the candles didn't look right.

"They run on batteries," said Christopher, following my perplexed gaze. He gestured toward the hay bales. "It's inadvisable to mix open flames with combustible materials. Phillip removed the candles and the matches from the candle stand for the same reason."

"Better safe than sorry," I said, nodding.

"Bishop? Is that you?" A stocky, gray-haired man with a stubbly chin emerged from the shadows beside the altar, carrying a camping lantern. He wore a thick woolen sweater, and his canvas trousers were tucked into a mud-caked pair of black Wellington boots. A smile creased his weathered face when he saw Christopher. "Aye, I thought it was you. Covering for the rector again tonight? I'm thinking you won't have many takers for evensong. Nothing personal, mind. Folk are sick and tired of getting wet."

"Who can blame them?" said Christopher. "Mr. Turner, please allow me to introduce you to my friend Lori Shepherd, who prefers to be called by her Christian name."

"Joe Turner," said the man, offering his callused hand to me.

I shook it, saying, "You're the man with the famous terriers. I believe I met your father earlier today at the village hall."

"Aye, so you did," said Joe. "I heard all about it from Becky Hanson. You've no need to confess your sins tonight, Lori. You've already done your penance." He threw his head back and let out a hoot of laughter that rang from the rafters. "He's an old rascal, my dad, but he's the only dad I have, so I put up with him."

"He's quite a character," Christopher agreed. He turned his head to scan the church, then asked, "Where is everyone, Mr. Turner? I didn't expect a large turnout for evensong, but I thought a few of the farmers I saw last night would be here again tonight."

"They're either feeding themselves or tending to their livestock," Joe replied. "The rector's lending a hand—both hands—with the milking."

"Bless him," said Christopher. "Do you know if he'll return to the church when he's done?"

"I expect so," said Joe. "The less time he spends in the rectory, the happier he is. Lonnie Baker's cockatoo is driving him mad."

"I'll say a special prayer for him," said Christopher.

"I think he's said a few already," said Joe. "Mostly asking Our Lord to give Lonnie's bird laryngitis."

"Poor man," said Christopher, smiling. "If you'll excuse me, Mr. Turner, I'll repair to the vestry to prepare myself for evensong." He tilted his head toward me. "I shall have at least one taker."

"Don't let the dogs loose," Joe reminded him, before turning to me to explain, "I keep my pups in the vestry during services—too many interruptions if I put 'em to work."

Trying not to imagine the kind of interruptions a pack of rat-hunting dogs might cause, I walked with Joe as he escorted me to a front-row seat.

"Jemima Hancock thinks highly of you," I told him. "She's very fond of the Gloucester Old Spot you gave her."

He sat beside me and placed his lantern on the floor.

"Jemima's a grand girl," he said. "Likes to feed the pigs when she visits the farm. Always scratches their backs. They run to the fence when they see her because they know she'll scratch their backs." He rubbed his stubbly chin thoughtfully. "Have to rebuild the fence when I get home. The sty held up fine, but the wind knocked the fence to pieces."

"I'm so sorry," I said. "I hope your pigs are all right."

"I got 'em out in plenty of time," he assured me. "They're living it up in Ted Fordyce's back garden."

"Good for them," I said, feeling more relieved about his pigs than

I'd felt about Bill's car. "Is that what happens to the smaller farm animals—the chickens, rabbits, ducks? Do the villagers take them in during a cyclone?"

"They do," he said. "Leaves a right old mess to clean up afterward, but we all pitch in."

"Cooperation seems to be the key to weathering storms around here," I said.

"You're right about that," he said, nodding. "Don't know what I'd do without my neighbors."

"How long have you lived near Shepney?" I asked, though I thought I knew the answer.

"I was born and raised on my dad's farm," he said. "It's my farm now, and it'll be my son's farm when I'm too old to manage."

"You'll know a lot about the town's history, then," I said, heeding opportunity's knock.

"I know a bit," he temporized.

"Do you know why The King's Ransom is called The King's Ransom?" I asked.

He squinted toward the ceiling, then said slowly, "I reckon it's something to do with smuggling."

"Smuggling?" I said, taken aback.

"Aye," he said. "Smugglers owned East Sussex back in the day. Not legally, mind, but in every way that counts." He inclined his head in the general direction of the high street. "Horatio Best's your man if you want to know about Shepney's history."

"The bishop and I plan to speak with him tomorrow," I said. "We tried to speak with him today, but—"

"Dennis Dodd fell off the step stool," said Joe. "I heard."

I was about to compare Shepney's gossip grapevine to Finch's when the bishop came rushing toward us. It was the first time I'd seen him in a cassock. It gave him an air of quiet authority that was undercut by his rapturous expression.

"Heavenly news," he announced. "I hadn't planned on a choral evensong, but four members of the choir have arrived, ready to sing."

"Folk are getting bored," Joe commented.

"Their boredom is our blessing," said Christopher. "It will take a little longer than a spoken evensong, but I didn't think you'd mind, Lori."

"I don't," I said. "I've never been the only worshipper at a choral evensong before. It'll be a service to remember."

"You're welcome to join us, Mr. Turner," Christopher said encouragingly.

"Thanks, Bishop," said Joe, "but I'll stay in the vestry with my pups. They're not used to music, and I wouldn't want 'em to raise a ruckus when you're halfway through the third collect."

"Before you go, Mr. Turner," I said, "can you tell us how badly flooded the roads are?"

"They're bad enough," Joe replied. "No one'll be going anywhere soon."

"Thanks," I said. I was neither surprised nor disappointed. The day's steady rain hadn't raised my hopes for an early departure from Shepney. "Give your pups a pat for me."

"Will do," he said.

Joe retreated to the vestry, the four choristers filed into the stalls, and the service began. I was completely absorbed in the readings, the music, and the chancel's candlelit beauty until a faint yip from the vestry reminded me that Joe Turner's terriers were not on patrol.

From then on, I couldn't help listening with half an ear for the sound of scurrying vermin.

I nearly jumped out of my skin when the rector slid into the chair next to mine. His cheeks were red and rain dripped from his yellow slicker, so I assumed he'd come directly to the church after he'd finished milking his quota of cows, without stopping at the rectory first. Lonnie's cockatoo, I thought, must have the lungs of a costermonger.

The service ended and the choristers dispersed. Joe Turner released his terriers and the four adorable little dogs resumed their search-and-destroy mission among the grain sacks. The vicar returned to the vestry to change into his civilian garb. I told the rector about the last-minute switch from a spoken to a choral evensong, and he told me proudly that he'd milked twenty cows in just under three hours.

"That's amazing," I said.

"I was raised on a dairy farm," he explained. "It was automated, of course, but my parents made sure that each of their children knew how to milk by hand, in case we lost power. Little did they know . . ." He nodded at the candles.

"Ah, Phillip," Christopher said as he walked toward us. "I'm glad to see you." He pulled a chair around and sat with his back to the altar, facing the rector and me. "I'm afraid I must speak with you about Trevor."

The rector's grin vanished as he let out a piteous moan.

"Oh, no," he said. "What's he done now?"

Fifteen

T he rector had the desperate look of a man pushed to his limits. "Every time I turn around, Trevor's up to something."

"We did hear that he had a slightly tarnished reputation," Christopher acknowledged.

"We heard about the church bell incident," I said.

The rector moaned again and buried his face in his hands. "He woke every dog in the village. Leona Dodd came tottering out of her cottage in her dressing gown, convinced that an air raid was imminent. Everyone else thought the church was on fire. The county fire brigade showed up, sirens wailing, along with an ambulance and two police patrol cars. Church Lane looked like a scene from a disaster film."

"How very distressing," said Christopher, eyeing the young man sympathetically.

"The emergency service workers were not amused," the rector continued, staring bleakly at the flagstone floor. "Nor were our neighbors. My wife and I were up until dawn, assuring Mrs. Dodd that she had nothing to fear from the Luftwaffe, answering dozens of phone calls, and brewing tea to pacify the furious few who banged on our door. I had to make a public apology from the pulpit the following Sunday."

"What happened to Trevor?" I asked.

"My wife suggested sending him to jail in one of the patrol cars," said Phillip, "but in the end we decided that the policemen had suffered enough, and we grounded him instead."

"For how long?" I asked out of professional curiosity.

"A month." Phillip released a dismal sigh. "The hours he would have spent at football practice were spent doing chores for Mrs. Dodd. He also wrote individual apologies to every living soul in the village, which he delivered by hand. It gave him a chance to demonstrate his remorse, and it gave quite a few villagers the chance to tell him to his face what they thought of his behavior."

"Brilliant," I murmured, conceding silently that Phillip Lawson had nothing to learn from me about dealing with naughty boys.

"His offenses have been relatively minor since then," he went on. "He's upset several teachers and irked a handful of parents, but he hasn't thrown the entire village into confusion. If you've come to speak with me about him, however, I can only assume that he's—"

"Taken a misstep," Christopher interjected gently. "As we all do."

Phillip seemed to brace himself before he asked, "What misstep has my eldest son taken, Bishop Wyndham?"

"Lori?" said Christopher. "Would you please tell Phillip about your encounter with Jemima Hancock?"

I had my story down pat by then, but I delivered it with more detail than I had before, describing Jemima's demeanor as well as her words and actions. When I finished, Christopher took over. He recounted Jemima's unhesitating answers to her mother's low-key interrogation and suggested in the kindest possible way that it was, perhaps, unwise of Trevor to tell stories about the walking dead to a child younger and more impressionable than himself.

As Phillip listened, he underwent an unexpected and inexplicable transformation. His shoulders lost their dejected slump, his eyes shone with relief, and his clenched jaw relaxed. By the time Christopher and I reached the end of our tag-team account, the young rector seemed to be suppressing a smile. I wasn't sure what to make of his reaction, and Christopher seemed equally confused.

"Are you all right, Phillip?" he asked.

"I'm better than all right," the rector replied. "Thank you. You've taken a great weight off my mind."

"How?" I asked.

He laughed suddenly. "It won't make sense to you because you don't live here, and it wouldn't make sense to Jean Hancock because she's new here. It didn't make sense to me when I first arrived, but I've gotten used to it."

"Gotten used to what?" I prodded.

"To one of Shepney's little peculiarities," he replied with a tolerant chuckle. "None of the villagers will frown on Trevor for telling a ghost story to another child, because it's done all the time. It's a cherished village tradition."

"It's a village tradition for children to tell ghost stories to other children?" I said, wondering if I'd misunderstood him.

"Adults tell them as well," said the rector. "I'm not saying that everyone does it, but most people do. The stories are passed down through families."

"They're a form of folklore," I suggested.

"They're the purest form of folklore," Phillip confirmed. "Some of the stories are hundreds of years old, and they're told nowhere else. An Oxford anthropologist collected Shepney's ghost stories in the late 1950s, but they've evolved since then. The best storytellers add their own special twists to the tales as they retell them."

"Remarkable," said Christopher.

"I'll speak with Jean Hancock," said Phillip, "but I doubt that she'll demand an apology from me or from Trevor. The parents she's ringing will exonerate Trevor by explaining the tradition to her. Jean may not like it, but she'll have to learn to accept it if she intends to stay in Shepney." He chuckled again. "Ironically, some of the most well-known ghost stories are set within The King's Ransom. Take the tale of the gray lady, for example."

"The gray lady in room twenty?" I said without thinking. When Christopher gave me a questioning look, I told him only that a woman at the inn had mentioned the apparition to me. I had no intention of introducing him to Aunt Dimity. He didn't need to know that there really was a dead lady in my attic and that I'd brought her there in my suitcase.

"The gray lady in room twenty was Grace Dunham," said Phillip. "Grace was the daughter of a tyrannical landowner who ordered her to marry a repugnant but wealthy neighbor. The girl fled before the marriage could take place, riding through a ferocious storm in the dead of night until, too exhausted to go on, she took a room at the inn. She found no rest there. Fear kept her awake and pacing until, tragically, she collapsed and died." He raised an eyebrow. "Believable?"

"Oh, yes," said Christopher. "Tyrannical fathers, oppressed daughters, and repugnant suitors are scattered throughout English history. That a corrupt cleric could be found to perform a nonconsensual marriage ceremony grieves me, but it's well within the bounds of credibility."

"So it is," Phillip agreed. "As time passed, however, the true story of Grace Dunham's tragic demise became less credible. At some point, a villager decided to make the tale more dramatic by adding a ghost. Instead of ending with the girl's tragic death, the legend ended with her spirit drifting perpetually from door to window, ready for all eternity to flee from the men sent by her wicked father to capture and return her to his estate, where she would be forced to marry a man she abhorred."

Against my will and my common sense, a shiver insisted on trickling down my spine. The weirdly flickering candles, the yawning darkness behind us, and the echo that chased the rector's quiet voice around the otherwise silent church gave the story a power it shouldn't have had.

"Has anyone seen the gray lady?" I asked. "After her death, I mean."

"Dozens of guests have claimed to see Grace Dunham's ghost," Phillip replied, "but I doubt that they were sober at the time, and I'm quite certain that they heard the story in the pub before they retired for the night."

"The power of suggestion creates the apparition," said Christopher, nodding.

"Exactly," said Phillip. "Like Grace, Captain Josiah Pigg was an actual historical figure. He was a shady character, but church and civil records prove that he did exist. He, too, died at The King's Ransom, but the coroner's report cites a putrid liver rather than exhaustion as the cause of death."

"He drank himself to death," I said.

"He drowned in an ocean of gin," Phillip said poetically. "It's a local expression, and an apt way to describe the death of an alcoholic sea captain. Sometime after his passing, a villager turned an all-too-common tale into an interesting one by inventing Captain Pigg's merry ghost. Whenever an accident happens in the pub—a spilled drink or a wayward dart—it's blamed on Captain Pigg's tipsy spirit."

"A spirit full of spirits," I commented. "Poor Jemima. I wonder if she knows that she named her pig after a clumsy drunk?"

"I'm sure her village friends will enlighten her, if they haven't done so already," said Phillip. "Come to think of it, they probably told her about the gray lady, Captain Pigg, and the rest when they found out where she lived."

"The rest?" queried Christopher. "How many ghost stories are connected to the inn?"

"A half dozen, at least," Phillip replied, "and each has some basis in fact. In addition to the gray lady and Captain Pigg, there's a chap who cries into his ale, a boy who sings lullabies, a pair of sword fighters, and a big black dog. I imagine Jemima has heard about all of them by now. It would explain why she wasn't unduly alarmed by Trevor's story."

"Jemima was somber when she gave Captain Pigg to me," I concurred, "but she wasn't quaking in her bedroom slippers."

"She didn't have to sleep in the attic," Christopher pointed out.

"She may be halfway between believing and not believing the stories," said Phillip. "If she'd grown up in Shepney, they wouldn't trouble her because she'd know where they came from. She'd know that a chum's great-granduncle or a chap's great-great-grandaunt invented them."

"I wish I'd known it," I said. "I didn't lose sleep over Jemima's warning, but it made me look twice at the shadows in the attic." With a sense of foreboding I asked, "What's the true story behind the lady who died in my bed?"

"I don't know," said the rector. "I haven't heard of her before, but I would never claim to be familiar with every one of Shepney's ghost stories. I wasn't born and raised here."

My heart sank. I could have told him that the dead lady was pure fiction, but I held my tongue. Though I believed Aunt Dimity, I doubted that he would accept her as an expert witness. I had no doubt, however, that his son had let him down again. It was clear to me that Trevor had invented the dead-lady story for one purpose and one purpose alone: He'd thought it would be amusing to frighten the little girl who lived in the inn.

"I'm glad I made it to the church in time for at least part of your lovely service, Bishop Wyndham," Phillip continued, "and I'm grateful to both of you for bringing Jean Hancock's concerns to my attention. As I said, I'll speak with her, but not tonight. I'm already late for supper. If my wife has to sit through another meal alone with the Bakers, I may find myself sleeping in the front parlor with their beastly cockatoo."

"Heaven forfend," said Christopher, smiling. "Shall I preside at evensong tomorrow?"

"Yes, please," said the rector. "Unless the floodwaters recede in record time, I'll be called upon to employ my skills as a dairyman for a few more evenings. I'd also appreciate it if you'd let the Hancocks know that we'll hold a service in the village hall at ten on Sunday morning. I can rely on them to post notices in the inn."

"I'll let them know," said Christopher. "Before you leave, Phillip, I wonder if you might help us with another matter related to The King's Ransom. Lori and I have spent much of the day attempting to ascertain the origin of the inn's name. Can you enlighten us?"

"Joe Turner thinks it has something to do with smuggling," I put in.

"It does," said Phillip. "You see—" He broke off as his cell phone rang. He pulled the phone out of his trouser pocket, glanced at the small screen, and jumped to his feet as he answered the call. He nodded several times and concluded the one-sided conversation by saying penitently, "I'll be home in five seconds." He shoved his cell phone into his pocket and gazed at us imploringly.

"Go," said Christopher.

"Run," I advised.

"We mustn't run in church," Phillip shouted over his shoulder as he race-walked toward the south porch. "As for your question—ask the bookseller on the high street. His name is Horatio Best. He'll tell you more than you ever wanted to know about The King's Ransom. Good evening! God bless you!"

A gust of damp air blew through the church as the rector opened and closed the stout oak door. I folded my arms and faced forward. I was beginning to feel as if our quest for information regarding the inn's name was doomed.

"If his wife had waited one more minute . . ." I groaned.

"If Phillip had waited one more minute," said Christopher, "he would have spent the night in the parlor with his head sandwiched between pillows."

"The curse of the cockatoo," I said, giggling. "I hope he makes it home in under five seconds."

"He will," Christopher said confidently. "Phillip is an excellent runner. He raises money for charity by running the London Marathon. He's finished five of them."

"No wonder he's so skinny," I said. "The mere thought of running a marathon makes me hungry, and I'm hungry enough as it is. Lunch was a long time ago, Christopher. I don't know about you, but I'm ready for dinner."

"Thankfully, we won't have to run back to the inn," he said. "Our table will be waiting for us whenever we arrive."

We stood. Christopher returned his chair to its place in the front row and I pulled up my hood. As we wound our way through hay bales to the south porch, Joe Turner emerged from the shadows to give us a progress report.

"No luck so far," he informed us. "Not like last night. We bagged a sackful of rats last night—what was left of 'em, anyway. The ones we missed must know by now that my pups mean business."

As the bishop and I left St. Alfege's, I sent up a silent prayer of thanks for the rat grapevine.

Sixteen

With its shops closed, its traffic at a standstill, and its streetlamps rendered useless by the power outage, the high street was almost as dark as Church Lane. The windows in the village hall shone like diamonds on black velvet, but the rest of the buildings appeared to be lit by lanterns or glimmering candles, if they were lit at all, which most of them weren't. A handful of flashlight beams bobbing along the sidewalks told us that, though pedestrians were scarce, a few stalwart souls were still out and about in Shepney.

"Well," I said, "we solved one of our mysteries today. We found out who told Jemima about the dead lady in the attic."

"Horatio Best will help us to solve our second mystery tomorrow," said Christopher. "He'll tell us more than we ever wanted to know about The King's Ransom."

"Unless his cell phone rings," I grumbled gloomily, "or a customer falls off a step stool."

"One must always be prepared for disappointment," he acknowledged. "I'm rather pleased that Trevor didn't disappoint his father. In this instance, at least, the boy didn't intend to cause mischief. He was merely upholding a time-honored village tradition."

I avoided lying to him about Trevor's intentions by focusing on the tradition. "It may be time-honored, Christopher, but it's pretty bizarre."

"Is telling ghost stories any more bizarre than chasing a rolling round of Double Gloucester cheese down a treacherously steep hill?" Christopher asked. "The Cooper's Hill Cheese-rolling is held annually in Brockworth, Gloucestershire. It attracts hundreds of participants, some of whom sustain serious injuries while chasing the cheese."

"I know about Cooper's Hill," I said. "If you ask me, the cheese chasers are certifiable, but they're not as crazy as the people who parade through Ottery St. Mary once a year with blazing tar barrels on their shoulders." I gave him a sidelong look. "Cheese rolling? Flaming tar barrels? You can't deny that some of England's finest old traditions are bizarre."

"The tradition of telling ghost stories seems tame by comparison," he observed.

"Unless you're a stranded stranger sleeping all by herself in an attic filled with creepy shadows and scary noises," I protested. "Trevor may be blameless, and Jemima certainly is, but the village isn't. I blame Shepney for spooking me last night."

"I suspect that Mrs. Hancock will agree with you," said Christopher. "I hope she adjusts to the town's peculiarities as well as Phillip has."

"So do I," I said. "It took me a while to get used to my neighbors' funny little ways, but once I did . . ." I paused briefly to examine my conscience before confessing, "Okay, I haven't quite adjusted to all of their peculiarities, but I've learned to live with them. I even enjoy them, most of the time."

"Perhaps Mrs. Hancock will learn the same lesson in forbearance," said Christopher. "It's better to be amused by one's neighbors than to be annoyed by them."

We fell silent as we approached The King's Ransom. The wet

sidewalk gleamed in the light spilling from the inn's ground-floor windows. Many of the windows on the upper floors were lit, too, but since they were fairly small and obstructed by grapevines, they shone less brightly.

The attic's dormer windows, by contrast, were an unwelcoming shade of pitch black. To distract myself from thoughts of creepy shadows and scary noises, I came to a halt and peered intently at the inn's perplexing sign. Christopher stopped, too.

"A wooden barrel filled with gold coins," he murmured. "What can it mean?"

"We have two votes for smuggling," I said. "Joe Turner's and the rector's."

"We also have five votes for five other explanations," Christopher reminded me.

"I could be wrong," I said drily, "but I think the rector is a tad more reliable than our lunchmates at the village hall." I let my gaze travel slowly over the sign until it came to rest on the gold coins. "Could it have something to do with smuggling counterfeit coins?"

"Possibly," said Christopher. "Coins have been counterfeited in England since Roman times, and there's a long history of smuggling in East Sussex. You must put the question to Horatio tomorrow. Even if you're wrong, you'll earn top marks for effort."

"Once a teacher, always a teacher," I said, smiling. "It won't be easy to ask a question once he starts talking, but I'll give it a shot."

The recessed door opened and Jean Hancock appeared, lit colorfully from above by the stained-glass lantern.

"I thought I saw you out there," she said. "Come in and warm up! Your table is waiting for you."

Jean escorted us from the front door to the dining room. As we crossed the foyer, I sensed a profound change in the inn's atmosphere. The foyer was no longer a chaotic crossroads of confused and frantic refugees. Though it was still a bustling central hub, the guests passing through it did so calmly and confidently, and no one pulled Jean aside to demand anything.

"Peace reigns," I commented.

"It's more like resignation," said Jean. "Gavin gave them a discouraging update on the flooded roads. Some of our guests—most of them, actually—thought they'd be able to leave town as soon as the rain came to an end. Gavin had to explain that, even after it stops raining, it'll take time for the saturated ground to drain and for the river to recede."

"Then the cleanup begins," I said.

"Cleanup and repair," Jean corrected me. "We know the roads will be blocked by debris, but we won't know if they've been washed out until we can take a good look at them, and we won't be able to see them until they're dry again."

"So I shouldn't count on leaving tomorrow morning," I said with a wry smile.

"Definitely not," said Jean as we entered the dining room.

"Not that I want to leave," I hastened to add. "I can't think of a better port in the storm than The King's Ransom."

"I concur," said Christopher. "Everyone who works at the inn should be commended for behaving with consummate professionalism despite the trying circumstances."

"I'll pass your commendation on to the staff," said Jean. "They're a stellar bunch. I don't know what Gavin and I would do without them."

"As it happens, I have a message to convey to you, too," said Christopher.

While he told Jean about the Sunday service at the village hall, I surveyed our fellow diners. Since they were speaking French, I assumed that they were with the tour group. They, too, seemed more composed than they had the previous evening, though their conversations might not have been entirely benign. I'd never seen so many dirty looks cast at one man.

Monsieur Renault was the only diner to have a table all to himself. The fat little Frenchman sat in splendid isolation, reading a book while sipping daintily from a demitasse cup, seemingly immune to the hostility directed at him by his disgruntled countrymen.

I doubted that they knew about his mysterious white packets. They were so angry with him for stranding them in Shepney that they would have jumped at any excuse to rat him out to the police. As an image of Monsieur Renault being led away in handcuffs drifted idly through my mind, I realized with a start that I hadn't yet told Christopher about Steve's unfortunate past. I tucked the tidbit away for sharing later, when we were alone. Jean might not wish to discuss her chef's unusual background with her guests.

Jean accompanied us to our table near the windows, then pulled up a chair and sat with us. Tessa appeared a moment later, bearing two cups of roasted cauliflower and white cheddar soup.

"With the chef's compliments," said Tessa. "Does your mobile need charging, Lori?"

"No," I said, prying my ravenous gaze from the soup. "I've used it only once today, so it should be okay."

"Enjoy," she said. "I'll be back in a minute."

"Give us ten minutes, will you, Tessa?" Jean requested.

Tessa nodded and moved on to a group of diners who clearly approved of her familiarity with their language.

"I won't keep you for more than ten minutes," Jean assured us. "I'd like to apologize for asking you to speak with the rector. It seems I was wrong about Trevor Lawson. In fact . . ."

As Phillip Lawson had predicted, the neighbors Jean had telephoned had explained Shepney's time-honored tradition to her. I felt as if I were betraying a maternal pact by not informing her that she'd been right about Trevor all along, but I couldn't figure out a way to present my evidence without presenting Aunt Dimity, so I said nothing.

"Jemima knew about the village's ghost stories," Jean continued, "but she never mentioned them to Gavin or to me because—"

"She thought you knew about them," I broke in.

"I'm afraid so," Jean said ruefully. "I sometimes feel as if I don't know what's going on in that busy little head of hers."

"You're not alone," I told her. "My children are constantly surprising me."

"My village surprised me," she said. "Apparently, The King's Ransom is the backdrop for quite a few of Shepney's ghost stories."

"It's a great setting for a ghost story," I said.

"Phillip told us two such tales after evensong," said Christopher.

"Which brings me back to how grateful I am to you," said Jean. "To show my gratitude, I've asked Steve to prepare a special meal for you this evening. I hope you don't mind."

"Mind?" I said incredulously. "My mouth is already watering."

"It will be a privilege to taste whatever Steve sends out to us," said Christopher, "but the gesture is unnecessary, Mrs. Hancock. In truth, I should be thanking you. My conversation with Phillip was one of the most interesting I've had since I first visited Shepney."

"Hush," I said to him with mock severity. "If Jean finds out how little we did, she'll cancel our special dinner."

"I wouldn't dream of it," said Jean. "I have just a few more items to tick off my list before I leave you." Her tone became businesslike as she turned to me. "You'll be pleased to know that Gavin oiled the hinges on the attic's downstairs door."

"I'm very pleased," I said. "I won't have to worry about disturbing your family or your guests every time I visit the powder room. Please thank him for me."

"I will," she said. "You'll find clean towels in the powder room as well as a laundry bag. If you leave your laundry in the powder room, we'll have it back to you, washed, dried, and folded, before you come down to breakfast tomorrow morning. Tessa will have another thermos of hot cocoa ready for you when you finish here tonight. Finally . . ." Her elated gaze shifted between Christopher and me as she announced, "Good weather news at last! The rain is supposed to end tomorrow. As I explained, we're not out of the woods yet, but it's a start. Please, enjoy your meal." She caught Tessa's eye and nodded, then left us to the pleasurable anticipation that precedes any fine dining experience.

The meal that followed fulfilled food fantasies I didn't know I had. The bread basket alone was heaped with the stuff that dreams are made on. Out of respect for Steve's culinary skills, however, I refrained from gorging on the buttery brioche, the savory fougasse, and the rustic sourdough known in France as *pain de campagne*.

My respect was rewarded. The soup and the bread were superb, but they were only the beginning of a fabulous meal. A shredded brussels sprout salad with a balsamic vinaigrette, shaved pecorino cheese, and bacon slivers was followed by a wild-rabbit terrine, which was followed in turn by the main course: local salt-marsh lamb served with roasted shallots, pickled carrots, and a porcini risotto so creamy, earthy, and rich I could have eaten it with a ladle. Fortunately, the portions Steve prepared for us were large enough to be satisfying but small enough to leave room for his very special dessert.

"Apple crumble," I said, laughing. "With custard *and* cream."

"Not both at once, surely," said Christopher, reaching for the small pitcher of custard.

"I prefer cream, thank you," I said.

I was too absorbed in the flavor fest to waste time talking while we ate. It wasn't until we were lingering over an after-dinner pot of chamomile tea that I relayed Kenneth Cartwright's tidbit about Steve's prison record.

"He wouldn't tell me the whole story," I concluded, "because his mother doesn't approve of hurtful gossip, but even the little bit I learned helped me to understand a remark Tessa made about Steve's lack of social skills. The transition from life behind bars to life in the big wide world must be incredibly difficult."

Tessa, who'd been hovering near us throughout the evening, stepped forward, hesitated, then said in a rush, "Steve may be rough around the edges, but he's all right. He must be. The Hancocks wouldn't allow him to live on the premises if they didn't trust him."

"He lives here?" I said. "In The King's Ransom?"

"He lives in Hastings," she clarified, "but when it looked as though the cyclone would close the roads, Jean and Gavin offered to put him up at the inn. He accepted the offer because he's absolutely devoted to his work. I shouldn't have joked about him this morning, Lori. He may not have polished manners, but he's a good man and a bloody great chef." She caught herself, blushed, and ducked her head. "Sorry, Bishop Wyndham, but I get sick and tired of people harping on about things that can't be helped. Would you like another pot of tea?"

"I'm fine," I said.

"So am I," said Christopher.

Tessa retreated to the stone fireplace, looking as if she wanted to kick herself for saying "bloody" in front of a bishop.

"A spirited defense," said Christopher.

"And a persuasive one," I said. "She's right about the Hancocks. They wouldn't let a convicted felon into their lives—and into their children's lives—unless they were convinced he'd turned over a new leaf." I looked down at my teacup. "But I have to admit that the insatiable gossip in me is dying to know what Steve did."

"Does it matter?" Christopher asked. "I'm afraid I agree with Tessa. There's no point in harping on about things that can't be helped. You wouldn't want a man's past mistakes to hang around his neck like an anchor for the rest of his life, would you?"

"It depends on the mistakes," I said.

"I don't think it does," Christopher argued. "Steve learned a valuable skill in prison. I believe it awakened him to his true purpose in life. To deprive him of the chance to use his God-given gift in an honorable manner merely because he served a prison sentence would be truly criminal. As long as he continues to move forward, his past mistakes are no one's business but his own."

"I'll tell my inner gossip that he took a misstep," I said. "As we all do."

Christopher smiled wryly, then raised a hand to cover a cavernous yawn.

Nancy Atherton

"Forgive me," he said. "It must be past my bedtime." He looked at his watch and sighed. "I must be getting old, Lori. It's only half past nine."

"With age comes wisdom," I said. "You've had plenty of fresh air today. You've earned an early night."

"I prefer the fresh-air excuse to the old-age one," he conceded. "It makes me seem outdoorsy instead of ancient."

"I'll go up, too," I said. "Though my sons refuse to believe it, an early night never hurt anyone."

Tessa handed my thermos to me as we left the dining room. She also reminded us of our nine o'clock reservation for breakfast the following morning, but when she began to apologize for intruding on our meal, I told her not to be silly and Christopher praised her for standing up for her friend.

Christopher did seem tired. As we climbed stairs and clomped through corridors, I wondered if he regretted his choice of a top-floor room. To allow him to conserve his energy, I kept my chatter to a minimum until we reached his door.

"I'll see you in the morning," I said.

"Breakfast at nine, bookstore at ten," he said.

"What if Horatio Best manages by some miracle to tell us why the inn is called The King's Ransom?" I sighed wistfully. "We'll have no more mysteries to solve."

"Oh, I'm sure we'll find something else to do," said Christopher. "Perhaps Phillip will teach us to milk cows."

Reassured by the twinkle in his eye that he wasn't on the verge of collapse, I said good night and headed for the attic. I intended to spend the rest of the evening curled up in bed with a good book.

Seventeen

fter testing the oak door to make sure that it was creak-free, I opened and closed it with gay abandon as I climbed up and down the U-shaped stairs, filling my laundry bag and returning it to the powder room. Once I'd made use of the clean towels, I went back up to the attic, where I changed into my long underwear, gave Captain Pigg an affectionate pat on his pink head, and hunkered down under my duvet.

The pattering rain, the fabulous meal, and the overdose of fresh air should have made me drowsy, but I hadn't retired early because I was tired. I'd done so because Aunt Dimity and I had a lot of catching up to do. Before I opened the blue journal, however, I reached for my cell phone. I knew that Bill would be waiting for my call.

He was.

"*Thank God,*" he said when he heard my voice.

"What's wrong?" I asked as a hundred heart-stopping scenarios darted through my mind. "Is it the children? I meant to call your father, but—"

"The children are fine," he interrupted, "but I'm not."

"What's wrong with you?" I asked, limp with relief.

"Terminal boredom," he replied. "Sir Roger Blayne must be the most tedious man on earth. He spent *all day* showing me his stamp collection."

"Stamps are educational," I said with exaggerated primness. "They're tiny little windows on the world."

"*All day*, Lori," Bill complained. "His butler served our meals *in the stamp room*. I used to think Sir Roger chose to be a recluse. I know now that he's a recluse because no sane person would choose to spend more than five minutes listening to him drone on about his favorite hobby—not if they wanted to stay sane, at any rate. Please tell me that you had an interesting day."

"As a matter of fact, I did," I said, "but I didn't charge my phone, so you'll have to make do with the highlights."

"Do they involve stamps?" Bill asked.

"Nope."

"I'm all ears."

Even the summarized version of my lunch at the village hall had Bill in stitches, as did my descriptions of Horatio Best's steamroller monologues and Joe Turner's rat report. Though I told him that Christopher and I were seeking an explanation for the inn's name, I didn't mention ghosts, ghost stories, ghost warnings, ghostly noises, or ghost-busting pigs. I loved the sound of Bill's laughter, but not when he was laughing at me.

I also refrained from mentioning Monsieur Renault, the suspicious white packet, and the tattooed ex-con in the kitchen. I didn't want my overprotective husband to get the idea that The King's Ransom was a den of iniquity.

"Thanks," said Bill when I ran out of highlights. "I needed that."

"Be of good cheer," I said. "It's supposed to stop raining tomorrow."

"And it may take a week for the floodwaters to recede," he said with a distinct lack of good cheer.

"The wind has died down," I said. "You could call for a helicopter to whisk you away from Blayne Hall."

"Don't think I haven't considered it," said Bill. "But Sir Roger means well, Lori. I may want to beat him over the head with a postage stamp album, but I wouldn't want to hurt his feelings."

It was my turn to laugh.

We talked for a few more minutes before saying good night. I set the alarm on my cell phone and exchanged it for the blue journal.

"Dimity?" I said as I opened the journal. "Believe it or not, I feel sorry for Bill."

I laughed again as Aunt Dimity's fine copperplate unfurled across the blank page.

Will wonders never cease? What brought about your change of heart?

"I had a million things to tell him tonight," I said, "but he had only one thing to tell me. You were right, Dimity. I have been lucky. I'd much rather be marooned in Shepney than in Blayne Hall." I recounted both sides of my conversation with Bill, then waited for Aunt Dimity's response.

You didn't really tell him that stamps are educational, did you?

"He deserved it," I said. "He frightened me half to death with his 'Thank God.' I thought Will and Rob had broken their necks."

You're a cruel woman, but I do understand.

"Thank you." I leaned back against my piled pillows. "And now for the unexpurgated version of my day."

I thought I detected a gap in your narrative. Your failed attempts to identify the king in The King's Ransom couldn't have taken more than a few hours, which leaves quite a few unaccounted for. I assume you had a good reason to omit certain items from the version you shared with your husband.

"I had a very good reason for not telling Bill about Monsieur Renault," I stated firmly.

Who is Monsieur Renault?

"He's a shady Frenchman who sneaks around the inn with white packets of an unknown substance on his person." I took a deep breath and launched into a comprehensive account of my night as volunteer parsnip peeler. I described the choice of doors that faced me as I hunted for the kitchen, the heated argument I inadvertently overheard, Monsieur Renault's abrupt departure, and my first impression of Steve.

"He looks like a pirate on steroids," I said. "He's about eight foot six, bulging with muscles, and covered in tattoos. He didn't have a parrot on his shoulder or a peg leg, but he has a goatee and he was wearing a bandana on his head. He looks so scary that I wasn't entirely surprised to learn that he's an ex-con."

Are his employers aware of his prison record?

"I imagine everyone in Shepney is aware of his prison record," I said drily. "It's not the sort of place where a secret stays secret for long."

In that respect, at least, Shepney is very much like Finch.

"A village is a village," I said.

And since villagers the world over like to gossip, you must have learned a few more things about Steve while you were out and about today.

"I didn't learn why he went to prison or how long he spent there," I said. "The mother of the young man who told me about Steve has given him strict orders to keep his mouth shut about the details. She doesn't want idle gossip to get in the way of Steve's attempt to turn over a new leaf."

Good for her. As you know, gossip is a double-edged sword. It can be quite useful, but it can also do great damage.

"It doesn't seem to have damaged Steve's reputation in Shepney," I said. "Our waitress overheard me talking about him and instantly came to his defense. She thinks he's a stand-up guy."

The Hancocks must think so, too, or they wouldn't have hired him.

"They've also given him a room at the inn," I said. "It's not a permanent arrangement. He has a flat in Hastings, but when it looked as though the cyclone would close the roads, the Hancocks offered to put him up. If they didn't trust him, they wouldn't let him sleep under the same roof as their children, would they?"

No, they wouldn't. Are the children fond of him?

"They're fond of his apple crumble," I said. "He made it for them as a reward for good behavior during the storm."

Steve has the support of a villager, a coworker, and his employers, and he makes special treats for Jemima and Nicholas. It sounds as though he's well on his way to redemption. Why, then, would he lose his temper with a French tourist?

"Monsieur Renault seems to have a knack for infuriating people," I informed her. "He's the reason the tour group was stranded here. Apparently, he vanished just before they were due to leave Shepney, and he didn't show up again until it was too late for them to get out of town."

What an inconsiderate thing to do. He must have known that the storm would make it imperative for them to leave on time. It would have served him right if they'd left without him.

"They may leave without him anyway," I said.

Has he done something else to irritate them?

"He has," I said. "While the rest of the group is camping out in the inn's public parlors, he's sitting pretty in a guest room."

How did he come by a guest room? I thought they were in short supply.

"He reserved his ahead of time," I said, "so he could take a nap while the group explored Shepney."

Bus tours can be tiring, but I suspect his foresight hasn't endeared him to his compatriots.

"Quite the opposite," I confirmed. "He must have nerves of steel, though. Almost everyone in the dining room was giving him the stink eye this evening, but he didn't seem to care, and he held his own in his argument with Steve."

I wish you'd understood more than three words of the argument.

"Sorry, Dimity," I said, "but I was listening through a closed door and they were talking very fast. *Le prix, un escroc,* and a string of emphatic *nons* were the only words I could make out."

The price, a crook, and no! It's not much to go on.

"According to our waitress, Steve routinely bars guests from entering his domain," I said. "I can't help wondering if he had a special reason to bar Monsieur Renault. Remember the white packet?"

The white packet filled with an unknown substance?

I hesitated, then said cautiously, "What if the unknown substance is drugs?"

Then Monsieur Renault would be a very dangerous man indeed.

"He'd pose a particular danger to an ex-con," I said pensively. "I don't think they're allowed to hang out with drug dealers."

Steve's parole may require him to avoid contact with criminals of any kind. But if Monsieur Renault is a drug dealer, why hasn't Steve reported him to the police? At the very least, I would expect him to tell the Hancocks that they're harboring a felon.

"The police can't reach Shepney until the floodwaters recede," I said, "so there'd be no point in notifying them right now. As for the Hancocks . . ." I frowned into the middle distance for a moment, then looked down at the journal. "Maybe Monsieur Renault has something on Steve."

Are you suggesting that Monsieur Renault is a blackmailer as well as a drug dealer?

"In for a penny, in for a pound," I said. "Christopher thinks Steve's found his true purpose in life at The King's Ransom. If there's a shameful secret in his past—a secret that would put his job at risk— he might do just about anything to hush it up."

How would Monsieur Renault have discovered Steve's shameful secret?

"They could have known each other in the bad old days," I said. "They could have been partners in crime. Or Monsieur Renault could have heard about it from one of Steve's cellmates or from an accomplice, if Steve had an accomplice. Criminals are probably as prone to gossip as villagers."

As underworld gossip can have terminal consequences, I would expect criminals to be more circumspect than villagers, but I take your point. Do you intend to tell the Hancocks about the white packet?

"No," I said, "not unless something else crops up. It's okay to speculate about Monsieur Renault with you, Dimity, but I wouldn't go to the Hancocks with nothing more than three words taken out of context and a glimpse of a packet that may or may not contain drugs."

Unless I'm mistaken, Lori, you have just refused to jump to a conclusion.

"Will wonders never cease?" I said, grinning.

Apparently not. I, too, will reserve judgment on Monsieur Renault, but I'm in complete agreement with your decision to exclude him from your conversation with Bill. Your husband would not have been pleased to hear that you were staying in the same inn as a drug-dealing blackmailer.

"My sentiments exactly," I said. "I didn't tell Bill about Jemima's dead lady, either."

Why not? Were you afraid he'd tease you about your skittishness last night?

"He wouldn't have understood my skittishness," I said, "because I also didn't tell him that I'm sleeping in a spooky, creepy, shadowy, dusty attic. And by the way," I added defensively, "I wasn't the only one who heard strange noises last night. Christopher heard them, too. We both heard my oak door creak and we both heard children laughing at half past two in the morning."

I believe we've explained the creaking door adequately, Lori. As for the children laughing, your room and the bishop's are situated near the Hancocks' flat. You both must have heard Jemima and Nicholas.

"That's what we thought," I said, "but Jean swears that her children were asleep at half past two. She blames the storm for the sounds we heard."

How does the bishop account for the laughter?

"He thinks we may have heard children on another floor," I said. "His theory is that the sounds funneled up to us through gaps in the inn's walls."

It's a reasonable theory. Old buildings often have architectural quirks. I once stayed in a house in which noises from the kitchen could be heard in the upstairs guest bedroom. I found it quite disturbing until I realized what was going on, just as you were disturbed by Jemima's dead lady until you spoke with me.

"I'm still disturbed by Jemima's dead lady," I said, "but for a different reason."

Was the bishop responsible for Jemima's macabre flight of fancy?

"He had nothing to do with the dead lady," I said. "Jemima heard the story from the rector's son, a ten-year-old troublemaker named Trevor. I'm disturbed because Trevor won't be punished for trying to frighten her."

Is the rector reluctant to punish his son?

"No," I said. "He's unaware that his son deserves to be punished, because . . ." I took another deep breath and explained Shepney's bizarre tradition of handing ghost stories down from one generation to the next. "The difference between Trevor's story and the traditional stories," I concluded, "is that the traditional stories were inspired by real people."

I see what you mean, Lori. Captain Pigg, the gray lady, the maudlin drunkard, the singing boy, the sword-fighters, and the angry man in room thirty-two once lived and breathed. The same can be said of the black dog who wanders The King's Ransom in search of his master. Trevor's dead lady, however, is pure fantasy. Her ghost doesn't exist because she never existed.

"I believe you, of course," I said, "but the rector would think I was nuts if I told him that a real dead lady told me the truth about the fake dead lady."

Yes, I'm afraid he would regard your testimony as somewhat unreliable.

"So Trevor won't be punished because I can't tell the rector why he should be," I said. "Trevor wasn't being a good little Shepney boy when he told Jemima about the dead lady. He made up the story because he wanted to scare her."

I wouldn't jump to that conclusion, either, Lori. It's possible that Trevor told the story in good faith. He may have heard it from a village child who was trying to scare him. It seems unlikely that he's the only troublemaker in Shepney.

"Anything's possible," I agreed. "But Trevor will remain my main suspect until I hear otherwise. Thankfully, Jemima doesn't seem to be losing sleep over the dead lady. In fact, she was aware of the storytelling tradition before her mother was." I shook my head. "Jean Hancock knows remarkably little about the inn or the village."

There's nothing remarkable about it, Lori. The poor woman is raising two children while running a demanding business in a new community. If she ever has a moment to call her own, I doubt that she spends it swotting up on Shepney's history. You and the bishop, on the other hand, had all the time in the world to search the bookstore's extensive history section for the answer to your question about the inn. Why didn't you?

"We . . . I . . . uh . . ." My voice trailed off into embarrassed silence while I scrambled for a reply that didn't make my foolish oversight seem like an imbecilic oversight. "The store was packed with people, Dimity, and the big guy fell off the step stool, and Horatio told us to come back tomorrow, and we wanted to talk with Jemima before evensong, and . . . and . . . I guess you could say we were distracted," I finished weakly.

You're not distracted now. I believe you mentioned a collection of books in the attic. One of them might contain information about the inn.

"There's a bookcase," I said, "but it looks as though it's full of boarding-school novels." I turned my head to scan the faded spines, then tilted the camping lantern to shed more light on the teak bookcase. The tilted lantern and my prone position allowed me to see a slender volume I hadn't noticed before. "Hold on a minute, Dimity. There seems to be something wedged between *Billy Bunter of Greyfriars* and *The Fifth Form at St. Dominic's*. I'll be right back."

I placed the blue journal on the octagonal table, got out of bed, and crossed to the bookcase. The slender volume I'd spotted wasn't a book per se but a worn and faded notebook. Since it looked as though it might be fragile, I removed the books on either side of it before pulling it from the shelf and opening it. After turning a few pages, I brought the notebook back to bed with me, crawled under the duvet, and laid it gently on my lap. I took the blue journal from the octagonal table and held it open with one hand while paging through the notebook with the other.

"I think it's a ledger, Dimity," I said. "An eighteenth-century ledger, by the looks of it. The paper and the writing style are Georgian, and the entries were handwritten with a quill pen."

Your background as a rare-book bibliographer is serving you well, my dear.

Aunt Dimity was referring to an informal position I'd once held at my university's library. Though I didn't have a degree in library science, I had a lot of experience handling rare books and manuscripts.

"Knowledge is never wasted," I declared. I pulled the camping lantern closer and studied the florid handwriting. "The first entry is dated"—I gave a low whistle—"19 September 1741. The rest of the entry reads like an alcoholic's shopping list: 61 gallons brandy, 120 gallons wine, 200 gallons rum, and 330 gallons g-geneva." I stumbled over the last word and looked questioningly at the blue journal. "What's geneva?"

I have no idea, but if it's listed with brandy, wine, and rum, I imagine it's another type of liquor.

I turned back to the ledger. "The second entry lists various amounts of tea and tobacco. The third entry is similar to the first: brandy, rum, geneva. The prices aren't listed, but—" I broke off as a sudden insight occurred to me. "What if this stuff is priceless?"

Do you mean rare?

"No," I said slowly. "I mean illegal. The ledger could be a record of smuggled goods, couldn't it, Dimity?"

It could. I believe smuggling was a common occupation in East Sussex at one time.

"Smuggled goods would be sold on the black market," I said. "The prices would vary, depending on the buyer, so they couldn't be recorded accurately until the goods were sold." I stared at the incomplete entries, thinking hard. "I believe I was mistaken, Dimity. The notebook isn't a ledger. It's an inventory."

I follow your reasoning, but I wonder what prompted you to connect the notebook to smuggling?

"Joe Turner," I replied. "And the rector, come to think of it. Joe reckoned that the inn's name had something to do with smuggling, and the rector backed him up." I laughed out loud as another insight struck me. "Smugglers would have transported liquor in wooden barrels, wouldn't they? I'll bet you anything that the barrel on the inn's sign refers to smuggling." My laughter died away when I realized that I'd solved only part of the riddle. "But I still don't know why the inn is called The King's Ransom."

I suspect that Horatio Best will be able to give you a definitive answer.

"I'm sure he'll give us a long one," I said, "but it will probably be definitive. I'll bring the notebook with me to the bookstore tomorrow. It'll knock his flashy socks off."

You may not have noticed, Lori, but tomorrow is fast approaching.

I looked at my cell phone and saw to my dismay that it was nearing midnight.

"I'd better call it a day, Dimity," I said. "I'll need to have my wits about me tomorrow. It's not easy to keep Horatio from wandering off into digression land. I'll let you know what we find out."

I look forward to hearing the unexpurgated version. Sleep well, my dear. If you hear children laughing again, put a pillow over your head.

"I will," I said, smiling. "Good night, Dimity."

The graceful lines of royal-blue ink faded from the page. I closed the journal and the inventory and placed both on the octagonal table.

"Were you named after a smuggler?" I asked Captain Pigg.

His gleaming black eyes seemed to suggest that I was on the right track.

Smiling, I touched a fingertip to his pink nose, turned off the camping lantern, and pulled the duvet up to my chin. I had no trouble falling asleep.

A short time later, when the sound of a creaking door pulled me from a pleasant dream, I cursed the inn's architectural quirks and followed Aunt Dimity's sage advice.

Eighteen

unt Dimity's advice worked. I wasn't awakened by a sound the following morning. I was awakened by shafts of sunlight shining softly through the grimy dormer windows. The rain had ended at last. If the U-shaped stairs hadn't been so treacherous, I would have tap-danced down them.

My laundered clothes were waiting for me in the powder room. After completing my morning routine, I decided to wear my hiking gear again. Though the sun's return had lifted my spirits, I wasn't convinced that it would shine all day. English weather was changeable at the best of times. In mid-October, it was downright flighty.

I toasted the cyclone's departure with a cup of hot cocoa, stowed the slender notebook in my shoulder bag, gathered my rain jacket and the thermos, and went downstairs. The dining room was less romantic with sunlight streaming through the wall of windows, but no one seemed to mind. I detected a definite uptick in the general mood. Whether it was due to the sun's presence or to Monsieur Renault's absence, however, was debatable.

Christopher had beaten me to our table. To my relief, he looked as fresh as a daisy as he waved at me with a pair of menus. After informing me that power had been restored in the village, he selected oatmeal, fresh fruit, and coffee for his breakfast. I went for the roasted butternut squash omelet and a pot of black tea.

Tessa, who seemed to work twelve-hour shifts, came to take our orders and to relieve me of the thermos. She approached our table shyly, as if she still felt guilty for speaking out on Steve's behalf, but we did our best to put her at ease. When she left, I asked Christopher if he, too, had heard a door creak in the wee hours. He had, but he'd noted a detail that had escaped my attention.

"I heard the door creak at half past two in the morning," he said.

"Are you sure?" I asked with a doubtful frown.

He nodded. "My travel alarm is quite reliable, and I was struck by the coincidence. I heard the sound of children laughing at half past two yesterday morning, and I heard your door creak at half past two this morning."

"You didn't hear my door," I told him. "Gavin oiled the hinges to within an inch of their lives. They don't creak anymore."

"There must be another door in need of lubrication," said Christopher.

"I hope the guest mentions it to Gavin," I said. "I'd like to make it through at least one night without playing 'What's That Noise?'"

"A game in which we are involuntary and most unwilling participants," Christopher commented.

"On a brighter note, take a look at this." I pulled the notebook from my shoulder bag and passed it to him. "I found it last night, tucked away on a bookshelf in the attic. I think it's a smuggler's inventory. Joe Turner told me that smugglers owned East Sussex back in the day."

"So they did." Christopher turned the notebook's pages with the light touch of a man accustomed to handling delicate documents. "It could very well be a smuggler's inventory, Lori. I believe brandy, rum, and tea were among the most common goods smuggled into

England in the eighteenth century." He handed the notebook back to me. "I congratulate you. You've made a remarkable discovery."

"The attic is full of treasures," I told him, returning the slender volume to my bag. "If the Hancocks auctioned them off, they'd be rich enough to seal the gaps in the inn's walls."

"The notebook is certainly a treasure," he agreed.

"I'll turn it over to Jean and Gavin," I said, "but not until after I've shown it to Horatio Best."

"I must admit that I'd like to hear his thoughts on it," said Christopher.

"I'm sure we'll hear his thoughts on a whole lot of things," I said, rolling my eyes. "I had a thought about the inn's sign last night. It occurred to me that the wooden barrel could symbolize the barrels smugglers used to transport liquor."

"I suppose the gold coins in the barrel could signify the smugglers' ill-gotten gains," Christopher said thoughtfully.

"Brilliant!" I exclaimed, beaming at him. "Wish I'd thought of it. I have a feeling we'll both receive top marks from Horatio for good guesswork."

"Even if we go to the head of the class," he said, "our guesses don't explain the inn's name. Who was the king? Who held him for ransom? Was the ransom paid? If so, by whom?"

"We have to leave *something* for Horatio to do," I said airily.

Our breakfasts arrived. Christopher's oatmeal looked like oatmeal, but my omelet was another culinary masterpiece. The butternut squash was cooked to tender perfection with a sprig of rosemary and an inspired drizzle of maple syrup. Though Christopher finished his simple meal before I finished my feast, we left the inn in plenty of time to get to Best Books by ten.

As we strode down the high street, I saw an elderly woman standing stock still with her face turned toward the sun. Her beatific smile said everything that needed to be said about Shepney's release from the cyclone's rainy grasp.

She wasn't the only sun worshipper. Though most of the shops were open, they were less crowded than they'd been the previous day. The sidewalks, by contrast, were as congested as a freeway at rush hour. It looked as though everyone in the village was celebrating the sun's return with a leisurely promenade.

We hadn't gone far when Christopher was accosted by an elderly man walking a yappy dachshund. While the two men chatted, I caught sight of an encounter that made me wish I could lip-read. Monsieur Renault and a red-haired woman stood in a narrow passage between two buildings, out of the main stream of pedestrian traffic. They appeared to be having an intense, and intensely private, conversation. The redhead kept glancing over her shoulder, as if to make sure that no one was eavesdropping.

My eyes nearly started from their sockets when Monsieur Renault drew a bulky white packet from inside his trench coat and exchanged it for a manila envelope the redhead thrust at him. Monsieur Renault stuffed the envelope in his coat pocket and strode hurriedly down the passage. The redhead was still tucking the white packet into her purse as she stepped onto the high street and merged with the sun worshippers.

"Lori?" said Christopher. "We can proceed now. Mr. Braithwaite was simply confirming the time for tomorrow's service."

"Did you see . . . ?" I began, but I let the question trail off. There was no point in asking him if he'd seen what I'd seen. It was clear that he hadn't noticed anything beyond Mr. Braithwaite and the yappy pup.

Christopher continued to greet and to be greeted by various villagers as we walked on. I smiled reflexively while my mind lingered on the white packet and the manila envelope. I couldn't swear to it in a court of law, but I was fairly certain I'd just witnessed a drug deal.

St. Alfege's bells were chiming the hour as we approached the bookstore. A pudgy hand flipped the CLOSED sign to OPEN, and Horatio Best stepped through the doorway in his monogrammed bedroom slippers to call a cheery hello to a family passing by. It took him a moment to recognize Christopher and me, but he smiled broadly as the penny dropped.

"My friends with the question!" he exclaimed in his deep, resonant voice. "I'm so glad to see you again. Do come in!"

Horatio was dressed in his familiar frock coat and pinstriped trousers, but he'd accessorized them with obvious tributes to the change in the weather: a yellow bow tie sprinkled with sunbursts, a yellow pocket square, a yellow-and-white striped waistcoat, and lemon-yellow socks. His colorful attire and his even more colorful manner helped me to set aside my unsettled thoughts about Monsieur Renault and the redhead, and to concentrate on the task at hand.

In keeping with the solar theme, the purple-haired young woman at the checkout counter wore a butter-yellow pullover and a pair of gold sunburst earrings. Horatio introduced her to us as the irreplaceable Ursula before leading us to his lecture hall in the history section. While we resumed our perches on the four-legged stools, he lowered himself into his high-backed armchair.

"How may I help you?" he inquired.

It would have been polite to ask him if Dennis Dodd had recovered from his fall, but I had no desire to listen to a lengthy discourse on the dangers of diabetes, so I stayed on the straight and narrow.

"Why is The King's Ransom called The King's Ransom?" I asked.

"Therein lies a tale," he said.

"I thought it might," I said under my breath.

Christopher disguised a snort of laughter with a cough.

"The inn was originally known as The Crown," Horatio began. "The name referred to its lofty position atop Shepney's limestone ridge, however, rather than to the monarchy. As we shall see, the monarchy has not always been held in high esteem in Shepney."

"Why not?" I asked.

"Taxation," Horatio answered with rare brevity. "From the Anglo-Saxon period onward, English monarchs have financed lavish lifestyles as well as a continuous series of wars by imposing taxes on their subjects. The taxes were particularly burdensome in rural areas, where the common people were desperately poor and frequently on the brink of starvation. To evade import and export taxes, as well as starvation, residents of coastal communities frequently resorted to small-scale smuggling."

"How burdensome were the taxes?" Christopher inquired.

"They became increasingly so," Horatio replied. "By the early eighteenth century, the import tax on tea added almost seventy percent to the tea's actual cost."

"Ouch," I muttered.

"As higher and higher taxes were placed on a wider and wider variety of products, smuggling became more and more profitable," Horatio continued. "When profits rose, small-scale entrepreneurs were replaced or absorbed by highly organized gangs running massive operations."

"What sorts of things did they smuggle?" I asked.

"In East Sussex," Horatio replied, "wool and sheep were smuggled abroad, where they were used to buy taxable goods, which were smuggled into England. Methods varied from place to place and from era to era, but I can, if you wish, paint a broad portrait of a typical eighteenth-century smuggling operation."

"Please do," said Christopher.

Horatio cleared his throat and settled back in his chair. "A fishing ship laden with wool would set sail from an out-of-the-way-port—a port unsupervised or inadequately supervised by the Crown's customs service—and return laden with luxury goods such as brandy, tea, and lace. Small boats would ferry the illicit goods from the ship to the shore. The cargo would then be transferred from the small boats to packhorses and transported inland."

"Where did they take the cargo?" I asked.

"The most common destination was London," said Horatio. "It was the biggest market for commodities of all kinds. Contraband goods were distributed from warehouses along the Thames and sold through fences, that is to say, purveyors of illegally obtained property."

"Sounds like a massive operation," I conceded.

"I did not choose the words for dramatic effect," Horatio informed me with genial tartness. "By the eighteenth century thousands of people living on or near England's south coast were involved in smuggling, either directly or tangentially."

"Thousands?" I said in surprise.

Horatio rested his elbows on the arms of his chair and tented his fingertips over his brightly colored waistcoat. "It may be helpful to think of a smuggling operation as an import-export business."

"Horatio?" said a vaguely familiar voice. The irreplaceable Ursula had left her post at the checkout counter to track down her boss. "Mongolian throat singing?"

Christopher and I exchanged mystified glances, but Horatio understood the cryptic query to be a request for help, which he instantly provided.

"Travel," he said. "Third shelf from the top. Beige cover, black type."

"Thanks," said Ursula and departed.

"Where were we?" Horatio asked.

"We were thinking of a smuggling operation as an import-export business," I said.

"Excellent." Horatio tapped his tented fingertips together as he continued, "Local fishermen were paid to carry out the Channel crossings, but a large network of employees was needed to load and to unload the cargo, to transport it overland, to run warehouses and other storage facilities, and to sell contraband goods. The gangs also employed lookouts and spies as well as armed guards who protected not only the contraband cargo but those handling it."

"Those people were directly involved," I said. "Who was involved tangentially?"

"Nearly everyone who lived near the coast was involved," said Horatio, "whether by choice or through coercion. Contrary to popular belief, the smuggling gangs of the eighteenth century had little in common with Robin Hood's merry men. They were vicious thugs who engaged in murder, torture, theft, and extortion to achieve their ends."

"What happened to those who refused to cooperate with the gangs?" I asked with some trepidation.

"They were beaten brutally," said Horatio. "Informers were singled out for special treatment. They were subjected to unspeakable torture before they were put to death."

"To serve as an example to others?" Christopher put in shrewdly.

"Precisely." Horatio nodded. "By the mideighteenth century, the rule of law had been all but abandoned in coastal regions. The gangs were often better armed and more numerous than the dragoons sent to arrest them. Corrupt magistrates would sometimes order the arrest of an arresting officer, and jailers were easily bribed."

"If you can't arrest criminals or lock them up," I commented, "law enforcement can get a bit tricky."

"Collusion and corruption were rife in the customs service as well," Horatio went on, "even at the highest levels. Some of the most prominent men in the kingdom—including prime ministers—stocked their cellars with wines acquired through the so-called dark trade."

"Yet the era came to an end eventually," said Christopher. "What brought about the gangs' downfall?"

"A convergence of events," Horatio replied. "The establishment of an effective police force, the creation of the coast guard, and the wholesale reform of the customs service diminished the gangs' power. It must also be said that public opinion turned against them."

"Horatio?" Ursula had returned. "Sir Francis Dashwood?"

"The Hellfire Club," said Horatio. He stretched out a hand to remove a small yellow paperback from a shelf at knee level and handed it to Ursula.

"Thanks," she said and left.

Horatio favored me with an interrogative look.

"Public opinion turned against the smuggling gangs," I prompted.

"So it did," he said. "As smugglers became more arrogant and more violent, they were no longer regarded as cheeky rascals picking the king's pocket, or as impoverished men justly rebelling against iniquitous taxation. Victorian villagers viewed smuggling as a criminal enterprise that undermined morality, terrorized the innocent, and endangered the economy."

"I'm pleased to hear that morality played a role, however small, in the gangs' demise," Christopher said drily.

"Morality was a contributing factor," Horatio allowed. "By far the greatest factor, however, was the implementation of free-trade policies in the nineteenth century. When the government abolished or significantly reduced taxes on imports and exports, the smuggling gangs lost their raison d'être."

"When smuggling ceased to be profitable," I said, "the gangs went out of business."

"Smuggling still occurs," said Horatio, "and smuggling gangs still exist, but today's smugglers do not sit in The King's Ransom, waving carbines and cutlasses while they quaff flagons of ale and snap their fingers at the law." He raised his eyebrows and looked from Christopher to me. "Have I answered your question?"

"No," I said, shaking my head.

"Not at all," said Christopher.

Horatio looked baffled.

"You answered lots of questions we didn't ask," I explained, "but you didn't answer the question we asked."

"Which was . . . ?" Horatio coaxed with a perplexed frown.

"Why is The King's Ransom called The King's Ransom?" Christopher and I said together.

"I do apologize. I shall provide an answer forthwith." Horatio folded his tented hands and rested them on his round belly. "The King's Ransom was known as The Crown until its major expansion in 1732, at which point the new owner, a brash man named Godfrey Shuttleworth, renamed it The King's Ransom. It was an inside joke, referring to the amount of gold that changed hands among the smugglers who used the inn for business as well as for pleasure. Godfrey boasted that each deal made under his roof was worth a king's ransom."

"So the inn's name doesn't refer to an actual king," I said.

"Quite the opposite," said Horatio. "Godfrey Shuttleworth was thumbing his nose at the king and at all those tasked with enforcing the king's laws. He decorated the inn with carpets and draperies festooned with golden roosters. The roosters were a blatant reference to the *coq gaulois*, a symbol of France, and another in joke. The *coq gaulois* was Godfrey's salute to those customers who paid their bills with money derived from goods smuggled to and from France."

"The carpets are still festooned with golden roosters," I said.

"French tourists still visit Shepney," Horatio reminded me. "Godfrey created a new sign for the inn as well."

"A wooden barrel filled with gold coins," I said. "We wondered what it meant."

"Wonder no more," said Horatio. "The wooden barrel is, in fact, a half-anchor spirit cask, the vessel used by smugglers to transport contraband brandy, cognac, and gin. The gold coins represent their illicit profits."

"Godfrey advertised his inn as a smugglers' hangout," I marveled. "The customs men must have wanted to wring his neck."

"The honest ones did," said Horatio. "The rest overlooked his brazen tribute to the dark trade in exchange for free drinks."

"Why would smugglers hang out at The King's Ransom?" Christopher asked abruptly. "Surely it would have been more convenient for them to patronize inns closer to the coast. The Mermaid Inn in Rye was, I believe, a favorite haunt of the notorious Hawkhurst gang. As you so kindly informed us yesterday, Rye was, at the time, a busy and prosperous port town."

"Coastal inns were popular among smugglers," Horatio acknowledged, "but Shepney's elevation gave them a distinct advantage. Lookouts positioned in strategic locations, such as St. Alfege's bell tower, could spot customs patrols long before they reached the inn. By the time the patrols rode up the hill, their quarry would be gone. Godfrey Shuttleworth made it possible for the smugglers to vanish, seemingly into thin air, and to appear again when the coast, so to speak, was clear."

"How?" I asked.

Horatio smiled. "You may have noticed the inn's labyrinthine interior."

"It's hard to miss," I said.

"It served a purpose," said Horatio. "When Godfrey expanded the inn, he created a maze of passageways and stairways in order to increase the time it would take to search The King's Ransom. The customs patrols had neither the manpower nor, in most cases, the will to conduct a thorough search of every convoluted inch of the inn. Most gave up out of sheer frustration."

"One can hardly blame them," Christopher observed, as if he were recalling the long trudge to his room.

"Godfrey was also responsible for the network of bolt-holes and escape tunnels hidden throughout the inn," Horatio continued.

"Horatio?" Ursula was back again. "Siamese fighting fish?"

"Hobbies," Horatio informed her. "Second shelf from the top. *Betta Fish Owners Manual.*"

"Thanks." Ursula was gone again.

"Bolt-holes and escape tunnels," I said.

"Thank you." Horatio paused to collect his thoughts before continuing, "Upon spotting a patrol, the lookout would send word to the inn. Guests wishing to avoid an unpleasant confrontation would dive into the nearest hiding place, secure in the knowledge that they were unlikely to be discovered by men already frustrated by the inn's confounding architecture."

"Do the Hancocks know about the inn's secret passages?" I asked, recalling the creaking door that had twice disturbed my sleep. "If they don't, they should be told. Hidden tunnels could present a security problem, not only for their guests but for their family."

"I can assure you that the escape tunnels do not pose a security threat to the inn's residents," Horatio stated authoritatively. "The tunnels were permanently sealed when the inn was refurbished in 1897."

"Good to hear," I said.

"I believe I have provided you with the answer you were seeking," said Horatio. "Have you any other questions?"

"Yes." I drew the notebook from my bag and handed it to him. "I found it in the attic at The King's Ransom. Is it a smuggler's inventory?"

Horatio fell silent as he examined the notebook. After leafing through the pages, he pulled a small magnifying glass from his watch pocket and studied each page minutely. The glass was, I knew, a tool used by booksellers who dealt in rare books. Horatio studied the notebook's faded covers as well, then tucked the magnifying glass into his pocket before pronouncing judgment on my discovery.

"Insofar as a cursory examination will allow," he began, sounding more like a lawyer than my husband ever did, "I can confirm that it is indeed an authentic smugglers' inventory."

"Why would anyone make a fake inventory?" I asked curiously.

"For the same reason smugglers smuggled," Horatio replied. "The reason being: money. There's a collector's market for everything, and items related to smugglers have become very popular over the years." He returned the notebook to me. "I reiterate, however, that your document is almost certainly authentic. I hope the Hancocks will donate it to a museum. Once it is properly analyzed, I have no doubt that it will contribute greatly to our knowledge of the history of smuggling in Shepney."

"Do you think it was Godfrey's?" I asked.

"I do not," said Horatio. "While Godfrey Shuttleworth facilitated the dark trade, he did not participate in it."

"I wonder if it belonged to Captain Pigg?" I said, slipping the inventory into my shoulder bag.

"Most unlikely," said Horatio. "The inventory lists contraband goods from a number of different sources. Josiah Pigg would not have recorded anyone's cargo but his own."

"So he was a smuggler," I said. "I wasn't sure. Jean Hancock referred to him as a brigand, and her daughter called him a pirate."

"Josiah Pigg was neither a brigand nor a pirate," said Horatio. "He was a mild-mannered fisherman who made a small fortune from the smuggling trade. He wisely retired before he ran out of luck, but the rather splendid home he bought in Shepney was wasted on him.

He preferred the pub's hearth to his own. He spent his sunset years at The King's Ransom, telling tall tales about his maritime adventures while drinking himself into an early grave."

"Did he drink geneva?" I asked. "If geneva is a drink. It's included in almost every list in the inventory, but I don't know what it is."

Horatio knew.

"Geneva or, to give it its proper name, *jenever*, is the traditional liquor of the Netherlands and Belgium," he said. "It's an early form of gin, and it was enormously popular in eighteenth-century England. I suspect that Captain Pigg drank an astonishing quantity of jenever, though legend has it that he favored brandy."

"One moment," said Christopher. He'd been silent for so long that I'd almost forgotten he was there.

"Yes, Bishop Wyndham?" Horatio said in the tone of voice he must have used to encourage a shy student to speak up in class.

"While Shepney's elevation was advantageous to the men making deals at The King's Ransom," Christopher said, "it would present a daunting obstacle to those transporting heavy kegs of liquor by horseback, would it not?"

"It would," Horatio agreed, "but smugglers didn't haul their cargo up the ridge, Bishop Wyndham. The packhorse drivers either carried on along the road through the valley or transferred their cargo to river boats at the base of the ridge. From time to time, they would store full or partial loads in the caves."

"Caves?" I said blankly.

"Ah, yes," said Christopher with a knowing nod, "limestone."

"I see that you have a grasp of geology, Bishop Wyndham." Horatio gave Christopher an approving nod before turning to address the class dunce. "Caves are a common feature of limestone formations.

Shepney's limestone ridge is riddled with them, but most are quite small. Smugglers used Shepney's larger caves as temporary storage facilities, just as they used haystacks, church crypts, table tombs, concealed cupboards in private homes, and holes dug in sand dunes."

"They hid their loot in table tombs?" I said, appalled. "What did they do with the remains?"

"I imagine they shoved them to one side to make room for the loot," said Horatio, with a touch of asperity. "They regarded the sanctity of the churchyard as nothing more than good cover. By now it should come as no surprise to you that smugglers were not regular churchgoers."

I heard only half of what he said because the phrase "good cover" had triggered a sequence of words in my mind: *bus tours, ghosts, escape tunnels, caves* . . . I wasn't sure what the sequence meant, or if it meant anything, but when I put it together with the exchange I'd witnessed in the narrow passage off the high street, I began to have my suspicions.

"Are the smugglers' caves still accessible?" I asked. "Or have they been sealed off, like the inn's tunnels?"

"A few caves have collapsed," said Horatio, "but none, to my knowledge, have been sealed."

"Horatio?" Ursula sounded as frustrated as a customs officer searching The King's Ransom. "There's a French bloke up front. I can't understand a word he says, but he won't stop pestering me. Will you talk to him?"

"*Bien sûr! On parle français ici,*" said Horatio. "My friends, if you will excuse me, I must attend to a customer."

"Of course you must," said Christopher. "We've taken up more than enough of your valuable time."

"Not at all," said Horatio. "It was an honor to review Shepney's checkered past with you and your friend, Bishop Wyndham. Please feel free to drop in for a chat whenever you're in Shepney." With a flash of lemon-yellow socks, he got to his feet and followed Ursula to the front of the shop.

Christopher stood as well, but I remained seated on my four-legged stool, staring intently at a bookshelf without seeing it.

"Lori?" said Christopher. "Have you another question for Horatio?"

"No," I said, "but now that we've discovered the meaning behind the inn's sign, I've thought of something else for us to do—something a little more interesting than milking cows."

Nineteen

Ursula's French bloke was none other than Monsieur Renault. As soon as I clapped eyes on the fat little Frenchman, another word popped into my head: "Marseille." When we reached the sidewalk, I swung around to face Christopher.

"I need Kenneth Cartwright," I said urgently. "He told me he'd be at the village hall again today, doing volunteer work. Do you think you could persuade Rebecca Hanson to let him leave early?"

"I can try." He cocked his head to one side. "I sense that you've had a revelation, Lori. Would you care to share it with me?"

"Not yet," I said. "Not until I'm sure it's worth sharing."

"Very well," he said. "I shall speak with Mrs. Hanson."

He crossed the high street. I stayed behind, pacing up and down in front of the bookstore while keeping a weather eye on the village hall. Ten minutes later, Christopher and Kenneth trotted down the stairs, the latter looking as though he'd been sprung from jail.

"*Crook,*" I muttered as still another word fell into place.

"Success!" Christopher announced as he and the gangly teenager stepped onto the sidewalk. "Mrs. Hanson was only too happy to release her volunteer into our care. She said it was the least she could do to repay the debt she owed us for, in her words, 'putting up with the old rascals yesterday.'"

"Hi, Lori!" Kenneth said cheerfully. "What's going on?"

"I need someone who knows Shepney like the back of his hand," I said. "You told me yesterday that you hunted for bones all over the place when you were a kid. Did you ever look for them in the smugglers' caves?"

"Lots of times." His eyebrows shot up expectantly. "Do you want to see the caves?"

"Yes, please," I said. "Will you take me to them?"

"Absolutely," he replied before adding a word of caution. "We may not be able to get into them just now. Three of the big caves are close to the river. They're probably flooded."

"Let's find out," Christopher proposed.

"Is it a strenuous hike?" I asked, giving my white-haired friend a sidelong glance.

Christopher caught my glance, clucked his tongue, and rolled his eyes heavenward. He lifted one foot to display his walking shoe's rugged sole, then pulled a slender black flashlight from his coat pocket.

"You needn't worry about my hiking skills, Lori," he said. "As you can see, I'm an experienced rambler."

"I'm worried about your stamina, not your skills," I told him frankly. "You dragged your feet when we climbed the stairs last night."

"I wasn't fatigued," he explained. "I was the victim of my own greed. Put simply: I overindulged during dinner. Happily, I did not make the same mistake with breakfast."

Kenneth intervened. "It's an easy hike, Lori. My granddad can do it, and he uses a cane."

Christopher put an end to the debate by sweeping his hand through the air and saying, "To the caves, Kenneth!"

Kenneth bounded up the high street like a happy puppy. When he realized he'd left the old folks behind, he kindly slowed his pace to match ours, and together we turned onto Church Lane. Bill's car looked less forlorn in the daylight than it had in the evening gloom, and St. Alfege's shone like a faceted gem. The flint shards in its walls had gleamed in the rain, but in sunlight, they glittered.

The houses beyond the church weren't as postcard-pretty as Finch's golden stone cottages, but they were, like the high street's buildings, an interesting jumble of architectural styles. As we passed a tile-roofed redbrick cottage, it wasn't hard to imagine poor old Mrs. Dodd tottering out of it to scan the night sky for bombers, and I could easily envision Captain Pigg looking down on his neighbors from the rather splendid Tudor house across the lane.

When I heard chickens clucking and caught sight of geese eyeing me beadily from a back garden, I recalled the villagers' willingness to shelter farm animals during the flood. Nothing prepared me, however, for the sight that met my eyes when we left the houses behind.

The village occupied only a third of Shepney's limestone ridge. The rest of the ridge was a grassy expanse of rough, open ground. The open ground was dotted with gnarled trees and a handful of windswept bushes that looked tough enough to survive a hundred cyclones. It had also been transformed into a veritable menagerie.

The farmers and their village allies had used temporary fencing to create spacious enclosures for cows, goats, pigs, horses, donkeys, alpacas, and llamas. The sheep, on the other hand, had been given free rein to graze wherever the grass was greenest. Their owners had no reason to fear that they might wander off into parts unknown, because a broad swath of farmland surrounding the ridge resembled an inland sea.

"Sheep island," I said dazedly, as I took in the wondrous scene. "Remember, Christopher? Horatio told us that 'Shepney' means 'sheep island' in Old English."

"I remember," he said, sounding equally stunned, "but I didn't fully comprehend its meaning until now."

"It's like a castle with a moat," I said.

"No, Lori," Christopher said softly. "The ridge is an ark."

Kenneth, who was not quite as bowled over as we were by a sight he'd seen many times before, was studying the ridge's north slope.

"The river's gone down a good bit since yesterday," he informed us. "They dredged it after last year's flood, so it can handle more water. We may be able to enter one of the caves after all. It's higher up than the others."

"How do we get to it?" I asked, tearing my gaze from the marvelous ark to give him my undivided attention.

"Follow me," he replied confidently. "You'll want to watch your step as you go downhill. It'll be slippery where the sheep have been."

"Thanks for the warning," I said.

I could tell by the way Kenneth spoke that he was proud of his knowledge and pleased to have two adults he respected depend on him. I hoped our outing would show him that in the wide world beyond his village, weirdos could find a place where they were valued.

I slung my shoulder bag crosswise in preparation for the hike, then followed Kenneth as he led us to the trailhead. The trail switchbacked downhill in long sections from the ridge's flat top to its rocky, irregular base. Christopher's knees must have been in good shape, because he had no trouble keeping up with Kenneth and me. Even so, I wasn't ready to give him full marks as a hiker. The descent would test his knees, I reminded myself, but the ascent would test his lungs.

As we descended, Kenneth pointed out small caves I wouldn't have noticed if I'd tackled the trail on my own.

"You don't want to crawl into those," he advised, with a certainty born of experience.

"Why not?" I asked. The answer was obvious, but I wanted him to have the pleasure of giving it.

"You don't know what might be in them," he said. "Floods drive all sorts of animals into the caves. You wouldn't want to come face-to-face with a badger."

"I certainly wouldn't," I agreed.

The river's roar wasn't nearly as loud as it had been when I'd stopped on the bridge, wondering what I should do to avoid being swept off the road by the gusting wind, but it was still loud enough to make me thankful that I didn't live near it. The road I'd chosen as my shortcut to Rye was partially submerged, and the dry spots were littered with tree branches, fence posts, and tangled piles of miscellaneous debris. I would have felt worse for the farmers whose homes were inundated had I not known of the support they would receive from their neighbors.

The lowest stretch of the trail was a waterlogged mess, so Christopher and I tagged along behind Kenneth as he scrambled across a rock-strewn slope to a point directly below the village. I had no idea where he was leading us even after he came to a halt.

"Here we are," he said.

"Where are we?" I asked, mystified by his triumphant expression.

"A smugglers' cave," he replied. "The only one that won't be knee deep in water."

He had to take me by the shoulders and turn me in precisely the right direction before I saw the cave. I pitied the customs officers assigned to find it. The cave mouth was camouflaged by scrubby shrubs as well as a fold in the hillside, and it was smaller than I'd anticipated, at least six inches shorter than I was, and no more than three feet across. Horatio Best would have been hard pressed to squeeze himself through it. Dennis Dodd would have been foolish to try.

Kenneth the proto-paleontologist pulled a flashlight from his jacket pocket. I imagined he never left home without one.

"Wait here," he instructed us. "I'll take a look inside to make sure it's unoccupied."

"What will you do if it's occupied?" Christopher asked.

"I'll leave," he replied.

"Sound thinking," said Christopher, with the faintest hint of a smile playing about his lips.

"The trick is to make a noise as you go in," Kenneth explained. "Most animals will hide when they hear a noise." Lit flashlight in hand, he bent low and entered the cave, calling softly, "Hello? Anyone at home? I'm not here to hurt you, and I won't stay long."

While we waited for him to return, I wondered what I would tell his mother if he was attacked by a badger. I hoped that convincing him to forgo tattoos would count in my favor, but it was a wan hope at best. I felt limp with relief when his very young face came into view, unmarred by tooth or claw.

"It's all right," he said. "You can come in."

I drew my earthquake survival flashlight from my pocket, and Christopher drew his black flashlight from his. We switched them on simultaneously, but he motioned for me to enter the cave ahead of him. If I hadn't known him to be a gentleman, I might have suspected him of being a coward.

A musty smell and the squelch of mud beneath my boots indicated that the rising river had reached the cave, though its waters had since drained away. I quickly discovered that I could stand upright, and that Kenneth, the tallest of us, had plenty of headroom. The cave wasn't a cathedral-like cavern, but its diminutive entrance belied its size.

The patch of daylight falling through the cave mouth looked like an illuminated welcome mat, but the rest of the cave was drenched in a darkness that made our flashlight beams seem like searchlights. When Kenneth began to describe the cave's features with the help of his flashlight, I felt as if I were in a primitive planetarium.

"Chisel marks," he said, shining his light on a row of deep gouges in the limestone ceiling. "Smugglers enlarged the cave by hand to make more room for their stashes." The beam slid sideways to a black stain on the scarred ceiling. "Carbon deposits from a smuggler's lantern." The beam jumped to the cave mouth. "They would have hung a black curtain over the opening, to keep the lantern light from giving them away." The beam traveled from the narrow entrance to a rockfall at the rear of the cave. "No one knows how big the cave was before the back part of it collapsed, but I've heard rumors that it was part of a tunnel system that ran up through the ridge to the village."

My pulse quickened, and my mouth became so dry that I couldn't speak. Unwittingly, Christopher spoke for me.

"Horatio Best told us that The King's Ransom is laced with escape tunnels," he said. "Were they part of the same system?"

"So they say," Kenneth replied. "When I was little, I used to tap on the cave walls, hoping to locate a smugglers' tunnel. I never found one. As far as I know, no one else has, either."

"Perhaps they're mythical," Christopher suggested.

"The tunnels in The King's Ransom are real," Kenneth stated

firmly. "James, the owner's son, proved it to me. The previous owner, I mean, not the Hancocks."

"Understood," said Christopher.

Even with my brain whirling at ninety miles an hour, I was aware of the surreal scene unfolding before me. A bishop and a schoolboy, their pleasant faces transformed into grotesque masks by three wavering flashlights, stood in a dank, dark cave, calmly discussing escape tunnels once used by ruthless criminals. It wasn't a situation I'd foreseen when Bill and I had set out for Rye.

"James took me down to the cellar once," Kenneth was saying, "and he showed me a tunnel entrance. It had been bricked up good and solid, but we could tell what it was. The bricks didn't match the rest of the wall and the outline was shaped like a tunnel. We wanted to tap on the paneled walls in the dining room, but his dad wouldn't let us. He wouldn't let us tap on the walls in the pub, either."

"How very shortsighted of him," Christopher commiserated. "He could have turned the tunnels into an attraction, had you and your friend found any."

"That's what we told him," said Kenneth. "But his dad wouldn't listen."

"I suspect he had his hands full running the inn," said Christopher.

"Our mums said the same thing," Kenneth said dejectedly, "so we gave up."

"You saw the tunnel entrance in the cellar," Christopher reminded him. "Since the Hancocks keep the cellar door locked, you've seen something I'll never see. I must confess to feeling no small amount of envy."

"I could find out where they keep the key," Kenneth offered eagerly.

"Best not," said Christopher. "Bishops aren't supposed to borrow things without asking permission."

"Sorry," said Kenneth. "I forgot you were, uh, you."

"I'll never forget today's excursion," Christopher declared. "You're an exemplary guide, Kenneth, and an excellent teacher. I knew nothing of the caves until you showed this one to me."

"Does anyone—" My voice cracked, so I cleared my throat and started again. "Does anyone use the caves now?"

"For what?" Kenneth asked.

"Storing things," I said with forced nonchalance. "Hiding things."

"Not that I know of," he said. "But I wouldn't be surprised if Steve used them. He has to have some place to stash his—" He broke off, and although I couldn't see him clearly, I could almost hear him blush. "To . . . to stash his stuff."

"What sort of stuff would Steve stash in a cave?" Christopher inquired in perplexed tones.

"Wine?" Kenneth ventured. "And . . . and cheese?" He must have known how unconvincing he sounded, because he made a beeline for the cave mouth. "We should get going. My mum will be expecting me. She worries when I'm late for lunch."

I thought for a moment that he would leave Christopher and me alone in the cave while he sprinted for home, but he waited patiently while our dazzled eyes adjusted to the sunlight, and he led us back up the trail at a pace that didn't cause Christopher's lungs—or mine—to burst.

Kenneth was silent until we reached the trailhead, when he swung around to face us, saying in a semipanicked rush, "What I said about Steve—I didn't mean anything by it. I was only joking, but if my mum finds out I was making fun of him, she'll kill me." He gazed at us beseechingly. "Do you think you could, well, keep it to your-selves?"

"It's against the bishops' code of conduct to lie," said Christopher, which I thought was a novel way to describe the Ten Command-ments. "Unless your mother asks me about our conversation, how-ever, I will keep it to myself."

"Your mum won't hear about it from me," I promised.

"Thanks," Kenneth said fervently.

"Thank *you*, Kenneth," I said. "I couldn't have asked for a better guide."

"Run along now," Christopher told him. "I believe Lori and I can find our way back to Shepney from here—and we wouldn't want your mother to worry."

Grinning from ear to ear, Kenneth nodded and took off.

Christopher opened his mouth to speak, but before he could ut-ter a word, a tall, slender figure stepped forward from a group of men mucking out a cow pen.

"I have wonderful news!" Phillip Lawson shouted. "My son is innocent!"

Twenty

The young rector sauntered toward us, looking every inch the dairyman. His cheeks were ruddy, wisps of hay clung to his coveralls, and his Wellington boots were caked with a substance I could smell from ten feet away.

"I'm glad I ran into you," he said. He hooked a thumb over his shoulder to indicate the livestock enclosures. "What do you think of our operation?"

"It's ingenious," Christopher replied.

"We penned the large animals in the lanes at the height of the storm," Phillip explained, "but when the wind died down, we moved them out here."

"I hope someone has recorded your procedures," said Christopher. "It would be an invaluable template for other communities to use when faced with a similar emergency."

"It's all in the master plan," said Phillip. "We've made the plan available online, and we update it regularly as we work out better ways to do things." He inclined his head toward Christopher. "Before I forget, Bishop Wyndham, you don't have to take evensong for me this evening. I've canceled it. As you may have noticed, it wasn't drawing a crowd, and the choir asked for extra time in the church to practice before tomorrow's service at the village hall."

"The members who participated in last night's service sang beautifully," said Christopher. "I look forward to hearing the full choir."

"Now, about Trevor . . ." The rector folded his arms and explained that he'd had a heart-to-heart with his son. "He claims—and I believe him—that when he delivered the parish magazine to the inn on Wednesday, he found Jemima Hancock sitting all by herself in Captain Pigg's parlor. She was crying her eyes out. He asked what was wrong, and she said she didn't want to live at the inn anymore because she kept hearing strange noises in her bedroom at night."

Christopher and I exchanged glances.

"Trevor had already heard about the inn's ghosts," Phillip continued, "so he told Jemima not to worry because everyone heard strange noises in the inn. He told her the noises were made by ghosts who'd lived there for many years, and as long as she left them alone, they wouldn't bother her." His gaze shifted from Christopher to me and back again. "You see? My son wasn't trying to frighten Jemima. He was trying to comfort her."

"If he was trying to comfort her, why did he make up a new ghost?" I asked. "Why did he tell her that a lady died in my bed?"

"He didn't," said Phillip. "Trevor insists that he never mentioned a specific ghost. Jemima must have taken the basic idea of ghosts and embroidered it to account for the noises she heard."

"She thought the noises came from the attic," I said reflectively, "so she figured a ghost must roam around there at night." I recalled Jemima's somber expression as she handed Captain Pigg to me. "No wonder she was afraid for me. After listening to Trevor, she must have thought that her ghost would object to a real, live human being spending the night in the attic."

"Did Jemima describe the ghostly noises to Trevor?" Christopher asked.

"More or less," said Phillip. "Trevor had the impression that she heard footsteps, laughter, and another noise she had to imitate because she couldn't put a name to it. It sounded something like . . ." He proceeded to do a fairly accurate impersonation of a creaking hinge. Then he smiled. "The inn must be an uncanny home for an imaginative seven-year-old, especially during the kinds of storms we've had lately."

"It must," Christopher agreed. "I'm pleased to hear that Trevor had good intentions, Phillip. He can hardly be blamed for Jemima's embroidery. Have you cleared his name with Mr. and Mrs. Hancock?"

"I filled them in first thing this morning," said Phillip. "They weren't thrilled to learn that their daughter had confided in Trevor instead of sharing her fears with them, but they understand that children sometimes find it easier to talk to another child than to their parents."

"And parents can't keep tabs on their children every minute of every day," I put in. "We aren't all-seeing, however much we try to be."

"Very true," Phillip said ruefully. "If we were, the church-bell incident wouldn't have happened."

"A lot of incidents wouldn't have happened," I said with a sympathetic chuckle. "Remind me to tell you about my sons and the water balloons one day."

"I shall," he said. A pickup truck loaded with grain sacks pulled up to the edge of the open space. He jutted his chin toward it, saying, "My cue to get back to work. Will I see you at the service tomorrow, Lori?"

"I'll be there," I told him. "I have a lot to be thankful for."

"We all do," said Phillip. "Until then!"

He sauntered away to unload the truck, and Christopher turned his head to look at me. I expected him to quiz me about my revelation, but he simply proposed that we return to The King's Ransom for a late lunch.

Christopher had to carry the conversational burden while we walked back to the inn, because my mind was elsewhere. He chatted about Horatio Best's history lecture, Trevor's unexpected sensitivity, and Kenneth's potential as a paleontologist—"He has a retentive mind, and he isn't afraid to get his hands dirty"—but he never once mentioned my revelation.

I was grateful to him for not pressing me on it. I wasn't ready to discuss the suspicions Horatio's offhand remark had inflamed. I wanted to assemble the puzzle before I presented it to Christopher, and to do that, I needed a very specific kind of help.

We crossed paths with Jean Hancock in the inn's foyer. After admitting that Trevor had risen in her estimation, she asked if we'd had lunch in the village hall again.

"We haven't had lunch," Christopher informed her. "We were otherwise engaged."

"I'm afraid we're setting up for dinner in the dining room," she said apologetically, "but you could have a bite to eat in the pub, or I could have something sent up to your room."

"Thanks, but I'll pass," I told her. "I'm not very hungry." I was, in fact, hungry enough to eat the rooster-festooned carpet, but I was too preoccupied to enjoy a pub meal, and I wished to avoid a room-service intrusion while I was in the attic.

"I confess that the pub is a little too lively for me," said Christopher, "but a sandwich sent to my room would be greatly appreciated."

"I'll fetch a menu," said Jean.

"I don't need a menu, Mrs. Hancock," he said. "I'm willing to trust your chef's judgment."

"I'll let him know." Jean began to turn away, but I held out my hand to stop her.

"I have something for you," I said, pulling the well-traveled notebook from my shoulder bag and presenting it to her. "I found it in the attic last night. I hope you don't mind, but I showed it to Horatio Best this morning."

"I'm glad you did," said Jean. "I intended to show it to him, but with one thing and another, I never got around to it. Someone left it on a shelf in the old wardrobe. I stuck it in the bookcase for safekeeping and promptly forgot about it."

"It's a smuggler's inventory," I told her. "Horatio thinks it's authentic."

"He hopes you'll donate it to a museum," Christopher added.

"We'll ask an expert for a second opinion," Jean temporized, "but I'd like to display it in the inn. I think our guests would find it interesting."

"I know I would," I said.

"As would I," said Christopher.

"In the meantime, I'll put it on the desk in the office so it won't slip my mind again." She smiled. "And I'll order your sandwich right away, Bishop Wyndham, before it slips my mind as well!"

She hurried off to the kitchen. Christopher and I climbed the stairs more slowly, in part because we'd done a fair amount of climbing already, but mainly because Horatio's lecture allowed us to see the inn's convoluted innards in a whole new light.

Christopher didn't have to do the lion's share of the talking as we made our way through the zigzagging corridors, past the oddly shaped alcoves, and up and down the peculiar little staircases. We both commented on the cleverness of Godfrey Shuttleworth's layout, the difficulties it would present to a search party, and the valuable minutes it would afford a smuggler attempting to dart into a bolt-hole or to flee via an escape tunnel.

We parted ways at the door to Christopher's room. Again he refrained from grilling me about my revelation, saying only that he hoped to see me at dinner. His restraint made my admiration for him shoot through the roof. If our positions had been reversed, I would have pestered him as relentlessly as Monsieur Renault had pestered the irreplaceable Ursula.

"You'll see me at dinner," I assured him. "If you don't, send out a search party."

"Why?" he said. "They'd never find you."

I knew he was joking, but for a moment it seemed as though he could read my mind.

Twenty-one

The attic wasn't much brighter than it had been at dawn. Dust motes glinted in the gray light leaking through the dormer windows, and silence reigned, unbroken by ghostly sounds. I dropped my shoulder bag on the bed, but I didn't remove my jacket. The October sun was too weak to warm the attic.

I lit the camping lantern, took the blue journal from the octagonal table, and sat with it in the Windsor armchair. I paused to steel myself before I opened it because I was about to do something Aunt Dimity would deem foolhardy. I was determined to do it with or without her blessing, but I hoped to convince her that it was a risk worth taking.

"Dimity?" I said, opening the journal. "I've had a revelation."

I was too wound up to smile as the familiar lines of royal-blue ink began to curl and loop across the page.

Good afternoon, Lori. You seem tense. Would I be right to assume that you've had a disturbing revelation rather than a pleasant one?

"You would," I said. "It's also a bit complicated."

Disturbing revelations are almost always complicated, my dear, but I'll try to follow along as you attempt to untangle yours.

"Okay," I said. "Here goes . . ."

For my benefit as much as Aunt Dimity's, I began with a review of the conversation we'd had the previous evening. I repeated what I'd told her about Steve, the chef who'd served time in prison;

Monsieur Renault, the obnoxious Frenchman with whom Steve had argued; Horatio Best, the authority on all things Shepney; and Trevor Lawson, whose ghost stories had scared Jemima. I touched lightly upon Christopher's observations regarding the inn's architectural quirks and concluded with my discovery of the smuggler's inventory.

I then brought Aunt Dimity up to date on everything that had happened since I'd last spoken to her. I described the surreptitious encounter I'd witnessed between Monsieur Renault and the red-haired woman, emphasizing the exchange of his white packet for her manila envelope. I summarized Horatio Best's lecture on smuggling as well as his illuminating comments on the inn's smuggler-friendly features, including its shamelessly pro-smuggler sign. I told her about the impromptu expedition to the smugglers' cave, and I repeated Kenneth's tellingly truncated allusion to Steve's need for a place to stash "stuff." Finally, I recounted Phillip Lawson's spirited defense of his son, underscoring Trevor's assertion that Jemima had been frightened by the same noises Christopher and I had heard: footsteps, laughter, and creaking.

"Are you with me so far?" I asked when I completed my two-part preamble.

I'm hanging on by my fingernails, Lori, but I'm with you.

"Dig in," I advised, "because the story is about to get complicated." I took a steadying breath before continuing. "I had my revelation when Horatio told us that smugglers hid loot in table tombs. He said a churchyard's sanctity provided them with good cover. And it struck me that a famously haunted inn might work the same way. It might provide a modern-day criminal with good cover."

I presume that Monsieur Renault is the modern-day criminal.

"After what I saw on the high street, I'm convinced that he's a drug dealer," I said confidently. "Tessa the waitress told me he's from Marseille. Marseille is a busy port town, like Rye was in the eighteenth century. It's also a notorious venue for drug trafficking."

Vast amounts of illicit drugs passed through Marseille in my time as well. Such a pity. It creates all sorts of difficulties for the decent, hardworking people who live there.

"It creates business opportunities for shady characters like Monsieur Renault," I said. "He could smuggle drugs into England via the bus tour, and sell them in towns on the tour's itinerary."

Drug addicts in Shepney. It's a dispiriting thought, but sadly believable. Addiction is an equal-opportunity scourge—it can destroy lives as easily in a small village as in a big city.

"It's a scourge because of people like Monsieur Renault," I said. "According to Tessa, he's taken the same bus tour repeatedly. He's been to Shepney several times before, and he's always reserved a room—the same room—ahead of time."

Yes, you told me that he prefers to nap while the rest of the group explores the village.

"What if he doesn't take a nap?" I said. "What if he sneaks out of his room to sell drugs?"

How could he sneak out of his room, Lori? Someone at the inn would be bound to see him, unless . . . Oh, I see.

"I knew you would," I said. "Don't ask me how, but he must have found a connection between his room and one of Godfrey Shuttleworth's sealed tunnels. It would explain why he always requests the same room."

It would. If he could get into the tunnels, he could use them to slip in and out of the inn unseen.

"One of his deals must have taken longer than usual," I said.

"That's why he didn't board the bus on time. Under normal circumstances, his tardiness wouldn't have mattered all that much, but with the cyclone closing the roads, it mattered a lot."

He was stranded in Shepney, along with his compatriots.

"As long as everyone believed he was napping, he could keep his stash in his room," I said. "He didn't have to worry about a maid stumbling across it because his room wouldn't be cleaned until after he checked out. When he realized that he would be staying at The King's Ransom for several days, though, he must have decided to hide his stash in a place Housekeeping doesn't clean."

The tunnels.

"The tunnels," I repeated with a satisfied nod.

To recapitulate: Monsieur Renault obtains illegal drugs in Marseille, a city known as a nexus for the drug trade. He uses a bus tour to smuggle the drugs into England. He pretends to nap at The King's Ransom so that he can sneak out of the inn via a smugglers' tunnel and sell his detestable wares in Shepney. When the cyclone compels him to stay at the inn for several days, he hides his supply of drugs in a tunnel to avoid detection by Housekeeping. Did he make the noises that disturbed you, the bishop, and poor little Jemima?

"He must have," I said. "I can't explain the laughter, but the creaking noise could have come from the secret door he discovered in his room—the door that gave him access to the tunnel—and the footsteps are even easier to explain: We must have heard him sneaking through the tunnel to get to his stash."

Why would Monsieur Renault visit his stash at half past two in the morning?

"Because sleepy people are more likely to believe in ghosts than wide-awake people," I said triumphantly.

Hence your revelation about a famously haunted inn providing good cover

for a criminal. Monsieur Renault utilizes the inn's well-known reputation as a gathering place for ghosts to deflect attention away from any noise he might make in the tunnel.

"Jemima was the only one who believed he was a ghost," I reminded her. "You blamed the noises he made on the storm and a wandering guest; Christopher blamed them on an architectural quirk; and I shifted my blame from one thing to another because I didn't know what to think."

I suppose other guests might blame the noises on a similarly wide range of causes.

"Some guests probably slept through them," I said. "Monsieur Renault knew what he was doing when he chose to visit his stash in the wee hours."

Your story seems plausible, Lori, but you haven't yet explained Steve's role in it.

"I think he was a dealer, too, before he was put away," I said. "Why else would Kenneth make a lame joke about Steve's stash?"

Kenneth's joke supplied you with the missing connection between Steve and Monsieur Renault.

"If they were in the same line of business," I said, "Monsieur Renault could know all sorts of ugly things about Steve. Remember the French words I overheard when they were arguing? *Le prix, un escroc,* and *non, non, non!*"

The price, a crook, and no, no, no! Yes, I do remember.

"Maybe Monsieur Renault offered to cut Steve in on a deal, for old time's sake," I said. "He'd sweeten the deal by reminding Steve of the high prices drugs fetch. When Steve called him a crook and told him to take a hike, Monsieur Renault used blackmail to guarantee his silence."

It would certainly explain Steve's rage. To be tempted, taunted, and threatened by a former associate would be a reformed criminal's greatest nightmare.

"To tempt, taunt, and threaten an ex-con who's trying to go straight is just about the most evil thing a man can do," I said darkly. "If I'd been in Steve's shoes, I'm not sure Monsieur Renault would still be walking around in his."

Let us be thankful that you'll never find yourself in Steve's position. I must admit that I'm impressed by your hypothetical version of events, Lori. I don't know whether it's true or not, but I can't deny its internal logic. Will you share it with the Hancocks?

"Not yet," I said. "Not until I have proof."

You're not going to search for Monsieur Renault's stash, are you?

"I have to," I insisted. "I can't dump a bucketful of unfounded suspicions on the Hancocks, not when they have so much on their minds. You said it yourself, Dimity: They're raising two children while running a demanding business, to which I would add that they're doing both during an emergency. I can't ask them to drop everything just because I've come up with a plausible theory. If they accuse Monsieur Renault of a crime he didn't commit, they might create an international incident, and that's the last thing they need right now. Before I go to them, I have to have some sort of proof to back up my allegations."

I realize that you feel a sense of obligation to the Hancocks, Lori, but I must urge you to reconsider what I believe to be a foolhardy course of action.

There was the word I'd expected to see, and I knew pretty much what would follow.

Please don't allow your natural stubbornness to keep you from listening to

reason. *If you learned nothing else from Horatio Best's history lesson, you should have learned that criminals are deeply unpleasant people. They do not care for unexpected company. They object strenuously to uninvited guests. What will you do if you happen upon Monsieur Renault and his stash? Beg his pardon and tiptoe away? Do you really think he'd let you leave?*

"I'm not crazy," I retorted. "I'm aware that Monsieur Renault may be armed and dangerous. I'd rather come face-to-face with a badger than bump into him in his tunnel. But I won't bump into him because he doesn't enter the tunnel during the day. I'm looking for evidence, Dimity, not a confrontation."

The pause that followed seemed to go on for several centuries, but Aunt Dimity's handwriting finally reappeared, scrolling across the page less frantically than it had during her attempt to divert me from my foolhardy course of action.

I apologize for underestimating you, Lori. You've clearly thought this through. I'd be happier if you left the investigation to the proper authorities, but I understand why you're reluctant to voice your suspicions. It would be unkind to trouble the Hancocks with them, and it would be unfair to Monsieur Renault to present them without any proof.

"Thanks, Dimity," I said, smiling for the first time since I'd opened the journal. "I would have gone ahead anyway—"

Naturally.

"—but I wanted you to understand why," I finished.

Do you have a plan?

"Sort of," I said. "It couldn't have been too hard for Monsieur Renault to open his tunnel. Someone would have noticed if he'd used a sledgehammer to break through a brick wall."

I agree. Ghosts aren't that noisy.

"He must have discovered a tunnel entrance that was overlooked during the inn's refurbishment," I went on. "As I said before, it must be an unsealed entrance that creaks when he opens it."

You'll need a key if you're going to sneak into his room to search for a tunnel entrance, Lori.

"I don't intend to sneak into his room," I said. "I intend to look for a tunnel entrance in the attic. There must be one. I wouldn't have heard his footsteps so clearly if the tunnel he discovered wasn't connected to the attic."

Allow me to suggest a starting point: The sound of footsteps seemed to come from your staircase.

I looked toward the staircase, but my gaze came to rest on the immense mahogany wardrobe.

"The wardrobe is right next to the staircase door," I said slowly, as the gears in my head began to spin again.

Are you about to have another revelation, my dear?

"I believe I am," I said, looking down at the journal. "My wardrobe at home is fitted with drawers and shelves and a bar for clothes hangers. The attic's wardrobe is just a big wooden box with a few hooks and a single shelf. The shelf is so high up I can barely reach it."

One would expect an older wardrobe to have a greater number of shelves and perhaps a few drawers. It is an old wardrobe, isn't it?

"It's very old," I said. "When I first met Jean Hancock, she told me it looked as if it had been in the attic ever since the inn was built."

Wardrobes as we know them didn't exist when the inn was built, Lori. They didn't come into fashion until the eighteenth century.

"So our wardrobe could have been made around the time Godfrey Shuttleworth owned the inn," I said, as the gears kept grinding. "Why would he put a wardrobe in the attic, Dimity? It's not a guest room, and I can't imagine him taking the wardrobe apart and putting it together just to store it up here. And he would have had to dismantle it because it's too big to bring up the stairs in one piece."

Perhaps he intended to use it for storage.

"Jean told me it was empty," I said.

It could have been emptied by anyone at any time, Lori, but its lack of contents may be significant. The pine chest of drawers was full of seashells, the teak bookcase was full of books, and the bandboxes were full of hats, yet the wardrobe was empty. One might describe it as conspicuously empty.

"It wasn't completely empty, though," I said. "Jean found the smuggler's inventory on the shelf."

I wonder why it was left there.

"So do I," I said, getting to my feet. "Excuse me for a minute, Dimity. I'm going to take a closer look at the wardrobe."

If the minute turns into hours, Lori, please be careful. Old tunnels can be dangerous places, even when they're unoccupied by dangerous criminals.

"I'll keep an eye out for badgers," I promised.

I placed the blue journal on the octagonal table and took the camping lantern with me as I dragged the Windsor armchair across the room. After removing my suitcase from the wardrobe, I used the chair as a step stool and held the lantern high while I examined the solitary shelf.

I saw nothing, but when I extended my free hand all the way to the back of the shelf, my fingers brushed against an object that had escaped Jean Hancock's inspection. It felt like a short length of stiff wire. When I pulled it toward me, I saw that one end of the wire had been bent to form a hook. I couldn't work out a relationship between the bent wire and the smuggler's inventory, but I slipped it into my pocket before stepping onto the floor.

I pushed the armchair aside and climbed into the wardrobe, placing the camping lantern at my feet. I wondered if Kenneth would approve of my technique as I tapped the back panels. After a while, I began to wish that I'd asked him for a few tapping tips.

Though I listened intently for a hollow sound, the only sound I heard was the dull thud of my knuckles against solid mahogany. I tapped every inch of the back panels, from top to bottom and from side to side, but I might as well have been tapping on concrete. Stymied, I bent to pick up the lantern and froze as my heart did a backflip.

The lantern had picked out a deep knot in the wide boards that formed the bottom of the wardrobe. I'd noticed the hollow clunk of my hiking boots as I'd moved around inside the wardrobe, but I'd assumed it was due to the space between its floor and the attic's. The knot suggested a different explanation.

I climbed out of the wardrobe and knelt before it. With a trembling hand, I pulled the stiff wire from my pocket and inserted its hooked end into the knot. It fit perfectly. I gripped the wire firmly, tugged, and gasped as a trapdoor swung up to reveal a staircase descending into utter darkness.

Twenty-two

The trapdoor was fairly heavy, but it wasn't hinged. With an effort, I lifted it out of the wardrobe and laid it and the bent wire beside the armchair. It seemed prudent to leave clues for a search party to follow in case I became lost or injured while hunting for Monsieur Renault's stash. Gripping the lantern securely, I stepped onto the staircase and began my descent into the smugglers' tunnel. Kenneth, I thought, would have given his eyeteeth to come with me.

Apart from the darkness and a few low-hanging cobwebs, the escape tunnel wasn't particularly spooky. It was warmer than the attic, and it smelled better than the cave. As far as I could see, which, admittedly, wasn't very far, it was a highly sophisticated piece of engineering. The walls and the ceiling were clad in what looked like ship's planks, and the wooden stairs were in much better shape than the stairs leading to the attic, though they were shallower and considerably steeper.

At the bottom of the stairs I came to a level passage that forced me to turn right or left. I turned right and walked on until I reached a dead end. With a sigh, I retraced my steps, hoping that a second dead end wouldn't bring my investigation to an abrupt and ignominious conclusion. I'd gone no more than ten feet past my staircase when I heard a sound that made my blood run cold. Somewhere behind me, and not far away, a door opened with a nerve-shredding creak.

I wheeled around, wishing I'd brought my shoulder bag to use as a weapon. There was no place to hide and it was too dark to run, so I stood my ground, ready to roar at the top of my lungs while I swung the camping lantern at Monsieur Renault's head. A flashlight blinded me as a figure appeared in the passage. I could almost hear the fat little Frenchman pull a cosh from his pocket as I tightened my grip on the lantern and waited for him to attack.

"Lori? What are you doing here?" said a voice that was unmistakably British.

"Christopher?" I put a hand out to support myself while my heartbeat slowed from a gallop to a moderate trot. "What are *you* doing here? And I think we should keep our voices down so we don't freak out other guests."

The bishop lowered his flashlight and crossed to where I was standing.

"Forgive me," he said quietly. "I didn't mean to startle you."

"You said the same thing in St. Alfege's," I reminded him, "and yet here we are again. Where did you come from?"

"My room," he replied. "I was reading the Venerable Bede's account of St. Aidan's remarkable life when I heard footsteps similar to those I'd heard late at night. Since I was awake this time, I had no trouble determining that the sound emanated from my wardrobe."

"Godfrey Shuttleworth must have spent a fortune on trick wardrobes," I murmured, shaking my head.

"I beg your pardon?" Christopher asked.

"Never mind," I told him. "Go on."

"To make a long story short," he continued, "I discovered a

sliding panel in the back of my wardrobe. It evidently hadn't been used for quite some time, because when I opened it—"

"It screamed like a banshee," I interrupted. "I know. I heard." I looked down at my hiking boots. "You must have heard me walking to the dead end and back."

"The dead end?" he said.

I pointed over his shoulder. "Behind you, a few yards past the secret staircase I discovered in *my* wardrobe. Now that I think of it, the dead end must be near Jemima's bedroom. Her room is on the same floor as yours and across the corridor. If you go one way in the tunnel, you come to her room. If you go the other . . ." I swung around to peer into the shadows beyond our circle of light. "Well, I don't know where the tunnel goes after it passes your room, but at some point I think it goes down."

"To a cave?" Christopher suggested.

"Possibly," I said. "I won't know until I get there."

"What prompted you to look in your wardrobe?" he asked, frowning. "You couldn't have heard your own footsteps."

"It's a long story," I said, "and I can't make it short."

"No matter," he said. "You can tell it to me after we've finished our journey of exploration." He ran his hand along the wall. "Marvelous construction. I'll wager Godfrey Shuttleworth hired local shipbuilders to construct his tunnels, perhaps the same shipbuilders who constructed vessels used in the smuggling trade."

"Are you sure you want to come along?" I asked, remembering Aunt Dimity's words of caution.

He looked taken aback. "You must have a very poor opinion of me if you think I would pass up a chance to explore a smugglers' tunnel. Besides, we have a responsibility to the Hancocks to find out who else has been using it. They'll wish to have a word with the culprit who frightened their daughter."

"Yes, but the tunnel could be partially collapsed or full of rabid bats," I pointed out. "I don't mind putting myself in danger, but I'd rather not drag you into it with me."

"What kind of friend would I be if I allowed you to face danger alone?" he demanded indignantly. "And how dare you suggest that I require dragging? I'm here of my own volition, and I have no intention of turning back. I will, however, fetch my coat and hat. The tunnel's subterranean section—assuming it has one—may be cooler than the section that traverses the inn. I do not wish to attend tomorrow's service with the sniffles." He spun on his heel and marched back to his room.

"And people call *me* stubborn," I muttered.

When I saw him in his black overcoat and his homburg hat, I had to admit that I was glad of his company. Though the tunnel wasn't overwhelmingly spooky, it wasn't the sort of place I'd choose for a picnic. I felt better knowing that I wouldn't have to face its shadows alone.

I led the way through level passages, down steep staircases, and across small landings. We didn't run into any more dead ends, but we occasionally heard muffled voices in places where hidden doors had been replaced by brick walls during the inn's refurbishment. Christopher must have thought I had a passion for fine carpentry, because I scrutinized every nook and cranny we passed. Instead of mysterious packets of powder or pills, however, I saw nothing but cobwebs.

A subtle waft of cool air prepared us for the change in decor we encountered when the tunnel went underground. Rough-hewn stone replaced ship's planks as we descended a long, straight staircase carved out of the living rock. If we were following in Monsieur Renault's despicable footsteps, I thought, he was in better shape than I gave him credit for.

The farther we went, the more keenly aware I became of the great weight bearing down on the tunnel. Far above us, Jemima and Nicholas played with their toys; Jean and Gavin attended to their guests; Steve prepared exquisite meals in the kitchen; and Monsieur Renault continued to infect Shepney with his filthy trade. Would he betray Steve as well? I asked myself. When he realized that the game was up, would he reveal Steve's ugly secret to the police? I could only hope that the Frenchman's crimes would overshadow the chef's.

The stone staircase delivered us to a stone passage that went on for a short distance before it opened without warning into a space ten times the size of Kenneth's cave. Boulders as big as bison littered the rock-strewn floor, and stalactites hung like hag's hair from the roof. The distant drip of water echoed faintly in the cavern, and a rustle hinted that we weren't alone.

I was about to ask Christopher if he knew how to deal with badgers when we came face-to-face with a much more fearsome creature. I caught a fleeting gleam of black leather as Steve reared up from behind a boulder, his face wild and his huge hands covered in blood.

"What have you done?" I cried, too paralyzed with horror to scan the ground for the lifeless body of Monsieur Renault.

"Be quiet," he growled.

With what little courage I had left, I protested, "I will *not* be—"

"*Quiet*," he cut in, "or you'll spook them."

"Spook whom?" Christopher asked with unfailing politeness.

Steve turned and nodded at a furry orange face with a pair of bright eyes that peered at us from between two jagged rocks. To my everlasting astonishment, the scary giant in the black leather jacket smiled angelically as he beheld the fox.

"She's a vixen," he said in a tender voice I scarcely recognized. "If you sit down and talk low, she may let you see her kits. She has three of them. They're used to me, but they don't know who you are."

My knees were so weak with residual fear that I had no choice but to sit. I sank onto a convenient rock, and Christopher found one of his own. Steve retrieved a flashlight from behind the boulder, then hunkered down across from us with his back to the vixen, as if to show her that he would protect her. He laid the flashlight on the ground, then stripped a pair of latex gloves from his hands, turning them inside out as he did so. They were the same kind of gloves he'd given me to use during my brief career as a beet peeler.

"Their den must have flooded, so she brought them up here," he said, shoving the gloves into his jacket pocket. "Then the lower part of the cavern flooded and she couldn't get out. I heard them on Tuesday night when I got back to my room." He pursed his lips and rubbed his chin, as if he were searching his memory. "Wednesday morning, it would have been, since it was past midnight. Thought it was the storm at first. Turned out the noises were coming from my—"

"Wardrobe," Christopher and I chorused, but softly, so as not to alarm the kits.

"Yeah, that's right." Steve nodded. "The back of it slid sideways. Made a hell of a screech until I oiled it."

I looked at Christopher, who nodded wordlessly. We'd identified the culprit who'd frightened Jemima.

"I followed the sounds all the way down here," Steve continued.

He glanced over his shoulder. "And there they were, the poor little mites, half starved and shivering. The vixen is still nursing, so I brought down a couple of blankets, a flask of clean water, and some raw rabbit meat from the kitchen. Foxes'll eat anything, but she looked like she needed meat."

"Nursing mothers need plenty of protein," I confirmed.

I'd thought the scene in Kenneth's cave was surreal, but it wasn't even in the same surreal ballpark as our little tableau. I'd never in my wildest dreams imagined that I would one day discuss breast-feeding basics with an ex-con in a cavern while a bishop and a mama fox looked on. It was almost disappointing to learn that the blood on Steve's gloves had come from raw meat instead of Monsieur Renault's mangled corpse. Literally as well as figuratively, he had no blood on his hands.

"A couple of days of good feeding put her back on her feet," Steve informed us. "She could hunt for her own food now if there was anything for her to catch, but there's nothing back here except for snails."

"No rats?" I said. "No bats?"

Steve shook his head. "You'll find rats near the cave mouth, maybe, but you won't find them back here, and I've yet to see a bat."

"It's just as well," said Christopher. "Otherwise, the inn would be overrun with rats and bats. There's no barrier to keep them from entering the tunnel."

"There's no barrier to keep thieves and murderers from entering the tunnel, either," I said.

"Yes, there is," said Steve. "There's a huge rockfall just inside the cave mouth. The vixen could get past it, but no human could."

"Why hasn't she gone up the tunnel?" I asked.

"Could be she doesn't like the way it smells," said Steve. He held up his outsized hands. "I wear gloves to keep my scent off the rabbit meat. She doesn't mind me leaving food for her, but I wouldn't want her to get too tame."

"It may be too late," said Christopher.

I followed his gaze and witnessed the miraculous sight of three kits, miniatures of their mother, standing beside her, eyeing us curiously.

"They trust you," said Steve.

"They trust *you*," Christopher said firmly. "If you weren't here, they'd hide from us."

"Maybe," Steve allowed.

"There's no maybe about it," I said. "We didn't save their lives. You did, and they know it."

"I reckon they'll be off soon," he said, with a wistful note in his gruff voice. "She'll know when it's safe to leave. She checks every day. But I'll keep feeding her until they're gone."

We sat in silence for a time, and the kits became bolder. Under their mother's watchful gaze, they began to tumble over one another and to make strange chittering noises as they played—noises that could, I thought, be mistaken for children's laughter when magnified and distorted by the cavern. I felt as if I were slicing through mysteries like a hot knife through buttery brioche, but a few questions remained unanswered and I didn't quite know how to pose them.

"You've done a wonderful thing, Steve," said Christopher.

"I've done nothing anyone else wouldn't do," Steve countered.

A green light flashed in my head and I saw my opening. "Monsieur Renault wouldn't have lifted a fat finger to save them."

"Him," Steve snarled, sounding like his old self again. "Renault doesn't care about anyone but Renault."

"He certainly knows how to irritate people," I said. "I overheard the two of you arguing when I came down to help in the kitchen. I couldn't understand what you were saying because I don't speak French, but you sounded angry."

"I could have wrung his neck," Steve acknowledged. "The guy who was head chef before me used to buy truffles from him——"

"He sells *truffles*?" I broke in, but it wasn't a real question. I was just putting off the moment when I'd have to admit to myself that I'd mistaken a truffle transaction for a drug deal.

"Renault gets them from his cousin in Provence," Steve explained. "He was willing to sell them to me, but when the storm hit, the rotten crook jacked his price up sky-high. When I refused to pay, he said he'd never sell his cousin's truffles to me again." He snorted derisively. "As if I care. I can make do with porcini until I source a new supplier."

"Porcini," I said dully, picking up on another clue I'd missed. "I think Monsieur Renault found a buyer for his truffles. I'm pretty sure I saw him selling them to a red-haired woman earlier today."

"That would be Samantha Johnson," said Steve. "She's one of our local gourmets. She wouldn't care what she paid for them, as long as she could outdo Jake Peters. Cooking's a competitive sport for some."

"They'd lose if they competed with you," said Christopher. "Your porcini risotto was *absolument magnifique*."

"*Merci*," said Steve, sounding gratified.

"Where did you learn to speak French?" Christopher asked.

"A French chef taught classes at my, uh, cooking school," Steve replied with only the slightest of hesitations. "I learned the lingo from him." He leaned forward with his elbows on his knees. "As long as we're asking questions, I have one for you: Why did you two come down here?"

I was relieved that neither he nor Christopher was looking at me, because the blush that suffused my face would have outshone Kenneth's. Eating a handful of raw rabbit seemed appealing compared to telling them I'd entered the tunnel in order to prove that Monsieur Renault was a dope dealer. I would have lied through my teeth if Christopher hadn't stepped in.

"Lori and I heard your sliding door *and* your footsteps *and* your little friends through the tunnel," he explained. "Jemima Hancock heard the queer noises, too, and they upset her. When we discovered our own hidden entrances, we decided to look into the matter in hopes of putting Jemima's mind at rest."

"The poor kid," said Steve, sounding stricken. "I should have known that if I could hear the foxes, other people could, too. I'll have a talk with Jemima. I'll bring her and Nicholas down to meet the vixen."

"I would speak with their parents first," Christopher advised. "They may wish to conceal the existence of an escape tunnel from their children for fear of their children escaping."

"You're right," said Steve, grinning. "I could've done with an escape tunnel when I was a kid, but Jemima and Nicholas will never need one." He glanced at his watch and got to his feet. "My break has been over for twenty minutes. I'd best get back to work."

"The finest chef in East Sussex mustn't keep the dinner crowd waiting," said Christopher.

Even in the dim light, I could see Steve flush with pride.

Twenty-three

J made my confession to Christopher over another spectacular dinner. To his credit, he didn't laugh at me for being foolish or chide me for being overly suspicious. He unknowingly concurred with Aunt Dimity when he observed that my revelation had an internal logic, and he helped me to salvage a modicum of self-respect by reminding me that truffles bore a certain resemblance to drugs.

"Truffles are more difficult to procure," he said, "but they're equally addictive to those who love them. I've never cared for them myself."

"I prefer porcini," I said, trying not to drool over the bowl of creamy porcini soup that had been made, I suspected, with Christopher in mind. "Why do you suppose some of the secret entrances were left open during the refurbishment? The tunnel would have led the inn's owner to every entrance, including yours, mine, and Steve's. Why didn't he seal all of them?"

"Perhaps the inn's owner wished to retain a few escape routes for his own personal use," said Christopher. "One never knows when one will need to disappear in a hurry." He gazed thoughtfully at his soup spoon, then looked at me with a mischievous twinkle in his eye. "Then again, there is a bed in the attic."

"Are you suggesting that my bed was used for illicit trysts?" I feigned shock, then shrugged, saying, "It's better than a death."

"Mr. and Mrs. Hancock handled the situation well, I thought," said Christopher. "Jemima needed to see the dead end outside her room and to hear Steve's story about the foxes in order to understand that there was nothing supernatural about the noises she heard."

I nodded. "I'm glad they decided not to bring her down to the cavern, though. It was a bit much for me, and I'm a bit older than Jemima, though clearly not much more mature." I shook my head morosely, then grinned as a more pleasant thought occurred to me. "Kenneth was over the moon when you persuaded the Hancocks to let him take a run through the tunnel. You helped him to realize a childhood dream."

"He revised his opinion of Steve as well," said Christopher. "Never again will he make jokes at Steve's expense or hold his prison record against him."

"Well done," I said admiringly. "You tucked a life lesson in with the fun, you crafty old, uh, fox."

"The bishops' code of conduct requires it of me," he said. "Though the fun is optional."

"I'm glad you included it," I said. "Kenneth's a good kid, and he's worked hard during the emergency. He deserves a reward."

"He has the distinction of being the last person to use the smugglers' tunnel," said Christopher. "The Hancocks are determined to seal it once and for all."

"I can't blame them," I said. "Setting aside the fact that it's a security hazard, the Hancocks wouldn't be allowed to open it to guests unless they installed railings and lights and fire alarms and smoke detectors and all sorts of things they can't afford to install right now."

"Fortunately, the tunnel will still be there if they can afford to open it sometime in the future," said Christopher. "I hold fast to my belief that it would be an attraction."

Tessa arrived with our main course—roast chicken with saffron and lemons—and we ate in blissful silence, savoring the flavors, textures, and fragrances of a dish neither of us had ever had before. After Tessa cleared the table, Steve himself served the dessert I would always associate most closely with him and his enormous heart: apple crumble, with a pitcher of cream for me and a pitcher of custard for Christopher.

We didn't say much as we made our way upstairs after dinner—I think we were both feeling the effects of a spectacularly full day—but Christopher paused before he opened his door.

"We solved our mysteries, Lori," he said. "We identified Jemima's ghost and we deciphered the inn's sign, though it would be more accurate to say that Horatio deciphered it for us."

"A half-anchor cask brimming with ill-gotten gains," I said, nodding. "An invitation to smugglers to make a king's fortune in dirty money beneath the inn's roof. But we still don't know who recorded the smuggler's inventory or why it was left in the old wardrobe. Did the person who wrote it leave it there? If so—"

"Lori," Christopher interrupted, looking both amused and exasperated. "We can't solve *every* mystery. To paraphrase Mrs. Dodd: Some answers are lost in the mists of time." He smiled, turned the key in his lock, and said, "I'll see you at breakfast."

"I'll see you then," I said, and walked slowly up the corridor, pondering what I would say to Bill when I telephoned him. I had a feeling he would question my judgment if I told him I'd spent a few hours in a smugglers' tunnel searching for a stash of illegal drugs, so

I decided to tell him about Kenneth's cave instead. Some things, I thought, were best explained in person.

Sunday lived up to its name as Christopher and I—and hundreds of others—made our way to the village hall for the morning service. Though many of the French tourists were Catholic, all of them poured out of the inn to attend the service, except for Monsieur Renault, who remained in his room, presumably to count the money he'd earned selling overpriced truffles to foolish foodies.

Phillip Lawson greeted us at the door and Trevor ushered us into the dining hall, which had been transformed into a place of worship by the simple expediency of folding all but one of the folding tables and unfolding row upon row of folding chairs. Though Trevor offered Christopher a place of honor in the front row, Christopher declined, preferring to take a seat in the back row, where he would be less likely to steal the limelight from the conscientious young rector.

I preferred to sit in the back row because it allowed me to survey the room without craning my neck. I couldn't put a name to every face I saw, but I was surprised by the number of people I recognized: the men who'd hauled grain sacks into St. Alfege's; the women who'd aided flood refugees in the village hall; the choristers who'd sung at evensong; and assorted shopkeepers, farmers, and villagers I'd seen on one or another of my many jaunts down the high street.

There were also those I could name, even though I'd never laid eyes on them before. Despite the absence of a cockatoo, the family group consisting of two parents, two grandparents, four children, and two Labradors could only be the Bakers, and I was fairly certain that the woman who held two small children by the hand while bestowing a quick kiss on the rector was his wife. Kenneth Cart-wright simplified my guessing game by introducing his parents to me. His face shone like the setting sun when I thanked them for raising such a fine young man.

Tessa sat with the weedy sous chefs from The King's Ransom. Horatio Best, dressed as flamboyantly as ever, sat with the purple-haired and irreplaceable Ursula. Rebecca Hanson sat with her family, and the members of the geriatric gang sat with theirs. The Dodd, Fordyce, Bakewell, and Turner clans were well represented in the dining hall, though Joe Turner turned up without his terriers.

I'd thought it would be easy to distinguish stranded travelers from everyone else in the dining hall, but it was impossible. I could pick out the French tourists because of their accents, but even they were interspersed among the locals. What could best be described as an air of convivial bonhomie pervaded the dining hall, a splendid side effect of an emergency plan that treated refugees and residents alike with openhearted and openhanded generosity.

The Hancocks were almost the last to arrive, and Steve came with them, carrying Nicholas in one massive arm and holding Jemima's small hand in his somewhat larger one. He had no trouble spotting five empty chairs over the heads of lesser mortals, but the family needed only four, because Nicholas insisted on sitting in Steve's lap.

Jemima held Captain Pigg in hers. I'd returned the brave Glouces-ter Old Spot to her with my heartfelt thanks, and she'd accepted him without hesitation, knowing that no dead ladies would trouble me in the attic, even without his protection.

The stirring notes of the processional played on a portable key-board by a sturdy gray-haired woman brought the congregation to order. The choir raised their voices in heavenly song and the service commenced. When it came time for the lesson, the animal-loving rector didn't read about the ark and the flood. Instead, he chose verses from St. Paul's epistle to the Philippians.

"Do nothing from selfish ambition or conceit," he read, "but in humility count others more significant than yourselves. Let each of you look not only to his own interests, but also to the interests of others."

He built on the verses by stressing cooperation and a selfless concern for others as the qualities that would enable a community to weather any crisis, and he went on to cite the myriad of ways in which his community had exhibited those qualities since the cyclone had engulfed Shepney. He concluded by thanking God for giving his congregation the wisdom to face adversity together. He was about to give the blessing when an excited young boy dashed into the dining hall and whispered something in his ear.

"Glad tidings!" the rector announced, raising his arms in an all-encompassing gesture of joy. "Connie Fordyce has given birth to a healthy baby boy! And she's named him Noah!"

"That's my granddaughter!" Mrs. Fordyce bellowed.

"And your great-grandson, you old fool!" hollered Mr. Bakewell.

"Be still, the both of you," Rebecca Hanson roared. "The service isn't over!"

Phillip Lawson was wise enough to bring the service to a speedy conclusion, at which point refreshments were served. Those who could stay stayed, and those who had to return to businesses, families, or volunteer activities dispersed. No one left, however, until everyone had raised a teacup to toast little Noah.

Christopher and I stayed. We chatted and mingled, sipped tea and helped ourselves to the seemingly endless supply of cookies that poured forth from the kitchen. While we sipped and nibbled, a team of volunteers unfolded the folding tables, rearranged the chairs, and readied a table for the lunch buffet. Despite the festive atmosphere, Shepney remained in a state of emergency.

"If the river continues to recede at its present rate," Phillip informed us, "the roads should be dry in two more days."

"It'll take two more to clear 'em," said Joe Turner.

"Let's hope for sunny weather," I said.

"There's no rain in the forecast," said Rebecca Hanson.

We all looked up as we heard the *whup whup* sound of a helicopter flying low over the village.

"Must be the BBC," said Tessa. "The Beeb loves to get aerial shots of Shepney during floods."

"Who can blame them?" I said. "It's one of the most amazing sights I've ever seen."

"I hope they don't spook the livestock," Phillip said worriedly, but when he took a step toward the door, his wife restrained him.

"The animals are being well looked after," she said. "Your human flock needs you right now."

"The service was wonderful," I said, and the others chimed in with comments and compliments that distracted the rector, at least for the moment, from his other responsibilities.

As the rich aromas of roast beef and Yorkshire pudding began to spill into the dining room, talk turned to Sunday lunch. Rebecca Hanson invited Christopher and me to dine at the village hall, with the assurance that we wouldn't have to share a table with "the old rascals." I was on the verge of accepting when someone tapped me on the shoulder. I turned to find my long-lost husband smiling down at me.

"Bill!" I cried, and threw myself into his arms.

"Hello, love," he said, lifting me from my feet in a hug that went on for quite some time.

"How did you get here?" I demanded, when I hit solid ground again.

"Sir Roger's chopper," he said. "The man may be a dead bore, but he's very kind. When I told him that I absolutely, positively couldn't live without you for another minute, he put in a call to his pilot and off I went."

"The cows——" Phillip began, but Bill raised a hand to calm him.

"We saw them," he said, "and we avoided them. The pilot landed at the bottom of the hill and I walked up the road." He smiled down at me. "Otherwise, I would have been here sooner."

"I'm glad you're here now," I said, returning his smile with interest. "Everyone? Meet my husband."

I spent the next several minutes introducing Bill to the assembled throng, but I waited until the others slipped away to introduce Christopher.

"Bill," I said, "meet my guardian angel."

"Bishop Wyndham, I presume," said Bill, shaking Christopher's hand.

"Christopher, please," said Christopher.

"I can't thank you enough for taking my wife under your wing," said Bill.

"I could hardly turn my back on her," said Christopher. "We share an interest in ecclesiastical needlework."

When I started laughing, Bill smiled uncertainly. He wasn't familiar with Christopher's sense of humor, but I was. I was also familiar with my friend's thoughtfulness, so I wasn't surprised when he excused himself to give us a moment alone.

It was then that the things I hadn't told Bill began to topple through my mind like dominoes. My husband didn't know about the attic or the dead lady or the ghostly noises or Steve's prison record or the plot I'd hatched to expose a drug-dealing blackmailer by descending to the depths of the earth in a three-hundred-year-old tunnel built to help cutthroat villains escape the long arm of the law. While I was wondering whether there would ever be a right time to reveal all, he was making things worse by apologizing to me.

"Forgive me for not noticing how badly you needed a break, Lori," he said. "I'm sorry we didn't make it to Rye, but Shepney has clearly done you a world of good. Your eyes are bright, your cheeks are rosy. . . . Whatever you've been doing, it's recharged your batteries."

"Well," I said, "I haven't been bored."

Epilogue

J waited until Bill was staring in dismay at my bed in The King's Ransom to make a clean breast of everything. By then, it was too late to avoid telling him that the only way I could have spent my first night in Shepney closer to the cyclone's ravaging winds would have been to climb out onto the roof to catch a few *z*'s. He took it as well as could be expected, accepting that the attic, while not an optimal storm shelter, had offered me more protection than his car.

Once I told him about the attic, the rest of it came spilling out in a surprisingly orderly narrative that he didn't take quite as well. To say that he questioned my judgment would be to put it mildly, and while he eventually acknowledged my argument's famous internal logic, it wasn't enough to keep him from being furious with me for risking my neck.

Rabid bats were mentioned, as were steep drop-offs, gaping holes, poisonous gases, knives, guns, cave-ins, and blunt instruments. Though I didn't dare ask, I assumed that the poisonous gases would have killed me by accumulating in the tunnel, because they didn't strike me as a practical murder weapon.

Thankfully, my husband was nothing if not resilient. After he vented his anger, he began to see the humor in my imaginative interpretation of events. I endured his laughter stoically, knowing that it,

too, would fade in time, though it might be several years before he let me forget my miscue regarding the truffles.

As Phillip Lawson and Joe Turner had jointly predicted, it took four days to restore the roads around Shepney to their preflood conditions. Christopher and I spent those four days taking Bill on a grand tour that included St. Alfege's—where he finally got Christopher's joke about ecclesiastical needlework, and I finally got to see the French coastline from the bell tower—as well as Best Books, the livestock enclosures, and Kenneth's cave. Since the Hancocks had already declared the smugglers' tunnel off limits, Kenneth retained the distinction of being the last human being to enter it.

On our final day in Shepney, while Bill was hauling my luggage down from the attic, Steve caught up with me in the foyer. The gentle giant gave me his parsnip soup recipe as well as the bittersweet news that the vixen and her kits had moved on. Their freedom, I thought, would bring a particular kind of joy to a man who knew what it was to be imprisoned, but I could tell by his tone of voice that he would miss them. For him, as for everyone else in Shepney, service had been a privilege, not a sacrifice.

Christopher called to us to join him at the dining room's window wall, where Tessa, Jean, and Gavin had gathered with assorted guests and staff members to watch a phalanx of grim-faced French tourists escort Monsieur Renault to the tour bus. A cheer went up in the dining room as the bus pulled out of the parking lot, but I doubted that it was as heartfelt as the cheer that must have gone up among the French tourists.

Even with Jemima and Nicholas back in school—their proper school—Jean and Gavin didn't have time to spare for a prolonged

good-bye, but they urged Bill and me to come back soon, promising to provide us with their finest room, which turned out to be the one favored by the dashing rogues who engaged in sword fights when the mood struck them. It would, we decided, make for a lively stay, if not a restful one.

While Bill fetched the Mercedes, I said a fond farewell to Christopher. I hadn't expected to find a friend when I'd staggered into St. Alfege's, but I'd found one, and while our mystery-solving days appeared to be over, I would always cherish the time I'd spent in his congenial company.

Fittingly, his was the last face I saw as we drove away from The King's Ransom, though I caught a glimpse of Trevor Lawson coming out of the candy shop when he should have been in school. To my relief, he was followed by the rector, who was carrying two very full shopping bags. Trevor's classmates, it seemed, were in for a treat. I suspected that his teachers would regard his reformation in the same light.

As it turned out, I saw Christopher again in mid-November. Bill's regret at missing the symptoms of my dolorous doldrums led him to plan a second getaway close upon the first. It wasn't an adjunct to a business trip, but a long weekend dedicated to the principle that every parent deserves time off for good behavior.

We went to Winchester, where Christopher gave us a guided tour of the cathedral, showed us the town's manifold highlights, and finagled permission for Kenneth to join us for a thoroughly enjoyable lunch. Our next getaway, so I'm told, will take us to Rye and to Winchelsea, but only as day-trippers. We'll spend our evenings at The King's Ransom. It wasn't as famous as The Mermaid Inn, but we

had friends in Shepney, and in our book, friendship beat fame every time.

I was at home one evening, shortly after our return from Winchester. Too restless to sleep, I sat in the study, with the blue journal open in my lap, while the rest of my family slumbered.

Memories of Shepney drifted through my mind as a fire crackled comfortably in the hearth and a cold wind ruffled the strands of ivy that crisscrossed the diamond-paned windows above the old oak desk. When Aunt Dimity's fine copperplate began to loop and curl across the page, I saw that she, too, was thinking of Shepney.

I've been meaning to ask, my dear: Did you ever find out why Steve went to prison?

"No," I said. "I didn't try to find out, because it's none of my business. Whoever he was then isn't who he is now, and who he is now is a stand-up guy."

Wonderful things can happen when a man is given the support he needs to make the most of a second chance.

"Christopher would agree with you," I said.

It sounds as though you had a delightful time in Winchester.

"We did," I said. "Everything went according to plan."

Quite a contrast to your previous getaway.

"Yes, but . . ." I sighed. "I don't mean to be perverse, Dimity, but if it hadn't been for the cyclone, I wouldn't have met Christopher. I wouldn't have seen the floodwaters stretching out beyond the ridge, or the expression on Steve's face when he looked at the vixen. I wouldn't have heard a choir sing for a congregation of one. I wouldn't have learned about smuggling in East Sussex, and I wouldn't have watched a village come together to do things that mattered, whether it was tending someone else's geese, or making sure the old folks had hot meals, or providing a bed for a stranger like me."

On the other hand, you wouldn't have slept in a dusty attic without heating, plumbing, or electrical outlets.

"A small price to pay," I said. "The cyclone taught me a valuable lesson, Dimity."

Did it teach you to check the weather forecast before you leave home?

"Definitely!" I said, laughing. "But it also taught me to embrace the unexpected."

Some of life's greatest adventures happen by accident.

"One of mine did," I said, "and I wouldn't trade my accidental adventure for a king's ransom."

Steve's Apple Crumble

Serves four

Ingredients

For the crumble:

10 ½ ounces all-purpose flour, sieved with a pinch of salt
6 ounces brown sugar, packed
7 ounces unsalted butter, cubed, at room temperature
more butter for greasing pan

For the filling:

1 pound Granny Smith apples, cored and chopped into half-inch pieces
2 ounces brown sugar, packed
1 tablespoon all-purpose flour
½ teaspoon ground cinnamon (or to taste)

Directions

1. Preheat oven to 350° F.
2. Place flour (with salt) and brown sugar in a large bowl and mix well. Rub a few cubes of butter at a time into the flour mixture. Keep rubbing until the mixture resembles bread crumbs. Set aside.
3. Place the chopped apples in a large bowl and sprinkle with the brown sugar, flour, and cinnamon. Stir well.

4. Butter a 9-inch square baking pan. Spoon the apple mixture into the pan, then sprinkle the crumble mixture on top.

5. Bake for 40–45 minutes, or until the crumble is brown and the apple mixture is bubbling.

6. Serve with custard or heavy cream.